THE CLASH OF FATES
MICHAEL E. THIES

Writer's Block Press

WRITER'S BLOCK PRESS

CONTENTS

PROLOGUE

2 Year Earlier...

"Who do you think he is?"

"Who?"

"Him."

Putting his forearm over his eyes to shield them from the suns, Edwyrd Eska followed his sister's finger and noticed a figure lingering on top of the dune that overlooked the city. The figure remained there for a few seconds before swiftly turning and disappearing behind the dune. "The Recluse? How did you even notice him?" Edwyrd let his arm fall and continued walking back towards the center of the city. He had more important things to worry about right now than some mysterious man.

"While you were training with Lord Omyon and the other boys, something hit my eyes. I think he has a shield. And a staff, if my eyes are good."

"Many people have shields and staffs, Alicia."

"Those people are soldiers living inside the boundaries, brother. Or they come in groups from Orion. He's the only one that has ever ventured *into* town by himself."

"So, he's a foreigner."

"By himself," she emphasized.

"So, he's a lonely foreigner. What more is there to it?"

"A lonely foreigner that isn't afraid of the dragons prowling outside. Hello? Doesn't that fascinate you?"

Rolling his eyes, Edwyrd said, "Sure. He's a lonely man that has a death wish. That's who he is. It's not called fascinating, it's called suicidal."

Alicia huffed and folded her arms across her chest. "Jeez, you're certainly as hot as dragon's breath today, aren't you?"

Edwyrd stopped. Shoulders slunk slightly, he turned to his sister and exhaled. Crouching on the balls of his feet, he put his hands on her shoulders. "I'm sorry, sis. Training was rather difficult today is all. My head isn't—"

"Eddie, did your sister come to comfort you today? Is she here to give you *emotional* support?"

Edwyrd turned his gaze to two boys his age, Oscar and Aaron, coming out of the castle's training grounds.

"Or is it elemental support?"

"Nice one, Os." Aaron held up his hand for a high-five.

Oscar slapped his buddy's hand. "Don't cry. Although if you do, at least you wouldn't have ended the training session early."

Edwyrd sighed and returned his attention to Alicia.

"What was that about?"

"A comment I said earlier."

"Which was?"

"We were discussing the elements today, and I said something stupid."

"Like?"

"Lord Omyon asked us to list off elements in elimination style. We couldn't say an element the others had said previously."

"Wait. There are like one-hundred-and-fifty-four of those, though."

Edwyrd craned his neck. "How do you—"

"We're learning about them in school right now. Well, surely not as much as you are learning about them."

"They teach that at your age?" Edwyrd looked incredulously at his sister, who was seven years younger than him, not even a teenager yet. He bit his lip, trying to remember his own intermediate education. *Maybe the curriculum has changed.* Shaking his head and waving off his sister, he said, "Yes. There are. Lord Omyon's goal was to get us familiar with all the elements, not ones just found on Pyre. At one point, I had said emotions. Then the others burst out laughing. It ended there."

"Over that? What did Lord Omyon do?"

"He studied me for a while, and then we moved onto potions."

"What caused you to say emotions?"

"Oscar, the guy you just met. He mentioned tears. It was the element I was going to say, so stumbling to find a different answer, I said emotions instead." Edwyrd sighed. "Let's go." He stood up and began walking away from the castle grounds.

Alicia hurried after him. "And how did potions fare?"

"No better."

"Why is that?"

"You ask a bunch of questions."

"I'm curious about your training."

"Is that why you're here?"

"No."

"Then why?"

Edwyrd continued walking along, waiting for Alicia to say something but when she didn't, he stopped and turned back to her. "Alicia? Why are you here?"

"I..." She blushed. "I wanted to see where he goes."

"Where who goes?"

"The Recluse?" She forced a laugh and kicked the dirt. Lowering her head slightly, she looked up at him.

Edwyrd shook his head and threw his arms up in the air. "You are obsessed with him, aren't you?"

"Not obsessed," Alicia stressed. "I just think he's interesting, is all. He doesn't talk ever in town. Mother and Father say he's been living outside Steorra's boundaries ever since they were little themselves. What if the dragons weren't as deadly as legends make them out to be?"

Edwyrd laughed. "Care to try?"

"Ha-ha. Very funny."

"I thought so." He wrapped an arm around his sister and pulled her in close. When he roughed up her hair, she pulled back.

"Hey! Don't do that. I like my hair."

Edwyrd stopped for a moment. "Sorry, sis. I like it, too."

Alicia harrumphed.

"I like it so much I can't keep my hands off of it." Edwyrd maneuvered his body in front of his sister and this time roughed up her hair with both of his hands.

Alicia screamed and ran around Edwyrd. He chased after her all the way to their parents' home. Alicia never stopped screaming, and Edwyrd never stopped laughing.

"Mom, make him stop! He's ruining my hair."

Alicia had wasted no time in calling their mother to her defense as they entered their modest house.

"Edwyrd!"

Edwyrd stopped chasing his sister, and when his mother came around the corner of the entrance hallway his smile faded. "I'm just having a little fun with her."

"He's torturing me," Alicia exaggerated.

"Enough torture. Time to eat. Your father will be home any minute now."

"Okay," Edwyrd relented.

"Go get cleaned up. I don't want you smelling up the table after your training sessions with Lord Omyon."

"They weren't even that difficult," Alicia said.

"And how would you know, young lady?"

"Uhmmm..."

"Were you over by the castle grounds today? Edwyrd, was she by the—"

"She saw the Recluse today."

"Pah." Edwyrd's mother shook her head. "A strange old man he is. You shouldn't be chasing after him, little lady."

"But he travels outside the bubble barriers."

"Edwyrd, go get cleaned up," his mother said, changing the topic.

Edwyrd obliged his mother and went outside to a thermal bath spring that every Novian family had. It was naturally heated by the thermic currents underneath the planet of fire in the system. While the nation of Nova certainly wasn't as hot as the neighboring nation, Therus, it had a pleasant warmth about it. It was a nation tucked away behind the eastward mountains and full of numerous hotsprings.

He didn't know how long he spent in the thermal bath; the orange clouds gathering in the skies caught his attention, as did the dragons floating behind them, only noticeable by the bursts of light that swelled the air behind the clouds. Could the Recluse be right? Were dragons not as dangerous as Lord Omyon would have them believe? After only giving it a minute's consideration, he shook the thought off as ludicrous. The Recluse was an outlier, whoever he might be. And he would always remain outside the barriers of normality.

Dressing himself in a fresh pair of pants and shirt, he went back inside to the dining room. His eyes bulged when he saw his father sitting at the head of the table with Lord Omyon to his right. His mother was sitting to his father's left, and Alicia sat next to her. His sister, like usual, had been keeping Lord Omyon preoccupied with questions, but when Edwyrd wandered back in all eyes shifted to him.

"Lord Omyon?" Edwyrd stumbled.

"Edwyrd, come sit down and have a seat. We're waiting on you to begin. You can sit next to Lord Omyon here." His father raised an arm and pointed Edwyrd to the seat across from his sister.

Was this Lord Omyon coming to tell him he has been eliminated from the training program? Had his answer really been that bad? A knot formed in his stomach. This is where everything would end. This is where Lord Omyon would shame him in front of his family. Hadn't it already been bad enough stopping the entire activity after he had said his answer?

Trying to ignore his impending fate, Edwyrd obliged his father and settled into the chair next to Lord Omyon as comfortably as he could. After his father led them in the Twelve's Blessing prayer, a prayer that Edwyrd had noticed Lord Omyon didn't take part in, they dug into the food on the table: skewered lizards, gathered flora from the garden markets, and to Edwyrd's surprise, sliced and seared strips of imported wyvern meat covered in fire sauce.

After swallowing his first strip of wyvern, Edwyrd's father looked at him. "Edwyrd, Lord Omyon came to find me today as work was closing."

Edwyrd's neck tightened. He continued staring at his plate, slicing the strip of his own meat vertically to avoid meeting his father's eyes.

"You said something today while in your program that intrigued him."

Edwyrd's shoulders slumped. He knew it. This was it. Not even wanting to put the strip of meat into his mouth, he looked up at his father and then at Lord Omyon. "I'm sorry that I ruined your activity today."

Lord Omyon arched an eyebrow. "Ruined the activity? What makes you say that?"

"Because my answer made everyone else laugh."

"I wasn't laughing."

"That's because you never laugh."

"If I would have thought your answer was silly, I would have laughed." Lord Omyon flashed a smile. "Tell me, why did you answer that way?"

"I was going to say tears," Edwyrd said, avoiding the topic.

"But Oscar had said tears."

"I know. I couldn't remember any of the other ones, so I said the first thing that came to my mind."

"And that was emotions?" When Edwyrd nodded, Lord Omyon followed up. "And why do you think emotions are elements?"

"I..." Edwyrd looked around the table. Everyone held their breath, knowing their place amongst the lord of the nation. "What does it matter, anyway?" Edwyrd stabbed at his bed of flora and plopped it in his mouth.

"It matters to me a great deal. Now, why did you say it?"

Edwyrd swallowed and rolled his eyes. "I don't know. Just..." His mind raced, hoping an answer would come to him. He began speaking, hoping he could produce something intelligible and plausible for the lord to believe and give him another chance. "Just that we all seem to be made of different emotions."

"How so?" Lord Omyon's eyes flashed. He tilted his head forward in Edwyrd's direction.

"You're serious. My sister is always curious. My mother is the kindest person I know. My father is hardworking."

"And you?"

"I'm... I'm..." What was he? What was his dominant emotion? "I'm logical."

"Logical? That is an interesting word choice."

"I couldn't think of anything else," he admitted.

"What then makes you think that *emotions* was a logical answer today?"

Edwyrd was getting annoyed by the interrogation, but he tried hiding it as best as he could through his straightened posture and focused attention. "Because it makes sense to me that if tears of a blind person could be used to make theoretical invisible elixirs, or tears from a goddess could prolong life, then there has to be something more making those two things different. Something changes them."

"Could it not just be the fact that one person is blind, and the other is a goddess?"

"It could be. But that doesn't explain why we are all such vastly different beings, as I mentioned before. Some are more prone to anger, and others are more prone to love. It's almost as if we are built from our emotions."

Lord Omyon studied him for a long while. Long enough to cause goosepimples to cover Edwyrd's arms. Eventually, he took his eyes off of Edwyrd and then studied his father and mother for a long while. "Edwyrd's training program is finished."

"Lord Omyon, I promise to be—"

Lord Omyon raised his hand. Edwyrd stopped. "He will move on to be under my direct tutelage for the next three years."

Edwyrd coughed. His mother and father gasped.

"Does that mean?"

"Yes, it does. Edwyrd, you will be my mentee."

"For what?" Alicia's sister asked. "What's going on?"

"Your brother will be studying directly under me as I prepare him for a potential voyage off planet."

"Off planet?" Alicia looked at Edwyrd, confused.

Edwyrd's eyes twitched slightly before he forced a smile. His stomach knotted as his heart panged. "It's... it's nothing, Sis."

"Whoa, whoa, whoa. You are going to go off planet? I thought this training was only because of your academics at school. One of those things Mother called it."

"An internship, Alicia. It was. And Edwyrd has passed. Edwyrd, my boy, you did it." Edwyrd's mother stood up and maneuvered around the table to hug her son. "You did it. You did it."

"When were you going to tell me?"

"Alicia, I..."

It was too late. Alicia had already thrown down her linen and stormed outside. His mother massaged his shoulders and spoke into his ears. "I'll go calm her down, Son. You stay here. Alicia, please wait." His mother departed from the dining room.

"So, my lord, what does this mean for Edwyrd?"

"It means he will have regular training with me now. Only me. Even though the Trials are still a few years away, unless he becomes my mentee, he will not have the foundational training the others will certainly possess by then."

"Do you think that'll be enough time? I don't want my boy to get injured."

"Edwyrd has his own decision to make regarding the Trials, Max. But Edwyrd,"—Lord Omyon shifted in his chair to look at him now—"know that if you accept my invitation to train under me, I will be sponsoring you for the event. And the Trials you face will be dangerous."

"But if I win, I would be Guardian of the Core."

"Yes. In time, you would become Guardian of the Core."

The impending weight of that title caused his shoulders to slump now. He wanted to feel happy in this moment, that he had said something, albeit unintentional, that had caused Lord Omyon to look at him differently, and now he was on the path to the most renowned position in the system—the Guardian of the Core. A position who treated with the Twelve, who knew the mysteries of old, who lived longer than others, and who had unfathomable Power, at least in the stories he read. And wisdom, too. A position created to protect against foreign threats and the infamous Curse of Pirini Lilapa. And while all of that certainly should have made Edwyrd's heart skip beats and his imagination soar across fields, he felt as confused as Alicia.

"I need some time to think about it," Edwyrd forced out.

"Of course. If you want to start this path, come to my castle tomorrow morning. I will be waiting for you there. If you don't come, then I'll continue with the other boys the day after."

The three of them continued eating their food. For a while, Edwyrd thoughtlessly put food into his mouth and chewed, but took no pleasure in it. His mind was elsewhere. As was his heart. He excused himself from the table and went to go find Alicia and his mother.

He found them outside on the wooden bench swing that overlooked their backyard. It sat next to the thermal bath. Alicia was cradled in her mother's arms. Edwyrd put a hand on his mother's shoulders.

"Alicia, Edwyrd is here." She stood up. "I'll leave you two alone."

"Thanks, Mother."

Edwyrd took his mother's spot next to Alicia, who now sat rigid and upright on the bench next to him. They swung slightly back and forth, the only sounds the slight passing of wind, the creaking of wood, and the light scuffle of feet hitting dirt.

"So, you're going to leave?"

"Only if I accept."

"And why wouldn't you?"

"Because it all seems so crazy right now. I didn't expect this at all. When I saw Lord Omyon at dinner tonight, I thought he came to tell me I failed, not that I had passed some unseen test."

"And now you might become the Guardian of the Core?"

"Only if I pass the Trials, Alicia."

"Lord Omyon would make sure of that. You would be training under him."

"There will be others there."

"Cautious."

"Excuse me?" Edwyrd cocked his head.

"That's what you are, if you ask me. Cautious. Not logical."

"I could be risking my life in attending that event."

"And when has anything great ever come from not taking a chance?"

Edwyrd didn't have an answer. When did his sister become so sage-like? He sighed. "You're right."

"I know I am. And you should have told me earlier."

"I would have."

"When?"

"If I had actually ever been accepted. I just didn't think I would have been accepted like this."

"Why do you think Lord Omyon wants you to participate?"

"Because I'll be his trainee if I show up at his castle grounds tomorrow."

Alicia shook her head. She twisted her body, putting one leg up on the bench, letting the other one dangle off. "I mean, why do you think Lord Omyon wants anyone to do that?"

"I..." Edwyrd paused. Not wanting to appear unsure, Edwyrd quickly recovered and said, "Because it is a once in a lifetime opportunity." In truth, he had actually never thought about that. He just assumed that any instructor would want to see their student reach the pinnacle of strength in the system, and that is why he would agree to sponsor them. Could there actually be another motive?

"Well, when you become Guardian of the Core, you can take me all over the system to see how the others live. I heard there are planets of water, and even sky planets."

He scooted closer to his sister on the bench. "If I win, I'll take you there."

"You promise?" She held out her pinky finger.

Edwyrd looked at it, understanding the trust she placed in him. "I promise." He wrapped his pinky finger around hers. He kicked the ground underneath the bench, pushing the chair into its pendulum swing once more. There they rocked and rocked for more beats than Edwyrd could count.

CHAPTER 1

A pair of dragons soared in the air above the enormous bubble barrier that encapsulated the castle grounds. For those not native to the planet, the surprisingly equal dragon-to-people ratio would have incurred a great degree of angst, but for natives like Edwyrd Eska, it was normal. In fact, he had quickly learned over his past two years of studying exclusively under Lord Omyon's tutelage that everyone in Nova could have had their own dragon, if the beast would ever allow itself to be domesticated, though Edwyrd doubted that could ever happen. No, the only way one would have a pet dragon was to bond with it, but what that entailed, he didn't want to know. Nor had his mentor deemed it pertinent enough to teach him.

Regardless of those caveats, though, and his twenty years of living on the planet already, he couldn't help but stop and admire dragons whenever he saw them passing overhead. That is why Edwyrd usually was known for having his head in the clouds. A part of him wanted to fly through the air with one. See it up close. Not just through the protective bubble barriers that kept them from entering any of the cities in Nova, barriers constructed by their one and only lord, Garrett Omyon.

During his time under Lord Omyon's private tutelage, Edwyrd had learned that his interminable reign extended as far back as any history book could recount. Lord Omyon, for all Edwyrd had gleaned from the copious amount of studying he did in the library when he wasn't practicing his swordsmanship, potions, or Power with the lord, wasn't like anyone else in Nova. In fact, he wasn't like anyone on the planet as far as he knew. The lord had First Blood. That was one of the first things Edwyrd had learned from his mentor. And if that was true, then that meant he came from the fabled lands of Gladima, the center of their system. The place where the Twelve came from. Yet, he wasn't one of the Twelve. What *did* that make him, then?

Edwyrd had been hoping his mentor would reveal that to him on his own volition, but the man never much liked talking about himself. His humble deportment, his title, his mysteriousness, and his surprising adroitness in combat, made Edwyrd respect this man even more then when he accepted his invitation for studying. It made the man powerful, and so at the end of the day, his true background didn't matter as much to Edwyrd as did the education and training he was receiving. That is why Edwyrd never wasted a breath, except, of course, when he was staring at dragons roaming the sky above the castle grounds.

"How do you do it?" Edwyrd asked.

"Do what?" His mentor huffed.

Edwyrd took his gaze from the sky. His eyes bulged. Lord Omyon was lugging a basin of water to the stone court. "Let me do that for you." He rushed over and took charge of the situation, dragging the basin to the last of the four spots. The other three held the other elements: earth, fire, and electricity. With each of them present and visible, Power could be cast, and now the training could begin.

"I was wondering when you would help me and stop looking up."

"I..." Edwyrd blushed. "I'm sorry, my lord. My attention was—"

"Up in the clouds. I know. Like usual."

"It's just that dragons are just so... so..." Edwyrd struggled to find the right word. "Majestic."

Lord Omyon shielded his eyes with his forearm and glanced upwards. "These two are. But not all of them are so regal." He took his gaze away, and Edwyrd did the same. "Remember this, Edwyrd, they may look nice; you may think that you can control them, but they are dangerous beasts. Dragons are like Ether Weapons. Pretty to look at but will bite if you get too close."

Edwyrd's eyes lit up. "Ether Weapons? I've read about those! Have you seen one before?"

"I've done more than seen one. I used to own one, but I gave it to a friend who needs it more than me."

Edwyrd's eye doubled in size. He coughed at the incredulity of the idea. To give up an Ether Weapon? When there were only eleven of them ever created!? Not knowing what to say, he merely said, "Friend?"

"Yes, Edwyrd, I, too, have friends."

"Like who?" Edwyrd tried to think about everyone who he had seen during his time with his mentor but could only recall one instance when the marquis of Orion came down from the north to stay at the castle for a few days. The marquis hadn't appeared to be a friend, though, merely an acquaintance to the lord. And he didn't brandish an Ether Weapon. Edwyrd would have spotted that immediately.

"It doesn't matter."

"The Recluse?"

Lord Omyon eyed him for a long while. "I don't know who you're talking about."

"Sure you do. Everyone does. That strange man who always carries a shield wherever he goes and walks with a staff. He comes into town sometimes. I think he watches me train sometimes when I'm outside of the courtyard."

"Oh, you saw him spying on you, did you, hmmmm?" Lord Omyon arched an eyebrow.

Edwyrd blushed. "Well, maybe. He likes to roam about on top of that hill overlooking the grounds. My sister has even seen him a few times there. Is he searching for something?"

"How do you know it was him?"

"He is the only one crazy enough to go outside the bubble barrier you erected over the city. And I think I saw him leaning on that staff of his."

"Well, he is not much of a recluse then if he is so visible, is he?"

Edwyrd's mouth was agape. "I..."

"It doesn't matter who that man is. His business is his own. As should be yours. Learning to mind your business and focus on yourself will be your best ally should you be accepted for the Trials."

"Do you think I will be accepted?"

"You have my sponsorship. I have high faith that Guardian Crevon will realize how valuable that is."

The confidence in his mentor's voice placated Edwyrd's qualms, like usual. "Thank you, my lord." Edwyrd bowed his head.

"Do not be so anxious, Edwyrd. If you do become the next Guardian of the Core, you will realize how inconsequential a few years can be to one's life. The two years I have known you will be like nothing."

He blinked and blushed. "Of course. My apologies. Patience is a virtue."

"And it's something all of us First Blood have since leaving Gladima."

"What happened there?" Edwyrd's chest tightened. Would today be the day he learned about the lord's past?

"The Great War."

"I know. But what was it?"

Omyon's eyes surveyed his trainee. "A story for another day. If you want to know about it, win the Trials. The Twelve will explain it to you."

Edwyrd deflated. Once again, the man refused broaching the topic of his past. But he wouldn't push him. Patience was a virtue, as his mentor had taught him many times before, and so he would hold out hope that eventually Lord Omyon would reveal the rest of the mystery.

Thinking of a way to continue the conversation, he laughed, hoping to disguise his disappointment.

"So you never answered my question. How do you create the barriers?"

"You never truly asked me. You got distracted. Distractions are always your biggest weakness. Make sure you don't have any during the Trials. It will be the difference between losing and winning, and maybe even life and death."

Another nervous laugh escaped Edwyrd. He put his arms back to his side. "Of course. No distractions." He leaned his body forward and arched an eyebrow. "So?"

"Potions. But we are not here today to discuss potions. We are here for Power. So let us begin."

Without letting Edwyrd have any more time to talk, his mentor flung a fireball at Edwyrd, who rolled to his right to avoid it. He jumped as the earth trembled under him, escaping the hand that came from the floor to grasp at his ankle. And when electricity assailed him from his left, he fought for control of earth with his mentor, managing to carve out enough control of the Power to raise a shield. And this pattern of striking and defense and evasive tactics continued until he finally succumbed to a mistake when Lord Omyon enveloped both of them and the basin of fire inside an earthen dome. Then, the man cast the spell for fire and it crept towards Edwyrd. Try as he might to combat the earth with his own earth spell, this time his mentor wouldn't allow him the ability to co-control the Power, leaving him defenseless. Edwyrd tried drawing upon the basin of fire, but his mentor held an even greater control over that spell, a control that would have required a great deal of energy to overcome. The drill ended when Edwyrd surrendered to the flames slowly encroaching on his position.

"How did I do?" he asked through panting breaths.

"More competent than yesterday."

Edwyrd's heart stung. Lord Omyon supplied him with the same answer daily. And it told Edwyrd nothing. "Will it be enough?"

"Enough?" Lord Omyon hummed.

"For the Trials."

Lord Omyon inclined his head. "Edwyrd, what you think is Power now is truly nothing but a geyser when compared to the eruption of a volcano."

Edwyrd blinked at the comparison. Was there truly such an extravagant difference in strength? "What will the caliber be like in the Trials?"

"Like you. Or better."

"Better?"

"Yes. Better. I've done my best in accelerating your skills to a level competent enough to compete in the Trials, but there are people who were born into this lifestyle. People who can cast blue flames, not just red flames. People who are more mentally adroit than you. And maybe even individuals who are stronger than you. I heard Lord Haco nominated a fireson to compete."

"A fireson?" Edwyrd gulped.

"And not just any fireson. Cyrus Oraine if rumors hold true. He is strong and will be a contender."

He had never heard about this particular individual before, but he knew of the reputation of the firesons. They were the personal guards for the Lord of Therus. The fact alone that he was from Therus made him formidable, but knowing he was a fireson on top of it, well, it caused shivers to run down his forearms despite the heat outside.

"What are the chances that he will be selected?"

"Assuming you are selected, he will be chosen too."

"How do you know?"

Lord Omyon opened his mouth and then closed it. He hummed. "Just a feeling I have."

"What can I do to improve?"

Lord Omyon chuckled. "You can continue to ask questions. It's good to have an inquisitive mind, but I do think you have reached your peak potential in terms of Power. That is, unless you win the Trials, become Guardian of the Core, and are imbued with the Power of the Twelve, or if you manage to bond with an animal."

"How would I go about doing that? Bonding I mean."

Lord Omyon scoffed. "You will have no say in the matter. If the animal intends to bond with you, it will seek you out, or fate will put you in each other's paths. Often it is in the most precarious of circumstances."

"Like when?"

"Like when you are at your lowest."

"How come you have never bonded?"

"I chose not to."

Edwyrd blinked. "You mean?" He stumbled over his words. "You... you met your animal? What was it?"

"A story for another day, perhaps. Follow me. It's time we practice your other abilities."

Edwyrd followed him inside the castle, leaving the courtyard. He knew what they were going to do next. They did it after Power training every day. And the monotony of every day was something that Edwyrd felt he needed to escape from.

Inside a canteen area on the first floor of the castle, Lord Omyon ushered Edwyrd into a room full of physical elements. This is where they conducted alchemy and practiced knowledge in the adored arts. While Blessed individuals who could cast Power fought and destroyed, those who were adored followed a path of peace and healing. Lord Omyon knew extensively about this subject, and it was only a byproduct of luck that Edwyrd's answer had caused his mentor to take interest in him.

The day after Edwyrd had gained that interest, he had made his way to Lord Omyon's castle to accept his training and his mentor brought him here. He had been in this room before; it was where he had trained with the others in the art of potion making. That day, however, Lord Omyon had revealed to him that these were simply physical elements. This is what comprised the worlds and the system they lived in. That day, Lord Omyon revealed that humans were first created out of what the Ancients had come to call emotions. These were the internal elements and the most important elements as they influenced the strength and potency of the other physical and natural elements.

Emotions gave too many people away, Lord Omyon had taught him, and so if he could master his emotions, he would surprise many. When asked how Lord Omyon knew this fact himself, the lord claimed to have trained under Ancient Lyoen. The rest of his training had made sense in Edwyrd's eyes, why he was so well-trained on the myriad of subjects he now taught Edwyrd, and why he was such an expert in alchemy.

So, like usual, Edwyrd spent the next hour learning about various combinations of herbs and liquids that went into potion making. How to heal. How to create poisons. How to create tonics for rejuvenation. Or even those that would slow down reaction times, jumble thoughts, or incapacitate individuals without killing them.

By the day's end, Edwyrd had finished Power training, his study of the adored arts, and even practiced physical endurance with a gauntlet of activities set up behind the castle.

With a sore body, Edwyrd walked home. While Lord Omyon could have given him ard leaves to heal him right away, his mentor thought it was good for his character to experience how such soreness felt. Moreover, it was to teach him not to rely on ard leaves to regain his vitality, and if anything, he would need to learn to transcend the pain if he wanted to make strides in his performance.

At home, Edwyrd entered into a scene that he didn't expect. His mother and his father sat on their couch of clay hunched over. His younger sister, Alicia, wasn't around. On the felsic table in front of them lay a blue envelope with his name written in silver.

His heart beat faster. *Could this be?*

One foot in front of the other, he inched forward, time seeming to slow. With a shaky hand, he picked up the letter and flipped it over. His breath hitched, and he choked. His mother looked at him with a tremble in her lower lip that she carefully nibbled away and his father with furrowed eyes, set and intent on the fate and destiny that lay before him. Now that this day had finally come, would they still be as accepting? Had they only ever thought the opportunity as a fairytale? Did Edwyrd even want this opportunity anymore?

He turned his gaze back to the seal and let his fingers slid over the embossed silver lion sigil on the back. He didn't have to open it to know what it said. There was only one reason why he was receiving a personally addressed letter from the Guardian of the Core—he was accepted.

When arms wrapped around him, his qualms subsided. His mother's angst had faded away, replaced with a bounty of appreciation. Her cheeks dimpled as she smiled. Bringing her son lower to her level, she kissed his forehead and then released him to grab him by his shoulders.

By this time, his father had come over, hand extended. "We knew this day would come eventually. Congratulations, Son."

Edwyrd took it.

"Does Alicia know yet? Where is she?"

"We haven't seen her all day," his mother said. She spoke with a smile that spread from ear to ear.

"And to think that this would happen. Truly, what fate is this?" His father mused.

Edwyrd began thinking about that too. Both his father and mother couldn't cast Power. Yet, for some reason, he and his sister could both cast. For all Edwyrd knew, neither family's side could cast Power, so Power suddenly being imbued to children of a Denied lineage was quite the interesting turn of fate.

"I'll find Alicia and tell her."

His parents nodded and returned to the sofa.

Because his father and mother couldn't use Power, Edwyrd searched within himself in order to find his sister. It was a process known as Blood Scrying, and only those with Power could use it accurately to track down others of their bloodline. As Lord Omyon taught him, he closed his eyes and focused on Alicia's pulse. Lips contorted in confusion, he opened his eyes.

"What is it?"

"Where is she?"

Without thinking, Edwyrd mumbled, "Outside."

His parents shot up to their feet again. "What was that?"

"Did you say outside? What do you mean *outside*?"

Edwyrd blinked. For once he wished he had been alone when he had decided to search for her. He fumbled for a way to calm his parents' mounting anxiety, apparent by the way they hovered around him.

"From what I could tell she's just outside the barriers. Probably wanted to see how different it is outside than inside the barriers. You know how curious she is. I'll go get her now and bring her back."

His mother went to the window and pulled back the maroon curtains. "It's getting dark. I do hope she hasn't wandered too far away." She leaned this way and that in a futile attempt to spot her from inside.

"Do you need me to come with you?" his father asked.

"No. But I should leave now. As Mother said, it's getting dark." Edwyrd gave the blue envelope to his father and immediately left the house, not wanting to wait to hear another word from his parents. While the answer he gave them sufficed, it was really only a half-truth.

If he had told them the truth that Alicia wasn't anywhere close to Steorra's barriers, they would have worried. If he had told them that Alicia was currently in the middle of Dragon's Ruins heading westward, they would have panicked. But if he had told them that Alicia's heartrate was high, that she was using Power, and that she was currently undergoing some sort of fight, they would have gone berserk. Edwyrd had a hard enough time controlling his emotions as it was, but he remembered how powerful of an element they were from Lord Omyon. If he showed fear, his parents would only buckle under the enormity of the situation. That is why he remained stoic. But as he walked out into the warm air of a settling dusk, his stolidity slipped into determination and apprehension, and he bolted forward, ready to save his sister from whatever predicament she was in.

CHAPTER 2

V ictor Zigarda stood alongside his younger brother in their father's attendance chamber where he would see the citizens as they voiced their
individual concerns about the nation. Duty brought them to this hall, and it was
their father's intention to groom them into well-respected leaders and carry
on the family legacy. Up until about three hours prior, that was Victor Zigarda's
fullest intent—to carry on his father's legacy—but now it seemed fate had seen
fit to grant him another path.

Hands behind his back, and keeping his torso partially turned from his
brother, he waited patiently for his father to finish seeing the last citizen
who had made an appointment with him, rotating in his hands a sealed blue
envelope that had come especially for him from the Guardian of the Core
himself. Oh, how proud his father would be and how jealous his brother. Or
maybe his brother would be happy for Victor. After all, once he won the Trials,
he would ascend to a title and rank far beyond their family station, he would
have the Power of the Twelve, he would live forever—or, at least until the next
Guardian was chosen—and his brother would inherit the throne that would
have passed to Victor through blood. Everyone would win.

"You have traveled far to be here today, Asher. Do not worry about the south.
Plans are finished, and a bridge is being constructed to connect the north with
the south. Soon the north will be of the south as well. You will have all the
amenities that we northerners have."

"But when will that be? The Chaons, my lord, they are expanding their
influence."

"As long as we control the isles off the side of Verimas, the city will continue
to be ours. Do not worry about Chaon."

"How can we be expected to meet our quotas with the crops we plant when
they steal what we sow?"

"Your story is not unlike others in the area. Perhaps I can reduce your load this quarter. Does that seem fair?"

Asher's eyes lit up. The flat line on his face broadened. "Yes. It certainly is good news, my lord."

"Go and let it be done. I will tell the marquis of Aeston the same as what I've told you."

Asher scrambled to his feet, bumbling his thanks all the while. After an elongated bow, he scurried out into the hallway, the double doors of the chamber resounding behind him.

From the throne to their left, their father looked at them. First at Victor and then at his brother. "Renaul, what would you have done if you were me in that situation?"

"I wouldn't have changed anything, Father."

Victor's stomach churned. His brother was always seeking his father's approval, destined to be a people-pleaser more than a pragmatist. Or perhaps it was just a lack of maturity? After all, he was seven years younger than Victor with time to eventually formulate his own opinions. But was never having an opinion worse than always mimicking the advice of another? Victor wondered if his father saw through his brother's adulation.

His father coughed into his fist. "And you, Victor? What do you think?"

"Why acquiesce to demands? They have a quota that isn't even high, and they should meet it. Survival of the fittest. If you bend the knee on this, what will they request next of you?"

His father studied Victor for a long while. He pushed himself off his throne. Before standing fully upright, he put a hand to his forehead as if balancing himself.

"Father?" Victor asked, stepping forward slightly.

His father stood upright and waved him off. "Got up too fast. Nothing to worry about." He shook his head and then carried his middle-aged body down the slight set of steps.

"I can find an adored from the apothecary to go to your chambers, my lord." His father's advisor, who had stationed himself off on the other side of the throne, moved to stand at the foot of the staircase.

"It's nothing, Darmus. I'm fine." Victor's father side-stepped his advisor and walked to stand before his two sons.

"Benevolence is a good trait to have, Victor."

"And I am not saying it isn't. Nor am I saying I do not have it. I just do not think this man's demand required any sort of benevolence."

"And why is that?"

"Well, if Chaon truly was disrupting Verimas to the extent of concern, it would justify a war, and I highly doubt the Chaons would want to go to war with us."

Renaul scoffed alongside him. "And why is that?"

Victor huffed. Did he have to explain everything to his younger brother? Why couldn't his brother read between the lines? Was he really that slow? With furrowed brows, Victor turned. "Because Empora is superior to Chaon. To war with us means to drag a razor along their own skin." He turned back to his father. "I say, let Verimas fend for itself and if it is truly an Emporian city worth having, it will rise to the occasion. That is what any good leader does, rise to the occasion, no matter the obstacle in his way."

A smile flashed across his father's face. "You always did have a way with words, Victor." His father inclined his head. "Yes, I do think you are right in these regards. It wasn't necessary to reduce their quota this quarter, but it is only ninety days of reprieve, and I feel generous today." His father patted the outer shoulder of each son and looked at each one in turn. "Do you know why?"

Now it was Victor's turn to cautiously survey his father. Had he already found out Victor's surprise? No, it was impossible. Victor had received it himself directly from a guard. Sure, the guard had delivered it to him, but he had told the guard to not mention it to his father, as he wanted it to be a surprise. Had the man disobeyed? Victor twitched his lips to the side. Feigning ignorance, he said, "I haven't the slightest idea."

His father cocked his head. "Victor, why so shy? Come on now. Show us. You have been waiting for some time now."

Victor cleared his throat and brought out the blue envelope to the forefront, revealing the letter to everyone in the room. "This arrived from the Guardian of the Core today. It is my acceptance letter to participate in the Trials."

His brother shifted his weight.

The eyes of his father's advisor doubled in size. "That is certainly worthy of quite the celebration. Congratulations, Prince Zigarda."

"With the Sages sponsoring me, I knew I would be accepted," Victor said triumphantly.

"They certainly are adequate sponsors. And, speaking of which, Byron tells me they are coming to the Web today."

"They are here?"

"They will be shortly. I suspect—"

Just then, the ceremonial doors to the chamber opened and in entered his father's receiver with four older men. Victor's eyes widened. *They're here.* He skipped a breath.

"Well, speak of good tidings." His father turned and extended his arms outward in a grand gesture of acceptance. "Sage Cronos, how nice of you to join us, especially today on such a historic occasion." With the help of the metal walling, his voice carried across the hall easily.

The Sages remained silent until they were closer to the group.

"My lord. I heard the news. Prince Zigarda is accepted?"

"He is."

"I am," Victor said simultaneously with his father.

"This is certainly joyous news."

Like his brother, his father's receiver was a people-pleaser as well. Although, in Victor's eyes, it was a little more acceptable. To be a receiver, one should be amiable and always show pleasantry as part of their duty. But the empty praise made Victor wonder. Did anyone use their minds nowadays? Why did it seem everyone was so bent on pleasing the others instead of telling individuals what they needed to hear?

"I wanted to surprise you today, Father. How did you find out?"

"You should know that there are flies all over this Web." He chuckled at his own joke.

Victor pushed his lips to his side. *Yes. Flies like undutiful guards. Hmmmm...* "Well, I cannot say that I tried keeping it from you."

"And it was of good intention, Son. I am proud of you." His father stepped forward and clapped Victor on both shoulders. "Truly you are going to bring even more Power to the Zigarda name." He kissed his son's forehead and stepped between him and his younger brother. He turned his body to the Sages, who had now finally joined their circle. "Isn't that right, Cronos? What has that staff of yours seen?"

Goosepimples popped up on Victor's skin as he looked from the bi-color eyes of Cronos to the Ether Staff in his hand. His family never had an Ether Weapon, and it has always been one of Victor's dreams to hold one in his hand, but that is all it ever would remain unless he became the Guardian of the Core. Then he would be granted the Ether Blade, Adonis. With it, he would have a weapon that could cut through any material in existence, or so the stories went. And when his mind thought about the weapon he would soon obtain, he wondered what other specialties it brought with it. After all, Cronos's Ether Staff could see the future, or so the sage claimed, and while he had certainly been right about Victor's acceptance, had there ever been any doubt? The real question was, would Victor truly win the Trials?

"Victor will win the Trials. There will hardly be competition for him."

"Is that so?"

Cronos nodded. "From what I've learned about the other Trials participants, he is one of four who can cast blue flames."

"There will be others there like me?" Victor asked.

"No. Only one other like you. The other two will be of no concern."

"Why is that?" his father asked.

"Because they won't have had Victor's upbringing."

"And the other one?"

"Plans are in place." Cronos bobbed his head. "How you've raised him will be his advantage, Hayden.

These Trials will be similar to the last one. They will test intelligence, leadership, Power, and combat skills. And I do believe out of all of those accepted, he has the making of a true guardian. That is why I sponsored him."

Victor couldn't help but beam. Leaning forward on his tiptoes, he gave a furtive glance towards his brother, who just stared silently in front of him, obviously annoyed at his praises. A simple victory, but certainly sweet, nonetheless.

"Knowledge is Power."

Victor chuckled at his family's motto. "Knowledge is Power." He repeated his father's words.

"Knowledge is Power," Cronos repeated. "And Foresight here tells me he will succeed. Very soon, Hayden, your son will be the next apprentice. And when he is Guardian, he can repay us for our faith in him."

"How could I possibly repay the generosity and confidence you have bestowed upon me?" Victor bowed a little.

"Win first; we can discuss later." A glint of mystery lay within the sage's bi-color eyes. "For now, we only came to congratulate you."

Victor itched with curiosity to understand why the Sages needed him. Him? What could he do for them? They were of First Blood. They possessed an Ether Weapon. They had a certain prescience he had never heard of before. And they were responsible for testing individuals for Power throughout the system.

They had tested him at five years old, after he cast his first spell of Power, a blue flame. Since then every time they came, they always said something that had been on his mind or had given some sort of vision that shortly came to pass afterwards. After noting his blue flames that day, they had told his father that his son was meant for greatness. He wondered if they had seen his future, this very moment, the moment before he became Guardian of the Core, in the blue flame he had cast for them that day, or if the blue flame had merely been the prerequisite to pique their interest.

Once he did become Guardian, as they foresaw, how much more powerful would he become under their guidance? And then how much more powerful would he become under the guidance of the current Guardian? And even the

Twelve? Victor's mind raced as he thought of all the possibilities his success would bring and only wished these Trials would start the day after.

As it were, the Trials would begin in seventy-two hours. The Guardian of the Core himself would be picking up Victor from his father's compound and from there would transport him back to the Core. How they would go without the use of a spaceship, he didn't know; or, maybe, the Guardian of the Core had a personal spaceship. Victor chastised himself. Of course, the Guardian had a personal spaceship. He was the Guardian of the Core, after all. But did the Sages have their own transport? How did they manage to get around? Or did they, too, have to subject themselves to the overwhelming swarm of people and long waiting lists for those wanting to travel by the interplanetary transport crafts fueled by the suns' solar power?

"You made quite the travel."

As if reading Victor's thoughts, Cronos responded, "Having our own vessel, we can travel easier than most."

The prescience of the sage sent shivers up Victor's skin. And a part of him wondered if his father's body shivered the same way his did whenever they spoke with clairvoyance. Did he put as much stock in their words as Victor did? Surely, he must. After all, these were the beings that had warned him of wife's death. Victor still had no idea what death meant at this point, and his father had refused to talk about it with him after they had left when they visited him at the age of seven, but it had come to pass. As everything they said came to pass.

"And we already had other business in Chaon to look into, so we—"

"Is Chaon planning something?" Renaul asked.

Victor turned towards his younger brother. The comment was out of place. One didn't just cut off the Sages, especially not one such as him. *Is he trying to show Father his attention and duty to the southern dilemma? Does he think that will help Father forgive him?*

Cronos swayed his head to Victor's younger brother. "What would make you assume that?"

Victor's father took over. "A few of the citizens today complained about increasing Chaon influence in Verimas is all."

"Verimas should be left alone. What is happening there is the rejuvenation of change."

"Change?" Renaul asked.

"It doesn't matter. We just came from there. Things will be fine. Trust us."

"I do. We do." His father stammered. "Sometimes it's hard to have faith in things we cannot see, especially since it's so far south."

"And sometimes to see is to be blind," Cronos retorted. He turned to Victor. "Put your faith in where your Power lies. Do not underestimate the others. And you will be successful."

"I will, Sage Cronos." Victor bowed, avoiding eye contact with the man's dual-colored eyes.

"Good. Then we are off. Happenings on other planets draw our attention away."

Without another word, the Sages turned around and left. The receiver led them out. The other three who stayed in the room remained silent. He didn't like it. Something felt off. He didn't know what it could be, but why had the Sages truly come there? Just to say thanks, or was there something more?

Victor jogged from the chamber, forgetting to make his formal goodbyes. He caught up with the receiver and the Sages outside of the Web. "Wait."

Cronos turned to look at him, as did the other Sages. "Yes?"

"I have a question for you."

"I already knew that." Cronos's eyes gleamed.

"Am I the first man you have ever sponsored?"

A sly smile overtook Cronos's face. "You certainly are."

"Why me?"

Cronos cast an eye at the receiver.

Victor looked at him as well. "Byron, go back inside. I can lead the Sages out of the complex."

The receiver left. Once the doors swung closed again, Cronos continued. "You have what it takes to win the Trials, Victor. That is why we chose you. And we very much need you to win."

"Why me, though?"

"You have incredible Power."

"But there are others who can cast blue flames just as well."

"There are, yes. But you have more than just Power. You have the right deportment. You do what needs to be done. And that is what Gladonus requires. A Guardian should be, decisive, assertive, focused."

"And the others aren't?"

"Not in a way like you." Cronos smirked. "You aren't afraid of bloodying your hands. And with you as Guardian of the Core, there will be much change to come and change sometimes requires sacrifice." Cronos turned around and left, leaving Victor with his thoughts.

CHAPTER 3

To Edwyrd's fortune, he didn't have to run far to reach the city limits, but it was still another ten minutes more than he would have liked. He considered stopping at Lord Omyon's castle and requesting help in navigating Dragon's Ruins, but time was of the essence, and he lived in the north of the city. As it was, Edwyrd would still have another few hours of daylight left. Summer in Nova meant that only six hours of each day were spent in true darkness.

Stepping past the city boundary, Edwyrd felt the oppressive heat of summer. Something blew across his face. Wind, if he recalled correctly. The only other times he had ever gone outside of the barrier were under the supervision of Lord Omyon while he trained with the others selected in his miniature apprenticeship. The wind pushed him west towards the ruins, and he wondered what controlled the wind's direction, or did it simply act according to its own whim? Regardless, he didn't need it to tell him where to go; he already felt Alicia's presence, and he continued holding onto it.

Solid, cracked pavement became loose sand that made his sprint even more strenuous. He left the city's borders and after another half hour came to first set of hoodoos, giant stacks of stone erected on arroyos of sand. The rocks were erected in such a way that they looked like giant fangs coming up from the sandy floor. Some of them even curved inward, breaking off at the top. From afar, Dragon's Ruins looked like the broken ribcage of a gigantic dragon. No one in their right mind would ever venture past here, so why had Alicia?

After an hour into his voyage outside of the barriers, he was deep within Dragon's Ruins. In the waning light of the suns, dragons flew overhead, scouring the land, looking for prey. Whenever Edwyrd would sense one above him, he put a shield of earthen Power over himself to blend in with his surroundings. All the while, he kept his attention on Alicia's presence. It had faded gradually in his westward journey, even though he had been coming closer to her location.

This meant she was in more trouble than he knew, but how she had even managed to keep alive for this long was a miracle Edwyrd still couldn't fathom.

But he soon realized why that was when he came across a thunder of dragons, four females and one male, if he guessed based upon the size. Each was perched on hoodoos or fallen boulders. A mix of flames constantly barraged a boulder in the center of the playa, slightly elevated and now completely dry of the water that must have, at one time, filled it. That water had tapered off into tiny rivulets running towards a lake another mile off with a gushing waterfall.

Edwyrd had the sickening realization that Alicia was trapped inside the boulder.

The other dragons hadn't noticed him yet. They were all focused on his sister, who had stowed herself inside the rock. Their fire hadn't been able to penetrate her barrier. Either that was a testament to her strength, or there was other Power he couldn't see within the hollowed-out shell of her protection.

Alicia.

Brother?

What are you doing out here?

Part of the boulder broke away. The half that still protected her was watery blue on the inside. She turned around, arms stretched out in front of her, keeping her spell active. Sweat and exhaustion blemished her face, her brown hair falling over her face, slightly covering her eyes. A smile spread across her lips. "Brother..."

In front of her, the fire stopped.

Movement to the right.

Alicia refocused. She twisted and threw up one of her hands, creating a large watery dome. Earth spread over the top of it, encasing it in a shell. A dual spell to stop fire in its tracks.

It never finished forming.

Sharper than the others, the male dragon, a large silver beast, had catapulted towards her, silver flames flowing. His hind legs picked up, bent at ninety degrees. Its torso fell backwards as if it was going to slow down. But it never did. Before Edwyrd could say anything, before he could even help his sister, the moment passed and the silver dragon stood on top of his sister, talons piercing her body. The dragon roared.

Alicia's barrier had crumbled.

The male dragon turned towards Edwyrd. Dark-red eyes the color of blood pierced him. It turned on its hind legs, grinding Alicia's body into the cracked barren pavement.

Tremors lurched through Edwyrd's body, bringing him to his knees. His sister lay motionless underneath the dragon's massive right foot. The dragon inhaled, the mythril-silver underbelly expanding to twice its size. It glowed. And the glow worked its way into the dragon's throat. It reared back its neck.

Underneath the dragon, Alicia reached out a hand towards him. Edwyrd blinked. *She's still alive.* Her fingers curled, trying to find something to hold on to. *She's still alive!*

Edwyrd got up from his knees.

The dragon roared and lurched its head forward. Mouth opened wide, it spat fire towards Edwyrd, inundating him in a deluge of silver flames.

CHAPTER 4

S ilver flames washed over Edwyrd. He had raised no barrier. He hadn't even given it a thought after seeing the large beast impale his sister and grind her into the cracked ground.

He expected to die. Just like Alicia.

But when the silver flames passed over him, leaving not even a touch of his clothing burned, he wondered what Power saved him. Was it the Ancients? The Twelve? *How am I not...* He patted his chest, feeling for something. Turning his head around, he searched out for whoever his savior must have been. Until a roar called him back to the present moment. Edwyrd pushed himself to stand, keeping his eyes locked on the dark-red eyes of the silver dragon before him. It flapped its scaly wings slowly. One beat. Two. Its mythril underbelly pulsed with each wing flap. Time stood still as both individuals faced off against one another, the beast and the man who had lived through flames.

My name is Vesel. I am yours should you choose to have me.

The thundering voice came straight into Edwyrd's mind. His heart was singed. He felt warm yet cold. The dichotomy left him in a frozen moment of disarray that he couldn't quite comprehend.

He dragged himself a little closer to the dragon, who still stood on top of his sister. "Why am I not dead?"

Because we are meant to bond.

"Wh... what?" Edwyrd shook his head, trying to shake away the rough male voice now inside of him.

I am yours should you choose to have me. We are meant to bond.

"Bah... bond?" Edwyrd sputtered the words. He clawed his way closer until he was one body's length away from the dragon. He looked from his sister's limp body to the dragon's garnet eyes. "And if I don't?"

Then you leave here and never come back. I will grant you safe passage.

"And her?" Edwyrd pointed to the body underneath its hindfoot.

Vesel removed its foot from her body.

Alicia gasped with newfound life, sucking in air as if she was a newborn. Edwyrd pushed himself up and dashed over to her. Going to his knees again, he cradled her body in his arms. Large holes defiled her, blood now spilling out of them without the talons to plug the wounds.

Wings flapped around him. Roars. Edwyrd ignored them as best as he could, focusing on his sister's russet eyes. But a tremor to his left caused him to look away. One of the other dragons, a red one, was flung down and crashed into a hoodoo. It crumpled away from him, still sending up a cloud of detritus in the aftermath of its collapse. The other dragons had scattered. Vesel touched back down in front of Edwyrd and his sister, landing with a soft thump.

Edwyrd turned his head back towards Alicia. "Why?" He choked out. Tears quickly swelled his face as he saw the life in her ebbing.

"I wanted to see where the Recluse lives."

"The... the..." Edwyrd had forgotten how to speak.

Alicia coughed up blood. She choked. "He lives... there." With energy she didn't have, she pointed towards the lake that filled in the blowout. A small mountain range lay behind it, the curtain of a blue waterfall, continually filling it. Her arm gave out. Her body became heavy. Limp. Dead.

His stomach churned. His strength faltered. A short gasp of breath, and he almost dropped her to the floor. But he held on. Determined to hold onto her and family. "Alicia?" Edwyrd cradled her in his arms, shaking her, trying to rejuvenate her. He tapped her cheek. "Come on, Alicia. Wake up. Wake up! Alicia!" *She's gone.*

Shifting in front of him and heavy breathing on his neck caused him to look up.

"You!" One knee still bent and crouching, Edwyrd shifted Alicia's weight to one arm and pointed at the dragon with the other hand. "This is all your fault."

She is the one who came into our home.

"And you killed her. Why?"

Are dragons not allowed to eat?

"And there are plenty of other things here to eat." Edwyrd looked around, hoping for something to prove him right, but there was no game in the dying light. He hung his head. "Why don't you eat me then, too?"

I am yours should you choose to have me.

Bond with you? Edwyrd thought how ludicrous that statement was.

Yes, bond with me.

Edwyrd jerked back, falling on his butt and letting his sister drop to the ground. Arms pillared behind him, he looked up at the dragon. Both breathed in the same cadence. Despite the loss of his sister, the warmth in his body hadn't dissipated. Warmth radiated around him, almost as if the dragon's aura caressed him, enveloped him—protected him from the harsher truths of reality.

"You killed my sister."

I did not know she was your kin. I killed one of my own for you. Vesel turned his long head towards the collapsed hoodoo where a red dragon lay motionless.

Edwyrd stood up. "You think that can bring her back? That we are even now?"

Vesel shook his head. *No life lost is ever equal, but it is what I offer, along with my strength, should you choose to bond with me.*

"And what is your strength?" Edwyrd asked, almost wondering why he asked it himself. He was speaking to a dragon, after all. Everything was its strength. What weakness did it have? It was the perfect creature. But the creature that had killed his sister.

We bond with the person, not their greed, Edwyrd.

Edwyrd didn't know what to do. *He knows my name?* His lip trembled. For all intents and purposes, he wanted to deny and rewind what had just happened. For the first time, he felt completely aimless. Is this what his life had come to? Is this what fate had in store for him? Bonding with the dragon that killed his sister? To what ends did that fate serve?

Questions ravaged his mind like wind eroding pillars of stone. Like time corroded youth. He stood there, never taking his eyes off of Alicia. Fisting his hands, he closed his eyes and breathed in deeply. When next he opened them, he stared directly into the blood-red eyes of Vesel.

"You will grant me your Power. I choose to bond with you."

Vesel roared. A pulse of silver light originated from his mythril underbelly and worked its way up his body, coruscating in another deluge of silver flames that washed over Edwyrd. Palms out, arms outstretched, he stood in the flames, basking in them, feeling their warmth yet again and being reborn in fire and blood.

After the flames died, his heart palpitated, wanting to come outside of his chest. His blood burned, heat gushing through him, surely reddening his cheeks. His skin itched, his focus and concentration heightened. He felt incredible, as if he could tackle an entire empire.

This new endowment of energy meant nothing to him. Not now. With somber steps he approached the corpse of his sister and picked her up in his arms. She felt lighter now.

May I help you, Edwyrd?

Body still in his arms, Edwyrd turned around and frowned. "Do not use my name, Vesel."

As you wish.

"I prefer to walk back. I will come back for you eventually." Edwyrd turned around and continued the trek towards Steorra. Vesel's voice caused him to stop.

I am sorry about her fate.

Edwyrd halted and peered over his shoulder. "You will repay me someday."

Tell me what I must do, and I will burn for you, Edwyrd.

It was the grave of night when Edwyrd returned to his home, carrying the weight of his dead sister. Vesel had silently flown above him. He assumed it was the dragon's way of showing his remorse for the incident. Perhaps it was even a gesture of safeguarding him from the others until he reentered the city's barriers. Through it all, Edwyrd was glad the dragon hadn't tried to speak to him; he was merely a shadow that Edwyrd could feel feeding him strength as his own diminished. Otherwise, how could he have carried Alicia's weight for so long without resting?

Using his shoulder, he opened the door and walked sideways through the narrow entrance, being sure not to break any of the clay pots his mother left as decorations. Were they still awake, waiting for him to return? The silence at his entrance told him no.

As quietly as he could, he laid her body on top of the coffee table in the living room. And then he went around the other side and fell into the clay cushion. He tilted his head back and closed his eyes, trying to find any modicum of comfort he could. Exhaling into the air, he stretched his long arms. Paper underneath his left hand caused him to readjust his position. Opening his eyes, he noticed the blue envelope. *As if this matters anymore...* He went to toss it away and the seal came apart and the back of the letter opened on its own accord. *Mother and Father must have opened it while I was away.* Edwyrd punched his tongue into his cheek and gave into curiosity, bringing the paper inside to his eyes.

Dear Edwyrd,

It is my honor to congratulate you on –

His heart ached like someone had wrung it of its warmth, replacing it with ice, leaving him as cold as his sister's body. Strength syphoned, sweat drenched his face and his body, causing him to shake. *What is –* Pain erupted in his lungs as if they were being torn apart. He gasped and fell facedown on the couch, seeing no more.

A wail of sobs awoke Edwyrd.

Groggy, light-headed, and with his strength severely diminished, Edwyrd pushed himself up with one arm.

"Ed... Ed... wyrd?"

Edwyrd blinked. His mother clung onto his father's shoulders, head halfway peeled back from his father's broad chest. Brown hair fell past her pale face, just like Alicia's. Her voice was cracked, no longer certain. Grief took any playfulness that had once been in her voice.

"Son?" His father stepped alongside his mother, cradling her with one arm. He looked at Edwyrd through russet eyes, the same eyes Alicia used to have, and close enough in color to Vesel's eyes. The deep dark red. Eyebrows the size and color of fireworms drew closer together as his father frowned.

Edwyrd tried standing but immediately collapsed again. His strength was still diminished. At his collapse, his parents rushed forward.

"Are you okay?" his mother asked.

Edwyrd coughed. Choked. He massaged his head, exhaled, and then inhaled. A gruesome odor bit the air and Edwyrd lurched over the clay couch, as the stench of his sister's corpse finally hit him. *Alicia...* Images of the altercation the night before came back to him.

"What happened?"

The tension and grief in the room halted any other of Edwyrd's senses from besting him again. He looked from Alicia to his parents and back down at his sister's body. He gulped and told his story but left out how he had bonded with Vesel. They wouldn't have understood what that meant. Instead, he told them how he found her ravaged by dragons by the Dragon's Ruins and that his presence alerted them and then after a quick show of Power, he had made them fly off.

"When did you get back?" his father asked.

"The grave of night. What time is it now?"

"A little past dawn. Why didn't you wake us up when you returned?"

Edwyrd tensed his neck and shoulders. "I was so exhausted I must have just passed out," he lied.

In truth, he wasn't exactly sure what had happened on the couch or why it had suddenly felt like every bit of strength inside of him had withdrawn, but it was something he would ask his mentor when he could.

"What was she doing out there? That isn't like Alicia! That..." His mother stopped, not knowing what more she could say.

It was obvious to both of them that nothing could be done for their daughter. And while Edwyrd wasn't entirely clear on why Alicia had ventured off in the first place, he wouldn't say it wasn't like her. She had always been curious. For years she had gossiped about the Recluse as much as anyone in the town. If Edwyrd had to guess, curiosity most likely had gotten the better of her and she had followed him, and then when she had seen that he lived outside the boundaries of the city, tried to track him down. But why had she been so foolish to go so far out? How did the man even live so far outside the city limits? How did he manage to make it into town without being mauled? These were more questions that Edwyrd would only get answers from one source—his mentor.

And so while he wanted to mourn the death of his sister, Edwyrd had shed his tears already. More than anyone, he had shed his tears. He had carried her burden. He had done his duty in bringing her here. Now, it was time to unburden himself and his curiosity. It was time to get answers.

Standing, he maneuvered around the table and bypassed his parents.

"Where are you going?" his mother asked.

"To Lord Omyon. If anyone can help us right now, it will be him."

"But your sister... she..."

"Lord Omyon is the most skilled adored that I know. He can help get her ready for the funeral. I will be back."

Clinging onto her husband, Edwyrd's mother nodded. His father gestured with his head to leave. Edwyrd wasted no time. Now that this tragedy had befallen him and his family, the hours were against him.

Across the wooden table located in the lord's extensive library, his mentor leaned back, his hand cupping his chin, massaging the jaw. He still hadn't spoken, even though Edwyrd had finished telling his story what seemed like an interminable amount of minutes before. Finally, he flicked his gaze to Edwyrd and leaned forward, as if he had decided where he wanted to begin the conversation.

"There is a lot to unpack."

Edwyrd blinked. His mentor didn't have to tell him that. He had lived it. What he needed were answers.

"I don't know where the Recluse lives."

Edwyrd stared at him long and hard. "And that is the truth?"

Lord Omyon shifted in his chair and waved his hand. "No. But that is not the issue here."

"How is it not the issue? My sister followed him out there."

"Under her own volition," Lord Omyon added. He put up a finger and repeated himself. "Under her own volition. Her curiosity got the better of her, and in turn, the environment bested her."

Edwyrd slammed his fist down on the table. "My sister was torn apart by a dragon. My dragon." Edwyrd pointed to himself.

Lord Omyon put his hand up in an effort to calm him. "Edwyrd, I know it is difficult losing a love one. I know. Trust me, I know."

"Do you? Who have you ever lost? All you ever have been is alone!"

"You know nothing of my past. I lost everything. My master. My home. My wife..."

Lord Omyon's voice tapered off at the end, as if he hadn't meant to say the word, but it had escaped him all the same. Wife? Lord Omyon had been married before? Immediately, Edwyrd hung his head, shamed at his outburst. Of course, Lord Omyon had lost something. Otherwise, why would a First Blood be on this planet to begin with?

Edwyrd sat down. Calmer, he said, "I'm sorry, but..."

"There is no need to apologize, Edwyrd. Each of us are made of emotions. That is how Ancient Lyoen wanted it to be. It is only natural to feel grief when we lose a loved one. It is only natural to feel anger."

Edwyrd sighed. "So you don't know?" He stared down his mentor.

"That information changes nothing, Edwyrd. He didn't make your sister go out and follow him. The dragons attacked her because she wasn't well-armed. She wasn't protected. And she was approaching their territory."

"But why would my sister lie?"

"She didn't. The Recluse does live outside of the city limits, but dragons do not bother him."

"How?"

Lord Omyon sighed now. He frowned. "That is a story for another day, Edwyrd."

"He's like you, isn't he?"

Lord Omyon's neck tensed. He cocked his head a little. "What do you mean?"

"First Blood. That Recluse is from Gladima."

"What makes you think that?"

"Because you know him."

"I told you I don't know who he is or where he lives."

"Yes, but those were lies. I can feel it. The way you defend him... He's your friend, isn't he? You gave him an Ether Weapon, didn't you? And that is why the dragons don't attack him!" Edwyrd stood up and pointed at Lord Omyon.

"You are intelligent, Edwyrd. And observant. It is a good trait to have in the Trials. It will fare you well."

"I..." Edwyrd hung his head. "I don't think I will attend."

"Why?"

"My sister just died. It wouldn't be right to just leave my family after her death."

"Sometimes life isn't fair. But that is fate, Edwyrd. What you have in front of you, though, is the opportunity of a lifetime. You would be a fool for letting it pass you by."

Edwyrd shifted in his chair.

"Tell me, what would staying here accomplish?"

"Well, uhmm, I could..."

He didn't get to finish his thought, for Lord Omyon continued on his own. "Would you be able to bring your sister back from the grave?" Edwyrd shook his head. "Are your parents so fragile they need your help around the house?" Although his parents were older than most children his age, Edwyrd shook his head. "Will the academy require you to fill in for Alicia in her absence?"

Edwyrd shook his head. "You make it seem that she is insignificant."

"By you staying here, Edwyrd, that is exactly what you are doing."

"What do you mean?"

"If you choose to stay here, life will continue, like normal. The Trials will continue like normal, except they will be missing one participant. The system continues to move forward, regardless of if you choose to stay here or not, but by participating in the event, you have the chance to change everything. In reality, it is the truest way of honoring Alicia's death."

"I—"

Lord Omyon continued, not letting Edwyrd finish his thoughts. "Because of Alicia, you bonded with a dragon, Edwyrd. A dragon. Do you understand how that never would have happened if Alicia had never stepped outside the boundaries of the city? Would you have ever traveled outside of the city limits if you hadn't needed to?"

"No," Edwyrd admitted.

"Then by staying here, you are making Alicia's sacrifice inconsequential. You think that you are honoring her by mourning her death, but you are doing the opposite. You are not acknowledging her sacrifice. You are not realizing the winds of fate that granted you the ability to bond. That most likely will give you an unparalleled advantage in the Trials."

Edwyrd arched his eyebrows.

"Sometimes you can be so dense; I really do not understand it." Lord Omyon sighed and shook his head in his hands. "It is very unlikely that anyone else who has been accepted has been bonded with an animal."

"So then I should bring Vesel with me to the Core? Will that be allowed?"

Lord Omyon scrunched his eyebrows. "I think it is best for Vesel to stay here."

"Why is that?"

"You and he will still have a bond and still have increased strength, just not as much. This way, though, there won't be any..." Lord Omyon pushed his lips to one side. "Disadvantages." He shook his head as if he was annoyed with the word he had chosen.

"Disadvantages?" Edwyrd arched an eyebrow. "Is that why—"

Lord Omyon cut him off. He nodded his head. "Yes. I told you I met my bonded animal once upon a time." Lord Omyon rapped his fingertips on the table in front of him. "It was a fox."

"Fox?"

"An animal the size of a dog but with cat-like features." Lord Omyon waved his hand. "I met it while still on Gladima. Before the Great War. At this time tensions were high between the clans." Lord Omyon looked at him, and when he realized the blank expression on Edwyrd's face, he continued explaining. "The Ancient's tribes in Gladima consisted of the Heavols and the Evolics and..." He bit his tongue. "Never mind. These two tribes were on the brink of war when I met Scarlett. That was her name. And she had come to me just after..." Lord Omyon sighed deeply. "Just after my wife died, due to rather unfortunate circumstances. Circumstances that led to the Great War. But, anyway, she came to me in my time of grief to help comfort me. To console me while I mourned for my wife. To bless me with an ability."

"What was that?"

Lord Omyon cocked his head. "I never found out. Animals do not give away their strengths unless you are bonded."

"So why didn't you—"

"I'm getting to that. I didn't bond with Scarlett because of the war that was to come. I felt it on the doorstep, and I knew that to bond with her may only cause me more pain." Lord Omyon looked hard at Edwyrd. He cleared his throat. "I'll spell it out for you then. When I lost my wife, it was the worst feeling I could have. Possibly the same feeling you encountered when you lost your sister. That shock in your stomach. That was it. But as Vesel's flames washed over you, he bonded with you, or at least, he began the process, and in what you have told me, in a much more accidental way." Edwyrd nodded and Lord Omyon continued. "I knew that by bonding with Scarlett, I could potentially lose her as well. If she were to die, then a part of my soul would die with her. Maybe I would survive. Maybe I wouldn't. And, if I did survive, what would the repercussions on my soul look like being severed from two bonds? I... well, no Power is good enough in my opinion to warrant that kind of potential heartache, so I said 'no.' And she left me, and eventually time healed me because that is what time does. You will understand that someday if you are Guardian."

"So I shouldn't have bonded?"

Lord Omyon shook his head. "I am not saying that at all. You made the decision you made, and there is no turning back on it now, but I believe you made the decision because you wanted the warmth that the dragon offered you. You wanted to be consoled and comforted."

"And I was. Until... well... until the time on the couch."

"Yes. We call that a 'withdrawal.' It happens to all first-time bondees. Your body was flooded, inundated with strength from your animal, and so after the animal leaves your proximity for the first time, that feeling fades away and you return to normal. Well, whatever normal that might be at that stage now. But it is sure to be different from how you feel when you are close together with a bonded animal."

"And will that always happen?"

"I imagine not, but I cannot say for sure."

"So then I need to bring Vesel to the Core."

Lord Omyon swiped his hand and leaned forward. "Do you pay attention?! The Trials will be dangerous. By bringing Vesel you are putting him in danger and therefore putting yourself in danger."

"But he's a dragon."

"And do you think that dragons cannot be killed?" Lord Omyon scoffed. "I had a friend... aahh never mind. It doesn't matter." Lord Omyon flicked his gaze to Edwyrd. "If anyone is likely to kill your dragon, it will be the competitors at the Trials. Now, how much time do you have left?"

Edwyrd blinked. Shivers crept alongside his forearms and the back of his neck. He sat there, idly tapping his fingers against the wooden table, reflective of what Lord Omyon had just said. *Competitors so strong that they can kill dragons? Dragons?* His stomach churned, thinking of who he would meet once the Trials began.

"Edwyrd?"

He blinked and shook his head. "What? Sorry."

"How much time do you have left?"

"Time?"

"You mentioned you received the letter. How long before the Guardian of the Core comes here?"

"I... I don't know? I never checked. I never even read the letter. With everything that has been—"

Lord Omyon stood up and waved off Edwyrd's excuse. "Enough. I will gather my things for your sister's funeral. Stay here." The lord stood up and darted off to other parts of the castle, leaving the library where they had convened.

Alone in the library, Edwyrd wandered the columns of books and scrolls he had ventured through before during his breaks from training. He wasn't strolling through in any particular manner. On the contrary, he felt like walking through the stacks of books in order to try and process everything Lord Omyon had just thrust upon him. *Competitors strong enough to kill dragons?* He still couldn't fully grasp or comprehend the idea. And he doubted any literature in this study would provide him anything of interest, but he wandered amongst the library all the same.

Eventually, he stopped among a wall at the far end of the library. Before him hung a painting of a large waterfall pouring into a blue lake. It sat as the doormat to a jagged range of mountains that looked like the backs of some lizards. He had seen it before many times when wandering about the library, but as he stopped before it now, it spoke to him differently. *The Falls?*

"He lives... there..."

Alicia's words came back to him in a sudden current. He stepped forward and fingered the painting, the memories of the past twenty-four hours inundating his mind. His sister's death repeating over and over again in his mind and the way she pointed to the place, using her last bit of strength to let Edwyrd know where he lived.

"Edwyrd, are you ready to leave?"

He didn't turn towards his mentor's voice. "Who is he?"

"Who?" Lord Omyon came to stand beside Edwyrd.

"Your friend. The Recluse." Edwyrd turned to look his mentor in the eye. "No lying this time or I won't attend the Trials."

Lord Omyon's neck twitched. His breathing hitched. "We really do not have time for this, Edwyrd."

"Then you can tell me while I stay here."

"Why does this man matter so much to you?"

"Why does he matter so much to you that you hide his identity and protect him?"

"There are things in this system that you couldn't possibly comprehend yet."

"Then help me understand them. My sister was obsessed with this man for years and he led her outside—"

"Your sister went and followed him on her own accord. Plato is of no—" Lord Omyon gasped. For the first time, he had made a mistake.

"Plato? Who is Plato?"

"He's no one. Not to you."

"Then I'm not going."

Locking his eyes with his mentor, Edwyrd stayed silent. It was a battle of wills, but Edwyrd knew he had the advantage. Lord Omyon wanted him to attend this event more than Edwyrd did now given the circumstances, and so he would let his mentor speak the first words.

Lord Omyon sighed. "Edwyrd, believe me when I tell you that Plato means nothing to you now. Even if I were to tell you who he is or why he is here, it would mean nothing."

"Try."

"To try would be to talk to you in a foreign language. You are not ready yet to comprehend."

Edwyrd searched his eyes, hoping to find some sort of false pretense to justify his stubbornness, but Lord Omyon spoke the truth. He sighed. "When will I be ready?"

"When you become the Guardian of the Core."

"Guardian of the Core?" Edwyrd muttered under his breath. Was the Recluse that significant?

"Now, are we ready to go?"

"If I become Guardian, you will tell me?"

"If you haven't already learned it by then, I will tell you. Now?"

Edwyrd acquiesced, bobbing his head. "Let's go."

Taking one last look at the painting, he followed Lord Omyon out of the library, out of the castle grounds.

Soon enough, Edwyrd would enter the unknown.

CHAPTER 5

Victor Zigarda stood inside the open courtyard of the Web. During his father's reign of thirty-five years, construction had been started and completed on one third of the Web, a domed building in a metallic black which had strands of red crawling on the sides like blood ivy. His father's vision called for three domes and an obelisk in the center of it all. The second dome was being built, but compared to the first dome, it was taking longer and that was because of all the interconnected webs of transportation the two would share in the future. The technology Empora had, to Victor's knowledge, was as contemporary as could be, no doubt the help and workings of the Sages who kept close with his father. In some aspect, Victor was quite surprised that the Sages were not here to see him off. Rather, only his brother and father were here, their mother having died in birth complications after Renaul was born.

"How much longer does the card say?"

"Only a few more minutes, Father," Victor replied. He had a hard time distinguishing whether or not he wanted him to leave, unlike Renaul who tapped his feet and had his arms crossed over his chest. He couldn't wait.

"This compound has trained you for the event. I know you will bring this family such pride than I could ever accomplish in building this Web." He coughed into his left fist and furtively looked at it before wiping it on his black tunic. His father twitched his neck and raised his arms, gesturing to the semi-completed Web in front of him. "It will be grand, but the life before you Victor will be even grander."

Victor ignored his father's praise. He flicked his gaze to the slight stain of red barely noticeable upon the black cloak. Victor's brows furrowed. *Father...*

"It would certainly be embarrassing for you to lose, considering all the advantages you have had in life," Renaul snickered.

Always like him to give a backhanded compliment. Jealousy is not a good trait, Little Brother. When his father's hand clasped him on the shoulder, Victor looked away from Renaul. "Regardless of any of that, Victor, you will do well. It is in your blood. Our blood." His father squeezed his shoulder.

Victor shot a glance to his father's hand. His father immediately withdrew his hand from the scrutiny of his son but not without leaving the faintest strain of blood on the red vest layered over his black tunic. The color would have been inconspicuous if Victor had not observed the earlier instances.

Victor's breathing hitched. He looked at his father with newfound concern. *What illness vexes you?*

Noticing Victor's studious gaze, his father stuffed the left hand inside the pocket of his pants. With a closed right fist, he brought it before him, flexing his arm in the process. "And our blood is strong. You know I've told you the story about how—"

Renaul rolled his eyes. "Yes. You've told us many times how grandfather took the throne from Lord Sedarthus."

"Right through the back." His father jabbed his arm through the air with a little twist. "You know he always told me, 'Take what is yours. Give what is theirs because...'"

Victor and his brother chimed in on the last line of the phrase. "Knowledge is Power." Victor patted his leg, wondering how the Guardian of the Core would arrive. He wanted to be off. Not because he didn't mind these last moments with his family, but because if he stayed here longer, illogical musings might make him reconsider the Trials. Was he needed more here? Or did his father need him to succeed there, to study, and to learn cures for his condition? Was his brother even keen enough to notice what his father's obsession with this Web was doing to him?

Most likely not.

The unfortunate death of his mother caused by Renaul's birth had stuck with Victor. It had engendered his own fear of death and given him the purpose of attending the Trials.

She had been young, yet she had died all the same. Only old people were meant to die, wasn't that it? Or the weak? They, too, were meant to die, but his mother wasn't weak. Nor was his father. She was young, beautiful, a strong-willed woman who had come from the Thieving Isles in the south, whom his father had met while in the old capital of Rydel. And his father was the strongest person he knew, respected greatly amongst all the cities of Empora. His father and mother had always joked it was fated for them to meet, for his family was meant to rule, and Rydel had been the first capital until

Zigarda's father had moved it to Mendeck, and she had come from the Thieving Isles and had truly stolen his heart.

"That is why you must listen to the others who will be competing, Victor. Find out what is theirs, give it to them, for knowledge is the truest Power we have. And when we use it, we take it for ourselves."

Victor sighed. "Yes, Father. Of course. I will do..." Before his eyes, a man appeared. "As you say..." His voice tapered off.

Blue and silver cape fluttering in the breeze, a longsword strapped to his back, the man clutched a dark cloth of fabric in his outstretched arm. Slowly, the man brought his arm inward and turned around, arching his shoulders back and straightening his spine at the same time. He couldn't have been past forty years old with cropped blonde hair so different than Victor's dark hair. A face chiseled and worn, one that had seen many years, yet no years at all for the lack of gray hairs on the goatee. Sapphire eyes like that of his cape shined upon him. Truly, this man was a lion. How was he so young?

"Victor Zigarda."

Victor cleared his throat and bowed. "Yes... yes, my Guardian." He shook his head. *Stupid. Stupid. You are making a fool of yourself. Act more composed.*

The Guardian of the Core chuckled. "You may rise. Thank you." When Victor faced him again, he asked. "Are you ready?"

Victor nodded his head frantically but didn't say anything.

"I take that as a *yes,* then. Come, I will take you to the Core, then I have to retrieve the others."

"Others?"

The Guardian turned towards Victor.

He blushed and chastised himself for the stupidity of the question. "I just meant, why don't we pick them up together? It would be less work for you, wouldn't it?"

"Perhaps, but I want to make sure all of my contestants arrive safely. I do not think you could handle multiple travels through the reimaje."

"Reimaje?"

Victor's ears piqued to his father's voice. He had forgotten his presence, lost in such a historic moment.

"You must be Hayden."

His father stepped alongside him. He bowed his head a little at his name, and it had been one of the very few times his father had ever been called by his first name. Many times no others outranked him, but here before the Guardian of the Core, he knew his father would respect such greetings.

"It is nice to meet you in person finally."

"It is an honor to meet you as well. All of us are honored by your presence here." His father shot a glance back at Renaul who came over to Victor's left-hand side and bowed his head as well.

"You are too kind." Guardian Crevon smiled. "There is no need to fear. I will be taking your son to the Central Core through this, the reimaje." Guardian Crevon held up the black cloth that hung limp from his gloved, left hand.

"Yes, but *what* is it?"

Guardian Crevon narrowed his eyes and furrowed his thin eyebrows. "Part of a Guardian's Power." He turned his gaze to Victor. "Are you ready to go?"

Victor's eyes gleamed. *Such Power.* "What other Power does it have?" he asked, lost in the awe of the object.

Guardian Crevon chuckled. "I'm afraid I cannot tell you that yet, Victor. But win the Trials, become my apprentice, and one day I will divulge everything to you. Are you ready?"

Victor looked from his father to his brother and then to Guardian Crevon. "I am." He bent down and picked up the bags of clothes, leather armor, and other trinkets on his left and right. Much like Guardian Crevon's sword, Victor had his longsword strapped to his back.

"Come." Guardian Crevon held up one arm, waiting for Victor to come under his wing. Victor obliged and felt the Guardian wrap his arm around him, holding him and protecting him like a father would. "You are going to feel a slight tug on your body when you enter. It may be a little painful."

Victor looked down at the black canvas spread out on the ground in front of the Guardian. Slowly brown replaced the black. A three-story estate stood upon the barren surface, forming and overtaking more of the black. It was as if the reimaje was painting a portrait by itself. Victor's eyes widened in awe at the beauty of the transformation. *So, this is the Power of the –*

He never had a chance to complete his thought. Guardian Crevon stepped forward, pulling Victor along with him, and together they dropped through the reimaje, through the very fabric itself. And in a snap of fingers, Victor left his old world behind and entered the domain of the Central Core, the place he would be spending the next two-hundred years of his life, or more, once he won the Trials.

CHAPTER 6

In the backyard of his parents' house, in between the thermal pool and the garden bed his mother would pick firebeets from or ashen potatoes, where flame lilies bloomed, that is where Edwyrd and his father dug a small hole for Alicia's cremains.

Lord Omyon had cremated Alicia's body and had carefully collected her remains into a bowl. To Edwyrd's surprise, he then crushed up a handful of ard leaves and sprinkled that in as well before mixing it with the soil that Edwyrd and his father had dug up. After this, the combination was reapplied to the hole. His mother then came and planted seeds given to her by Lord Omyon. Seeds from exotic plants not found in this area of Nova, and perhaps even some that were of Therus. How he had acquired the seeds, Edwyrd had no idea, but he assumed a man like Omyon would have his ways. His mentor had told them that they were seeds for red anthuriums, orange hibiscus, and yellow tulips.

Planted in the mixture of his sister's remains, Lord Omyon said that the crushed ard leaves within the soil would constantly rejuvenate the ground whenever it lacked life. For this reason, these flowers would last longer than any other, perhaps even for years before succumbing to the ravages of time.

This had been Edwyrd's first funeral, so he thought the gesture appropriate, considering Therus natives had the saying: "From ash to ash." It was only right, then, that Alicia would be cremated, and if what Lord Omyon said was true, then her beauty would endure for ages. It would continue burning bright even in whatever afterlife existed after death.

His mother did her best to hold back the tears, but eventually she broke in the moment of silence they offered after each of them gave their respective eulogies. None of which consisted of overdrawn statements because Alicia's life had been simple and sweet. In truth, it had been cut short; she hadn't been able to rise to the occasion that she had been meant for. Or maybe she had? Maybe her purpose was merely to be Edwyrd's impetus to compete in the

Trials. Edwyrd pondered that in the brief moments of silence that passed upon the closing remarks of his father.

"Let's go back inside, Son."

"I want to stay outside a little longer."

His father nodded, took his wife's hand, and led her up the slight incline into their house. "Don't stay too long. Time is short."

"I know."

Edwyrd hadn't expected his parents to be so accepting of his decision to attend the Trials, but as Lord Omyon had argued with him, by not participating he would be wasting Alicia's sacrifice. His parents didn't even know the half of that sacrifice, but they did know that they were strong and capable enough on their own and that they didn't need Edwyrd's help. For now, at least.

Before the funeral ceremony began, they had showed Edwyrd what Lord Omyon had called a telecard, an electronic messaging system designed by the nation of Mistral. After he had pushed a button, a little green man had appeared before Edwyrd, a hologram as Lord Omyon had described it, and had instructed him to make sure he gathered his belongings before the timer on the card reached zero. At that point, Edwyrd had noticed only three hours remaining on the accompanying card before they began the funeral arrangements. After packing his things and attending the abbreviated funeral, Edwyrd was sure he had little time left.

After a few minutes of extended silence, Lord Omyon asked. "Edwyrd, are you ready?"

"Where do they go?" Edwyrd asked, ignoring the question.

"Go?"

"After death. Where do we go?" Edwyrd turned his gaze from the soil to his mentor.

"Only the Ancients know that."

"But you studied under an Ancient, didn't you?"

"Lyoen revealed many things to me, Edwyrd, but I do not know all the mysteries of this universe she created."

"She?"

"Did you think Lyoen was a male?"

"Well... I... I guess I never really considered... We always... In school I mean..."

"Time distorts truth better than any silver-tongue I know. People want to believe she is a man because that would make sense of why the Great War happened. But even women can wage wars. Women can be warriors." He paused for a moment and then looked at the newly formed plot of soil. "Your sister knew that."

Edwyrd glanced at Alicia's flowerbed. "I believe that she would have been a great warrior."

"And I believe that her strength will become your own in the Trials."

A tear came to Edwyrd's eye at his mentor's comment. "Thanks." He snuffed the tear out while it cascaded down his cheek. "Emotions," he said, remembering his answer so many years ago. "That day, when you accepted me as your student, you mentioned we were all born out of emotions." When Lord Omyon nodded, Edwyrd continued. "How do you know that? She taught you that? Ancient Lyoen, I mean."

Lord Omyon nodded. "I saw her do it."

"You saw her form humans?"

He nodded again. "She formed my wife right in front of me. Right after she formed me."

"And when was that?"

"I was Ancient Lyoen's first."

Edwyrd blanched. "Fih... First?" Edwyrd shook his head, making sure he heard correctly.

"Yes, Edwyrd. I was her first."

"How come you never told me?"

"You never asked."

"And why are you telling me now?"

"Ed... Edwyrd?" His mother called from up top. Her voice was high-pitched with concern. "I... I think you need to come up here..."

Edwyrd twisted his ear. "He's here." He turned back to Lord Omyon. "The Guardian's here."

"Then we should leave, but I am telling you this now because I want you to understand just how valuable my training should be to you. Use it as your strength. The greatest warriors never just have one source of Power; they have many. So, use everything. My training. Alicia's death. Vesel. We have all shaped who you are right now, and we all, in some manner, have given you a part of us to take with you to the Trials. Now go and win them." Lord Omyon pushed Edwyrd's shoulder, turning him slightly. Together, they walked up the hill.

By the time he made it around the side of his house, his mother had already carried his things out for him. And there, in front of the house, stood none other than the Guardian of the Core himself, Matthau Crevon. Edwyrd took in the abnormally bright hair, the dark blue eyes studying him.

"Are you okay, Edwyrd?"

"I am fine."

"Lord Omyon, it is nice to see you again."

"Likewise, my Guardian." Lord Omyon inclined his head.

"Are you ready to leave, Edwyrd?"

"I am."

"Then let us go." Guardian Crevon threw the black bandana he had been clutching up into the air.

Edwyrd watched it reach its zenith, but he didn't follow it as it floated downwards. Instead, his attention stayed fixed on the sky as a large burst of silver flames spewed out from behind orange clouds. He thought he heard a roar, but that could have been only his imagination. But what he wasn't imagining was the fire pounding in his chest. The dragon flew amongst the clouds, but never close enough to make him out completely, but he didn't need to see the dragon now to know that it was him.

"Edwyrd?"

"Sorry, my Guardian. I am ready." Edwyrd hugged his parents once more, picked up the bags his mother had set out for him, and then joined Guardian Crevon beside the black hole that had appeared before the Guardian.

"We go through here. Together." Guardian Crevon raised his arm for Edwyrd to link together with his.

Edwyrd looked from the black hole on the floor, formed from the piece of black cloth, to the Guardian. The pure black canvas was slowly being replaced by brown and an image of a grand estate. Whatever this thing was, it was as if it painted itself a picture.

"You will learn about this in time. Now, if you will. Take my arm." Guardian Crevon motioned.

Edwyrd took a passing glance at everyone there once more, getting a nod from Lord Omyon before he turned his gaze to the orange clouds where he had seen Vesel not a minute before. The dragon had disappeared. The fire that had swelled in his chest had cooled. The energy he had felt dissipated, returning him to the exhausted state the last few days had brought about. Not wanting to have the Guardian ask him a third time, Edwyrd stepped forward and linked arms with the Guardian. Together, they stepped forward and instantly he felt his body sink into it as if it were a hole in the earth. And in a dragon's breath, the old life that he knew had been replaced.

CHAPTER 7

O n the Core, Victor stared at the palatial mansion in awe. It had a regality to it the likes of the Web could never exude. It stood as a haven on this melancholy terrain of dirt. Perhaps it was the silver bands that cut through the purple sky in the background that made the estate look somewhat heavenly, but Victor quickly wondered why the rest of the Core didn't match such expectations of beauty. Before he could ask about this, though, he realized the Guardian of the Core had left. And now he was alone, bags in his hand.

A dark-skinned lady with buoyant black hair came outside the estate. The golden necklace she wore matched the gown that came down to past her knees. Coated in scales, the gown hugged her like snakeskin. "Victor Zigarda, welcome to the Core. Come inside and join the others."

Others? Who else waited for the Guardian to finish collecting the contestants?

"Yes, Conseleigh Juniper."

Victor walked to the steps, smelling the flowered perfume on the conseleigh by the time he reached the first step. Already slanted, her eyes narrowed even further on him, almost squinting at him as he walked up the steps. Victor could tell that she was mixed blood, half-Ka'Chean and half-Chaon, an interesting combination. Coiled around her left forearm, she wore a wristlet of a golden snake, and on her other wrist were rings of varying colors. To Victor, lethal may have been too pleasant of a word for this woman just based upon first impressions, and it was no doubt in his mind that she had been chosen conseleigh because of such traits.

Inside the estate, two other women awaited him. Being the only male contestant in the room, both females surveyed him. Unlike the conseleigh, their blood wasn't mixed, each having dominant traits of their respective nations. The woman with black skin, coarse hair, and a thicker frame was from Ka'Che, and the petite woman with black hair tied into a short ponytail in the back and dressed in a fuchsia qipao was from Chaon. Neither spoke. After observing Victor, they turned back, clearly disinterested in him, preferring to focus their attention on the conseleigh who stood at the bottom of the staircase. Conseleigh Juniper had walked around the contestants to join the other three.

"I guess it is my turn now." One man yawned and pushed himself off the banister that led up to the second floor. Like Conseleigh Juniper, he too had darker skin, but his had been a result of the suns' kiss, rather than genetics. He stretched, pushing up his sea-blue tunic to expose a portion of his hairy potbelly. Victor would have immediately cast this man aside as unfit if not for two things: first, that he was, indeed, a conseleigh, and so would have earned his spot here on the Core like the other three, and second, the two halberds that were strapped on his back in the form of an x. The conseleigh stepped around the contestants and left the estate, only to return another minute later with a white-haired male with wide icy-blue eyes that seemed to pop out of the man's snowy skin.

Despite his cold appearance, the man entered the room with a pleasant deportment, standing alongside Victor and striking up conversation. He extended one hand, blushed, and then extended the opposite hand instead. "Christian Snowfield, you?"

"Victor." Victor squeezed his hand.

Christian nodded. "Nice to meet you. And you, ladies?" He extended a hand to each of them in turn.

"Iris," the Chaon woman responded.

"Kelis," said the Ka'Chean woman.

As he introduced himself to the ladies, Victor observed him more carefully. The original hand he had extended had rings on it. *Interesting.* Victor shot a furtive glance at the man's neck. A necklace hid beneath the collar of his white silk tunic. Victor smirked. *Well, well, well, another prince. Is this who Cronos had warned me about?*

Both women studied this newcomer as intently as he did, never removing their arms from the folded position across their chest. Victor wondered if each saw what he had observed. Constantly quizzed by his father after council meetings or after individual hearings with citizens, he had learned to read people as well as he had learned to read books. There was so much more to a person than just body language. Knowing weapon language, as Victor liked to call it, was just as useful. These two things, mixed with their demeanor, was often as informative as reading an autobiography.

Iris trained as an assassin. If the bow and knives that she carried didn't give that away, the fact that her hair was tied in a ponytail suggested she always made sure to see clearly. The bangs she had only went to her eyebrows, never over the pencil-thin lines, for that would obscure her vision. Kelis, a fighter. Her stature and weapon made that clear enough to see. While she wouldn't be as lithe as Iris, she would certainly have more endurance and perhaps a strength to match the men here, assuming she could wield the scimitar. And, finally, there was Christian. The rings on his finger and how he hid his necklace made it clear he didn't want the others to know he was a prince, and that is why the man had switched hands in the first place. It also meant that, while he was a prince, he was careless. Or was it simply a ruse? Victor tapped his foot as he contemplated the three of them.

Iris may pose a challenge, but where is the real competition?

His thoughts were disrupted when the conseleigh came back into the room with another man. A seaborn man by the looks of him, for he had blue hair with specks of white, as if he had been dipped into the ocean headfirst. His face was large, and compared to the others, the man was much stronger. But what concerned Victor about this man was that his strength was natural. The tan of his arms, how he wore sandals instead of shoes, and that he had a turtle shell as a shield strapped to his back all told Victor he was a born fisherman. In one hand he carried a whaling spear and in the other a fishing net that he had used in place of a bag, making all the contents he had brought visible to everyone. Physically, this man was a threat. But how strong was his Power? Victor bit down on his lip.

His presence dominated the room. So much so that Christian didn't even approach the man to introduce himself. Instead, the ice prince kept his distance, as if not wanting to be associated with such a rapscallion. That, in and of itself, told Victor a little about the climate on that planet. It was clear they weren't united. If he needed to, he could manipulate that distaste for one another in the future. His father had taught him that while it was good to keep your allies close, it was even better to know who your enemies were so you could keep them closer, gain their trust, and at the right time do what needed to be done. Sacrifices had to be made at times. His father had taught him the importance of that as well.

Before anyone spoke, the conseleigh returned with a woman with ravishing brown hair that curled down behind her frame. Her eyes were the greens of seaweed and her skin the color of pearls. Strung around her neck was a necklace with a single blue feather attached, and its barbs of electric yellow made it almost as attractive to look at as she. She carried two lances in her hands, and also strapped to her back was a shell of a smaller turtle.

She carried herself like royalty, but as Victor surveyed her fingers, he saw no rings, and the jewelry she wore carried no weight to it, save for the feather necklace. Her face wasn't worn, not like the Ka'Chean woman's, and it didn't hold the air of mystery like Iris's Chaon bloodline did. But that is what troubled Victor the most. Instead of being mysterious, it radiated a humble determination, as if the very thought of a competition excited her, and Victor could tell from her fit frame that she knew a thing or two about battle. Anyone who could wield a weapon in both hands did.

To Victor's surprise, Christian introduced himself to this water-born woman, which then made him reexamine the large fisherman who had come. Was he waterborn? Or did he merely live in a portside city near an ocean? Were there other dynamics that came into play? Victor frowned and listened intently as he heard the woman introduce herself as Cordelia. When she asked his name, he replied, and then she followed to introduce herself to the fisherman, Caspian.

"My turn." The conseleigh of Pyre, a man with orange skin and red hair, stepped down from the flight of steps that went up to the second floor, never unfolding the arms crossed on his chest.

Within ten more minutes, the remaining two competitors had entered. The first one was a tall man with brown hair. If it wasn't for the fact that the man was from the planet of Pyre, the man would have seemed almost insignificant. But, since he was from Pyre, he knew the man to be fireborn, and most likely had endurance and strength not natural for someone raised in less extreme climates. Like Christian, he introduced himself. Edwyrd was his name. Victor looked for signs of entitlement anywhere but found none; instead, he found the opposite, brown eyes with veins of red running through them, as if he hadn't gotten a good night's sleep for a few days. That meant he was tired, which boded well for Victor. However, it could also mean he had experienced a recent loss, and Victor was more inclined to think that way because, after the introductions, the man remained mute, lips slightly hung apart as if he was lost in another space and time. He was distracted, something that would work against the man if he wasn't careful, but if he learned to use the sorrow as fuel for these Trials, then the man maybe had a shot at gaining Victor's attention.

The last competitor was as large as Caspian. Out of all of the contestants who had entered, he had made it a point to engage in conversation with the conseleigh and even the Guardian of the Core himself as he entered the lobby.

"And here are the rest of the contestants, Cyrus."

The man turned to the conseleigh and shook his hand, bobbed his head towards Guardian Crevon, and then joined the others, placing himself alongside the other Pyrean and Victor. The man smelt of ash and sweat, but he was as clean shaven as his pate. Thick eyebrows, like fiery caterpillars, sat on top of his concave eyes, which were lit with the color of fire. Each forearm was flexed as he held two large sacks in his hands. When he caught Victor observing him, he looked down and smiled.

Victor furrowed his brows and smiled back, then he turned his attention to the Guardian of the Core, who had taken his place now in the center of his conseleigh.

"And then there were eight." Guardian Crevon let his gaze linger on each contestant. "It is my personal pleasure to welcome each and every one of you to the event. To an event of a lifetime. One of you will be my apprentice and will have the pleasure and opportunity of training under my conseleigh and I for the next fifteen years until the Passing occurs. Based upon observations of you and your application and sponsor letters, all of you have been hand-picked by my conseleigh, so congratulations for making it this far.

"Starting tomorrow, the Trials will begin. I will explain more then. Right now, focus on mentally preparing yourself and getting enough sleep. There will be three rounds and eliminations after each round. Eight will go to six, six will go to four, four will go to two, and two will go to one."

Victor pursed his lips. *Elimination?* That certainly made things more interesting.

"Good luck and goodnight." Guardian Crevon turned around and traveled up the stairs, the conseleigh following him up.

From the other hallways in the estate, eight maids and butlers came out. An older woman grabbed Victor by the arm and began carrying him off down another hallway. The same one as the two women and the fisherman. The others were escorted to the west wing. Victor glanced back behind his shoulder to take one last look at Cyrus, to make sure what he had first observed was correct. And it was. The man carried no weapon nor any shield. Nothing hung at his hips, nor was there anything slung over his shoulders and back. He carried nothing.

The fisherman to his left now didn't seem so intimidating. Victor had found the competition. It was that man. Cyrus. *That is who Cronos warned me about.* He had the confidence in him to talk to the Guardian of the Core and the conseleigh before the others. He had the confidence in his abilities to not need a weapon, and his physical size meant that he was good at brawling. If he broke Victor's defenses, he would win. Also, by not needing a weapon, Victor knew that man could cast Power, and he could cast Power quite well. And that troubled Victor more than he would like to admit.

CHAPTER 8

E dwyrd almost hadn't woken up that morning. If not for the servant knock-
ing at his door, he most likely would have still been sleeping, and if it
wasn't the first trial, he much rather would have been sleeping. He thought
the first trial would be something more grand, something more extravagant,
something dealing with the Power that the Guardian used to transport him to
the Core. He thought maybe there would be a battle or that he would have to
outwit his foe. But it wasn't any of those things. It was a paper test.

All participants took the test at the exact same time, spaced out at one
wooden table for each of them while in the library. The conseleigh were
responsible for overseeing their completion and collecting the exam when the
end of sixty-minutes had finished, regardless of where the person was in the
exam.

The test consisted of sixty questions, the first fifty being a format of
true/false, choosing the best option, yes/no or multiple choice. The last ten
were short answer responses. The time for completing the test was one hour,
which meant he could only afford an average of one minute per question,
but he knew that was unrealistic. After a quick flip-through of the exam, and
noticing that the last ten questions were different from the others, he made
sure to allow himself no more than forty-five seconds for each of the first fifty
questions so that he had time to record his answers on the last ten.

If the time constraint didn't make the assessment difficult enough, then the
fact that the test was sectioned off into six segments, each segment testing a
different ability, certainly proved to make achieving a high score near impossible. The first set of questions were true or false statements designed to test
his knowledge of the system and its workings. He smirked at the questions he
knew and frowned at the one or two that had him stumped.

"The Guardian of the Core position lasts for 200 years." True.

"Those who can cast Power are called Blessed." True.

"Power is hereditary." False.

"Only people who could cast Power could participate in the Trials." Edwyrd furrowed his brows but didn't award this question too much time. True.

"The origin of the system is known as Gladima." True.

"The only individuals with First Blood are the Twelve." Edwyrd grinned. False.

After the initial set of ten general questions, they became personal.

"If you were to choose between the death of a million innocent civilians or a single death of your loved one, which would you pick?" Edwyrd almost dropped his pen, thoughts of Alicia flitting into his mind. He squeezed his eyes shut, trying to force the memory of her away, locking it behind a vault he would never open. He chose the latter.

"A soothsayer allows you to ask about your death. Would you rather ask how you will die or when you will die?" When, Edwyrd chose. *Better to not know the details and instead know how much time I'll have left to make my impact.*

"You are determining your legacy. Would you rather die young yet be remembered or live a long life yet be forgotten?" Edwyrd's stomach churned. Had the Guardian picked these questions just for him? Did everyone receive the same type of questions? He took a casual glance at the other individuals, but when the conseleigh from Pyre, Pax Shadir, caught him looking around he buried his nose again in his test. He didn't want to be labeled a cheater. Young. He moved on.

After the second set of ten questions, they became downright ludicrous, forcing him to choose his preference in imaginary yes or no scenarios.

"Are the lives of ten people with no social standing but who can cast Power greater than the single life of one noble who can cast Power?" *How much is a life worth?* Edwyrd asked himself, knowing all too well the answer Lord Omyon would have given. The noble could employ those individuals and make sure they receive compensation. At the same time, ten people who died meant ten families affected by their death and that ripple could spread out to the city in unfathomable ways. As could the noble's death, he supposed, after thinking about it carefully. If the noble was well-loved his death would be felt by all families, not just the isolated families. Although he didn't like admitting that one life was worth more than ten, he said 'No.' Unsure if he could or not, he wrote the reasoning behind his answer. It had never said explicitly in this section to give a reason or not, but he did, knowing that it would cost him time in the long run.

The fourth question type tested his inference skills, drawing conclusions from supposed or observed facts. The concept of these were harder than the earlier question types as it not only gave him individual scenarios but also four plausible answer choices that he had to choose from. One of these inference questions had stated: A father and son were involved in an accident that required them to go to the nearest apothecary. By the time they arrived, the father had already died, and the son was barely clinging onto life. An adored came into the apothecary and looked at the boy who needed an operation, yet refused to operate on him, claiming "He is my son." The question then asked him to deduce who the adored was and gave a list of choices: The boy's godfather, the boy's pastor, the boy's mother, or the answer isn't given. Edwyrd had guessed a godfather, who may look at the boy as more of a son, especially given the information about the boy's actual father having died on the way to the apothecary.

The fifth set of questions were similar to the fourth but asked him to deduce conclusions based upon the information given and only that. Before that section of the test, it had in bold lettering: ***Do not attempt to draw upon your own knowledge to answer these questions.*** Those questions were the most difficult for Edwyrd for two reasons. First, he had to remind himself only to use information presented in the passage, not anything he may had learned from his tutelage with Lord Omyon or while in school. Second, sometimes conclusions couldn't be drawn from the information given and, if that happened, he would have to make that known.

After taking a mental pounding in this type of question, he approached the last ten with the mindset that they were absolute absurdity. These analytical questions placed him in the middle of situations and asked him to make a decision and explain why that decision was made. Edwyrd found that the actual scenario itself wasn't so hard, but the fact that he had to explain his choices, considering the little time he had left, and the fact that he had to first scrutinize the situation made this last question set nearly impossible. He didn't have time to think, he could only write what first came to mind.

One scenario had told him that he was a prisoner sentenced to death. The Guardian of the Core then offers him a chance to live by playing a simple game. The Guardian gives him fifty black marbles and fifty white marbles and two empty bowls. The Guardian then says, "Divide these one hundred marbles into these two bowls. You can divide them any way you like as long as you use all the marbles. Then I will blindfold you and mix the bowls around. You then can choose one bowl and remove one marble. If the marble is white you will live, but if the marble is black, you will die." He then had to choose how to split the marbles up so that he had the greatest probability of choosing a white marble and staying alive.

That one was relatively easy for Edwyrd, which is probably why he remem-bered it. He had recorded his answer, saying, "I would put one white marble in one bowl and the other ninety-nine marbles in the other bowl. By doing this, I would have a one-hundred percent chance of succeeding if I guess the bowl with only the white marble, and roughly a fifty percent chance should I choose the other bowl."

In fact, it most likely was the easiest question for everyone who attended the Trials. But while it may have been easy, the fact that he had to read the scenario and answer the question within a minute made it more challenging.

After relinquishing his exam to Conseleigh Shadir, Edwyrd sighed. He shouldn't have taken so much time on the third section. It had caused him to not finish two questions on the last part. And while he didn't know his exact score, he knew he had already beaten one individual, the blue-haired man from Sereya, who had engaged in a momentary tug-of-war with the conseleigh at the end of the hour, hoping to guess a few more answers correct. That meant he hadn't completed a majority of the exam, and Edwyrd knew the real trick to this exam, like any exam, was pacing. Questions he had no idea about were immediately guessed and not given much thought, saving him time for the other questions that were more likely to be solved correctly. Also, from what Guardian Crevon had said the day before, the Trials would function like a tournament, each round eliminating two contestants. This meant that Edwyrd didn't have to be the first done nor did he have to be the one with the most amount of answers correct, he just needed to beat two others. At the very least, that meant completing the test and hoping that some of his guesses along the way would turn out to be right.

At the end of it all, Edwyrd's head throbbed, and he was certain that others must have had been feeling the same way. The only person he had considered talking to was Cyrus. Edwyrd didn't know the type of training a fireson had to undergo to serve the lord of Therus, but he assumed it was intensive, and being from the same planet, it made establishing that initial connection with him easier.

"Is your brain hurting just as much as mine?" Edwyrd asked, massaging his temples at the same time while walking down the corridor, Cyrus at his side. He smiled a little, hoping to show warmth to a man that many would consider intimidating. To Edwyrd, he didn't know that word anymore. Not since his bonding with Vesel. After all, he had stared down an alpha silver dragon and lived to tell the tale. Not just lived but had bonded with the animal. Edwyrd was unsure anything or anyone could intimidate him anymore.

"I was expecting more."

"So was I. A paper test seems rather benign to me."

The man from Sereya butted in between the two of the fireborn, clearly still upset about his performance from the hint of annoyance in his voice.

Cyrus shook his head. "Paper test. Virtual test. It means nothing. All that matters is real-life. Those questions were not real life."

Edwyrd nodded. Cyrus had a point. "How would you change it?" he asked.

"If I was Guardian of the Core, I would throw my contestants into the fields of fire and see who could survive."

"Fields of fire?" the Sereyan asked. "Doesn't seem fair. Why not the plains of snow we have in Sereya and see who is brave enough to pass Peril's Passage?"

Edwyrd shook his head. "What Cyrus said is merely a saying. He just meant he would put them in an actual scenario where they could show their intelligence rather than having a test prove it."

Hope melted, the Sereyan retreated like a glacier. Edwyrd smiled.

From behind them, a woman laughed. "Honestly, Christian, you Sereyan need to see more of the world instead of ruling on icy thrones."

"At least we rule." He shot his chin up.

"And at least I will be advancing to the next round." She smirked back at him while at the threshold of her door.

Christian didn't have a remark to her words. Knowing he had probably forfeited his chance already, he disappeared into his room.

When his door slammed, Edwyrd asked. "So, you think you did well enough on the exam?"

"I did well enough to advance, and that is all that matters, is it not?" She winked at him.

Edwyrd smirked. "You're right. You seem to have confidence. You're from Acquava?"

She nodded. "Part of the Hart Isles."

"And you're royalty?"

"What makes you think that?"

"Your confidence."

She giggled. "Hardly. No one in my city is royalty."

"What do you mean?"

"I come from a city overrun by cats. They are the only true royalty there, and definitely have enamored us all." She cast a glance at Cyrus. "I will see you both later at dinner. Best of luck to you two."

"What do you think of her?" Edwyrd asked Cyrus.

"She is competent for a woman. I'll give her that. If she wasn't a woman, I'd say she would be a threat to us both."

"Why?" Edwyrd asked.

"Because she's waterborn. And we're fireborn."

"So, you can cast Power?"

"Of course." Cyrus laughed. "I believe everyone invited here can." He continued forward to his door.

"Right." Edwyrd forced out a slight chuckle. "What's your story?"

One hand already on the doorknob, door slightly ajar, he turned and asked. "Why do you care to know?"

"Because we are from the same planet. Being from Pyre, I don't meet many Therians, much less those who are part of the firesons."

"And I've never met someone born in the land of dragons."

"There aren't dragons in Therus?"

"Here and there, but only if they are scouting for wyverns."

"Wyverns?"

"The smaller, less lethal dragons. Come in." Cyrus opened his door the rest of the way, letting Edwyrd follow him in. Cyrus pulled up a chair for Edwyrd and leaned himself against the wall, preferring to stand rather than take the bed. Edwyrd quickly surveyed the room. It was identical to his but not as clean. It seemed Cyrus didn't take advantage of the hangers in the closet or the dresser close by the painting of a red spiral.

"Looking for something?" Cyrus asked.

Edwyrd's eyes bulged. Cyrus had caught him observing the room, trying to take in any information he could. Thinking of the least suspicious thing to say, Edwyrd said, "Your room. It's the same as mine. Even the painting." Edwyrd looked at the painting, glad that Cyrus could no longer see his face.

"What do you think it means?"

Edwyrd arched his brows and felt Cyrus come to stand beside him, admiring the painting, too. *Well, at least that worked.* Now he had to come up with an interpretation to keep his lie going. "It's just a hypnosis spiral, meant to calm our anxieties here before bed."

"Then why is it red and gold?"

Was this discussion really happening? He hadn't taken Cyrus to be an art connoisseur. Who exactly was this man? Hoping to avoid as much discussion on his part as possible, Edwyrd quickly confessed, "I hadn't thought of that. What do you think it is?" He turned the question onto Cyrus, suspecting this could be another opportunity to glean more information.

"The gold means victory. The red blood. Victory can only happen with blood; when we give everything we have. Die by fire, die with honor. Living in Pyre, nothing is higher."

Edwyrd winced when he heard the Pyrean mantra. He had never completely agreed with dying by fire, and seeing that his sister had just died from a fire-breathing dragon, he had even less reason to cling to the famous saying. Still, it was expected of him to say something. "Is any death more honorable?"

"Of course not. Not for a true fireblood. That's why I like this painting so much." Cyrus patted Edwyrd's shoulder and retreated back to his standing position on the wall. "Who are your picks for advancing to the next round?" Cyrus asked.

Edwyrd turned around, thankful that the discussion on art was finished. "The real question is, who won't be advancing."

Cyrus chuckled to himself. "The ice prince, that much is for certain. And if I had to bet, I would say Kelis, the Ka'Chean woman."

"I would have put my money on the fisherman."

"Caspian?"

Edwyrd nodded. "He's strong, but he doesn't seem mentally capable."

"Why not?"

Edwyrd couldn't produce an answer.

"You have to see the bigger picture, Edwyrd. I noticed the hostility between Caspian and Christian from entering. Caspian's goal is to beat him. Why, I don't know, but that type of ambition fuels a man. That's what rivalry does. Kelis seems like a lone wolf. A fighter, yes, but she only fights with a scimitar, meaning she hacks and relies on brute strength."

Edwyrd blinked, realizing that he was certainly outclassed here. Lord Omyon had been right and the people here would certainly prove challenging. He wondered if Cyrus was astute enough to know that he had bonded with an animal? Could anyone sense that?

"Speaking of which, I noticed you don't have any weapons."

Cyrus chuckled. "I do. These." He held up his fists.

"You're a brawler?"

"If you mean that I don't fight traditionally, yes."

"But how do you get past enemy weapons?"

Cyrus chuckled again. "I can't tell you that, my fireborn friend. Not yet. Maybe you'll see me do it in the finals when you make it there with me."

"You believe I will advance?"

"Well, you have made it at least past this first round, but who knows what the other rounds have in store."

"What makes you think I've made it to the second?"

"You ask questions. It's a sign of a thinker. And I believe there is more to you than meets the eye."

Edwyrd gulped. "And that is?"

"I don't know, but you came into my room to do more than establish a friendship."

"You think so?"

"You came to check out your competition as well, and if you believe that I am the largest threat in these Trials, then you are much more adroit than you appear."

"And do you believe you are the largest threat here?"

Cyrus laughed at that and folded his arms over his chest. "No. We are told as firesons never to be so proud."

"And why is that?"

"You have never heard of the story of the King of Fire before?"

Edwyrd thought on that for a while. "It sounds familiar, but I can't place it."

"Story goes that before the Great War, a King of Fire ruled over Pyre. He was bonded with Chantico."

Edwyrd's eyes bulged. "Chantico?"

"Well, at least you know about the fire serpent. Yeah. Her. Imagine being bonded to an animal that strong. How much Power would that give you?"

"Yeah. I'm sure it'd be a lot." Edwyrd avoided eye contact with Cyrus, feigning to be lost in contemplation, extrapolating the Power that would be invested into him. He already knew what it felt like to be bonded with Vesel, so Edwyrd had a pretty good idea of how overwhelming it would be to be bonded with a Creature of Legend.

"The King thought he was invincible, so he started expanding his lands and his reign. Eventually, he pushed his limits too far and a band of zubins destroyed him."

"Where was Chantico? What happened to her?"

"Hasn't been seen since. She had been at war with other creatures, though, and left her master to battle for himself. The weakest link got destroyed." Cyrus sighed. "That is how it always goes, doesn't it?"

Edwyrd gulped. He twitched his neck. "Yeah," he pushed out.

"But at least he died on the battlefield, and there is nothing higher in honor than that on Pyre." Cyrus looked at him. Once again, he began the mantra, which Edwyrd reluctantly spoke as well. "Die by fire, die with honor. Living in Pyre, nothing is higher." Cyrus chuckled. He kicked off from his leaning position and extended a hand towards Edwyrd, which Edwyrd took. "It's good to have another fireblood here. I hope I see you in the finals."

Edwyrd didn't respond. He didn't know what to say. Instead, he stood and flashed a smile at Cyrus with a quick head nod and left the room. Clearly the man was confident in himself, as he should be, being a fireson, but to hear the Pyrean mantra fall so effortlessly from his lips, and the way he had said it with such conviction when Edwyrd had only let it just spill from his lips due to reflex, meant one thing: this man was willing to die for his dreams. The man's interpretation of the painting told him that as well. And if he wasn't afraid of death, that made Cyrus the most dangerous contestant there.

For the first time since arriving to the Core the day before, all eight contestants ate together. While they had arrived at dinnertime yesterday, because of the need to get an early night's rest, individual meals had been brought to the rooms. Edwyrd imagined some had gone to breakfast in the morning, but he hadn't. He had preferred to sleep more and rest his mind rather than feed his stomach, and so with a dinner before him of steaks and fish and potatoes and fruits, he was salivating and ravenous.

He had been assigned a seat next to Cyrus, which he was thankful for, as the man certainly did intrigue Edwyrd on more than just a contestant level. Their Pyrean fireblood had created kinship to a degree, and he found himself talking with the man more than others. To his right sat the woman from Acquava, Cordelia. Alongside her sat Christian and then opposite of Christian sat the man Victor from Empora and alongside him Iris from Chaon, Kelis, and then Caspian.

Despite the delectable food on the table and the hunger he saw around the table, no one dared eat, eating for the Guardian of the Core to say something. He sat at the head of the table, two conseleigh sitting alongside each corner of the table, hands folded together observing them. Was he looking for something?

After a large bowl of assorted fruit was brought out, Guardian Crevon stood. "We are all finally together here at the table, for the first and the last time. After dinner, I will be announcing the remaining six contestants who will continue to stay on the Core. For the two that are not called, I will be transporting you back personally."

The room was brought to even further silence.

To be brought here just to be kicked out again? The idea was cruel, especially considering the first trial had been a mere exam. He wondered how much respect he would lose to Lord Omyon if he didn't advance. He hadn't performed poorly enough to warrant elimination, or so he thought, but the finality of everything caused his foot to tap on the floor impatiently. He slid one hand under the table to his knee to calm it and felt vibrations of the table rustle his forearms.

"Do not think of your time as a failure, though. Nothing should ever be thought of as failure but as a learning experience. Think to yourself, where did I go wrong? And then correct those inadequacies as you go about your life. Enough talk about those things, though. Please, let us begin." He gestured his arms upward, and individual servants came to each contestant. These were the same individuals who had taken their bags the day before. Each asked what the individual wanted and then leaned over the table to serve the person.

Edwyrd cocked his head at this and wondered why such a formality existed. He wanted more food on his plate than what his attendant had given him. Couldn't he just grab his own? Then he wondered why it truly mattered that he was thinking about these things at all. They were nebulous. But at the same time, they weren't. In all of Edwyrd's schooling, he had been taught that everything was done with intent. Intent plus action equaled results. And surely that was what the Guardian of the Core was hoping to get, results. Or was this merely Edwyrd overthinking again? He hated moments like this and was thankful for Cordelia's bantering to knock him from his thoughts.

"Are you going to stare at it or eat it? You looked ravenous as the food was being brought out."

"You saw that?"

"It's hard to miss when your mouth was drooling."

Edwyrd blushed. Quickly, he grabbed his fork and knife and shoveled food into his mouth, which only caused Cordelia to laugh even more. "I didn't eat breakfast this morning."

"I noticed. I was here."

Edwyrd straightened. "You were? Who else was here?"

"Everyone besides you firebloods," she joked.

Edwyrd looked to Cyrus. As if expecting the question, he commented. "Meditation and training are my breakfast."

Cordelia leaned back in her chair to look at Cyrus. "Or maybe you just don't have good breakfast options on Pyre, but it certainly was a delicacy. You should come next time."

Edwyrd gulped down his food and nodded. "I will do that."

"That is assuming there is a next time for you." She cut into a piece of steak and plopped it into her mouth while staring at Edwyrd.

The playfulness in her gaze caused Edwyrd to look away. The others were busy in conversations as well.

Victor maintained conversation with Iris and Kelis, but every so often short furtive glances towards his direction.

The hour-long dinner passed by quickly, Edwyrd gaining only a few more nuggets of information that seemed important. First, he had found out that he could order more food simply by calling to his attendant, who would then spoon more morsels onto his plate. Edwyrd did this five times. Second, while in the midst of his third plate, he found out Cordelia's parentage was rather unique. Her father had been the head guardsman to the baron of the city, but had since grown old and retired, passing along the necklace she wore now. He also passed along to her his title and so Edwyrd learned that she now had experience in combat, competent experience, too, if she was head guardswoman. Her mother couldn't swim, which was unusual for an Acquavan but not unheard of. In fact, it had been that quality that brought her mother and her father together.

Edwyrd stopped eating when Guardian Crevon stood up and Conseleigh Juniper handed the Guardian a folded piece of blue parchment paper.

"I am pleased to see everyone eating so well, especially you, Edwyrd." Guardian Crevon smiled.

Edwyrd blushed. He had drawn too much attention to himself because of his hunger pangs. He would need to control that better in the next round. But why had he felt so ravenous? Sure, he had not had breakfast, but he had eaten the day before, and it had been a rather large portion of meat and vegetables that had been brought to his room, so why the increased appetite? *What's going on with me?* He patted his stomach, quieting the last rumble it gave him.

"I will now announce the scores and the names of the contestants. The total score you could have received was sixty, but none of you received that. The highest score was a fifty-seven and the lowest score a twenty-six." Guardian Crevon took time to survey all the contestants and then continue.

"The contestant with fifty-seven answers correct is Cyrus."

Edwyrd straightened his posture but refused to look at the man next to him while everyone else did. After a moment, he leaned over and whispered. "Congratulations."

Cyrus nodded his acknowledgement.

"Second place goes to Victor with fifty-five answers correct."

Edwyrd looked at the man, who didn't balk in the glances cast his way. Instead, the man locked eyes with Cyrus, just for a moment, and then they turned their attention back to Guardian Crevon, who continued reading.

"Third place with fifty answers was Cordelia. Fourth place with forty-eight answers was Caspian."

Cordelia righted herself in her chair and flashed a smile. The large man across from Cyrus slammed his fist on the table and punched one fist up in the air. Edwyrd shifted in his chair. *What about—*

"Fifth place with forty-four answers was Edwyrd."

He let out a gasp of air. He had made it. His heart stilled, and he looked ahead towards the two women from Myoli. Those were the only two that would be making it; he already knew Christian to have failed the test. Both gave a nervous look at one another. The room lay silent for the most important number to be called, the sixth-place finalist.

The tension in the air was almost tangible as Guardian Crevon surveyed them all one more time, his gaze ending on Edwyrd, to whom he said, "Congratulations." Then, after a long moment of silence, he cleared his throat and then continued. "The sixth-place finalist, with forty answers correct, Iris."

The Chaonese woman let out a gasp of air and patted her chest. Kelis's shoulders collapsed. Before Guardian Crevon had time to call the remaining two contestants, Christian threw down his linen, stood up, and asked, "And how close was I to sixth?"

Guardian Crevon flicked a glance down at his paper. He shook his head. "Not at all. You were the last place with twenty-seven." The Sereyan prince melted back into his chair, saying nothing but casting eyes of contempt at Caspian from across the table, which the fisherman ignored in his jubilation. "Kelis," the Guardian continued, "You came in seventh with thirty-three."

Kelis bobbed her head respectfully. "Thank you for the opportunity, my Guardian."

"Kelis, Caspian, spend the next few hours packing. I will take you back personally. The other contestants, tonight and tomorrow is free to do with as you wish, but the day after tomorrow begins another trial. Another two contestants will be eliminated then."

Edwyrd stood up and wandered towards the exit with Cordelia. Christian had already left, in a temper-tantrum that only royalty could throw. While at the threshold, he noticed the others decided to stick around the dining hall: Caspian, Kelis and Iris all in conversation. Victor and Cyrus stayed locked in a battle of eye contact with one another.

"Go get him." Cordelia nudged.

Edwyrd went over to shake Cyrus. "Would you like to come back with us?"

Cyrus shook his head. "No. I have things I need to talk with the Guardian about. Go on ahead."

Edwyrd looked from the large Pyrean man to Guardian Crevon, who was in the midst of a conversation with his conseleigh. He wondered what the man would need to discuss with the Guardian but decided it didn't matter. Turning back around, he followed Cordelia out of the exit and to the rooms.

"Third-place. Congratulations," Edwyrd said.

"Fifth isn't so bad for you either." She nodded.

Edwyrd didn't know to take that as a slight or a complement, so he merely said, "Thanks. What do you think of those two?"

"They are in the battle that all top competitors show."

"And what is that?"

"The battle of intimidation." She laughed a little. "I'm glad I messed up a few answers in the test."

Edwyrd frowned, and he cocked his head. "You purposely missed answers?"

"Just a few. Maybe five or so." Cordelia winked.

"Like what?"

She hummed, thinking. "The one about the adored and the son."

"It was the godfather, right?"

Cordelia laughed even louder. "No. But that is what I put."

"Then what was it?"

"The answer was the boy's mother."

"But—"

"Who says adored can only be male?"

Edwyrd bit his lip. He stayed silent, unsure of how to recover such a loss of face until he forced a slight laugh. "Didn't you think the Trials would have been more than a paper test?" he asked, hoping to change topics.

"They will be. But this trial was rather well-designed."

Edwyrd cocked his head. "What do you mean? It was just a test. Something they could have given us on our home planets or a barrier to entry before coming. Why here?"

"To show how we perform under pressure, of course." Cordelia studied Edwyrd carefully. "

If you thought this trial was merely a paper test, you missed the point of it. It was to showcase our way of thinking. The question you missed about the mother and her son was meant to subvert expectations. My mother, she was an adored. And that is why she found my father so attractive." She stopped at her doorway. "She couldn't swim and he, a warrior, saved her. She who practiced healing and saving people's lives couldn't save herself. Irony is what brought them together. Maybe even fate, as they say. Do you believe in that, Edwyrd?"

"Fate?"

Cordelia nodded.

Edwyrd put a hand behind his head. "I'm starting to think about it more."

"And you should continue thinking about it as you sleep. Goodnight." She tucked herself away into her room and locked the door behind her.

Edwyrd went to his room and sat on the bed. *The adored was the mother. Of course!* How could he have been so blind to his biases? Lord Omyon had even told him of Ancient Lyoen before he came. She was the greatest adored.

Edwyrd sighed deeply, understanding that his lack of attention would cost him dearly if he wasn't careful. Laying back onto his pillow, he rested his hands on his stomach and pondered about what other surprises the Trials would bring in the events ahead. However, one thing was certain, there were more to these Trials than met the eyes.

CHAPTER 9

V ictor had stayed back at the table, trying his best to feign interest with the others in his wing. Iris was doing an ample job of pretending to care about Kelis's feelings, and Caspian was still in awe of his advancement to the next round.

"Kelis, do not worry. You are still strong for making it this far." Iris patted her back.

Victor almost let out a slight chuckle at the showmanship of such a manipulator. He liked her for that. If it hadn't been his acute perception of earlier, and knowing she was an assassin, then he would have thought it genuine. But could assassins actually carry genuine emotions? He doubted it. But they did carry death, and now she and Cyrus were more dangerous than he had once assumed. By passing this round, after all, they showed a hint of intelligence. More than a hint, actually, in Cyrus's case. It proved to Victor that he truly was indeed the main competition here. His previous thought about Christian being the only other here like him had proven false.

Victor bit his lower lip and shifted in his chair. *Only three wrong.* Victor swooped his vision along the table, passing quickly by Cyrus, who was in a short conversation with the other contestant from Pyre. Cyrus acknowledged his gaze and Victor held it for a time, hearing all the empty flattery coming out from Iris's lips and Caspian's condolences as well. When he got bored with the staring competition between him and the Pyrean, he looked away and focused his attention to Kelis. "Any achievement is better than none," Victor said, trying to offer some sage words.

"You're just saying that."

"Yes, I was." Victor shrugged his shoulders and took a sip of his wine. It didn't matter at this point if she liked him or not, she was gone.

Kelis huffed and threw down her linen. "Well, I suppose I should get packing." She sniffled and straightened up her shoulder and stood. She faced the head of the table. "Guardian Crevon, conseleigh, it was a pleasure to at least have been accepted. Thank you." She bowed her head slightly.

"I will make sure good words follow you into your next endeavors." Guardian Crevon acknowledged her with a nod of his own.

Kelis left. The fourth one to have done so, following the Acquavan and Pyrean out of the double doors. Caspian stood up soon after and put one hand into another hand and bowed. "My Guardian, I am glad to know I will rise tomorrow for another trial."

"Take care, Caspian. Hopefully, you'll have many more nights here as well." Guardian Crevon raised a chalice of mead and took a swig.

Caspian left, leaving just the three contestants—Victor, Iris, and Cyrus—in the room along with the Guardian and his conseleigh. Victor crossed his gaze back to Cyrus, the man who had beaten him in the first round. The man didn't acknowledge him at all. Instead, he looked towards the conseleigh and the Guardian of the Core, almost as if he already thought himself amongst them. But how could he think such a thing? Was he really that well versed and read and had that deep of analytical skills? Moreover, which questions did he get wrong?

Victor was reaching for another glass of wine when a squeeze to his thigh underneath the table distracted him. The hand drifted upwards on his thigh, the fingers pedaling their way to his manhood. Time slowed as she squeezed him, her fingers crawling over the bulge in his pants like a caterpillar on a leaf. Then it was gone. With a quick clearing of her throat, she finished her own glass of wine and stood to dismiss herself from the room, not giving him an ounce more of attention.

When the double doors closed, Cyrus stood up. Victor did as well. Both men narrowed their focus on the other and then strode forward simultaneously to Guardian Crevon. The Guardian chuckled to himself as the contestants approached. The conseleigh's eyes glowed, as did the Guardian's, and Victor knew they were using telepathy to talk about the situation occurring.

Without breaking the telepathic bond with his conseleigh, Guardian Crevon readjusted his posture in his chair. "What may I do for you both?"

"My Guardian, I wish to know the answers to the questions I got wrong."

"Me as well, my Guardian," Victor said, mimicking Cyrus. He had, indeed, wanted to know which questions he had gotten wrong, but he was more intrigued by the questions Cyrus had gotten wrong and if they could tell Victor anything about the man.

"Pax, Yun, the analysis of the results for these two men, please?" Guardian Crevon extended a hand to each of them. Each conseleigh put a slip of paper into his hand. With extraordinary fluidity, Guardian Crevon scanned both of their papers simultaneously, pausing only once. His lips bent into a smirk. "Each of the conseleigh here can discuss which individual questions you missed, but there is one question that you both seem to have missed. That I can explain here." Guardian Crevon handed back the papers to the conseleigh.

"I would be honored, my Guardian. I wish to learn from my mistakes." Cyrus bowed.

"Very well. You both missed the pen and the parchment problem."

Victor scanned his memory, trying to recall the phrasing of the problem, but it wasn't one that had stuck out to him. "Pen and parchment?" He muttered.

"Yes. A pen and the parchment used to write on cost one-hundred-and-ten copper cures in total. The pen costs one-hundred more copper cures than the parchment. How much does the parchment cost?"

Victor's eyes lit up. He had gotten that question wrong? How? It was so easy. "My Guardian, are you sure? It's ten. There must be a—"

Guardian Crevon shook his head. "Wrong. Both of you answered that way. If the parchment costs ten copper cures and the pen costs one-hundred copper cures more than the parchment, then the pen would cost one-hun-dred-and-ten copper cures, bringing the total to one-hundred-and-twenty copper cures. The parchment only costs five copper cures, bringing the pen to cost one-hundred-and-five copper cures, totaling one-hundred-and-ten."

Victor flushed. He wondered if Cyrus felt the same embarrassment. He couldn't tell due to the skin tone.

"It tells me one thing. Both of you ignore difficult problems and tend to downplay them into easier ones. You overlook things, despite how observant both of you think that you are."

"Thank you for the advice, my Guardian," Victor said.

"The same, my Guardian," Cyrus echoed.

"I hope you both take the advice to heart. Pax, go with Cyrus and discuss the other questions. Yun, take Victor aside."

Both conseleigh stood and beckoned the respective individual to follow them to a different part of the dining hall. Conseleigh Juniper ran a quick eye over Victor's exam, something he didn't really care about anymore. It's not like he could change the past. The reason he had wanted to approach Guardian Crevon was to learn the problems Cyrus got wrong, not learn about his own.

"Aahh, you missed this one." She pushed her shoulder up against Victor's and had him read the question again.

"There is this one man who killed his mother. He was born before his father and married over one hundred women without divorcing anyone. Yet, he was considered normal by all of his acquaintances. Why?" Victor bit his lower lip. He read the answer he circled to himself. "His acquaintances all had similar experiences."

"You are oversimplifying the problem again here."

"Well, it seems this man is anything but normal, but perhaps wherever this takes place, such a thing occurs regularly."

"What makes you think it occurs in a different system than our own?"

"The man was born before his father. Perhaps time travel has been invented there."

"It is not a riddle such as this, Victor Zigarda. It is asking you to think about possible scenarios."

"Well, then perhaps the father can give birth in this system?"

Conseleigh Juniper shook her head. "No, I assure you. Females are the only entities that have that right."

"Then what?" Victor huffed.

"The baby was born in front of the father, and the mother died from childbirth."

Victor's skin crawled. It already was too familiar of a situation. "That doesn't explain the last line."

"The man is a priest. That is his profession to marry people. A good profession, yes? Honest and true."

Victor chuckled to himself.

"What is it?"

He shook his head. "It's nothing. What were the others that I missed?"

While Conseleigh Juniper explained the other three questions Victor missed. He listened only half-heartedly, nodding his head and acknowledging her every so often to feign his interest. Inside, he was still thinking about the first question. That man the riddle spoke about was his brother. Well, nearly, but he may have been thought of as a priest for all the flattery he gave towards Father. His constant blandishments were probably the result of his childbirth killing Mother. Almost some biological reaction, as if he had to constantly rectify the damage he had done to the family for his birth. Prove himself. But didn't his brother know that he couldn't change the past? Didn't he know that he shouldn't hold himself captive to guilt? For a time, Victor had blamed his brother, but now, since his father's trainings and lessons, he'd learned that sometimes sacrifices had to be made, and sometimes those sacrifices were the things closest to us.

"Do you understand all of that?" Conseleigh Juniper asked.

"I do. Thank you for taking the time to explain the things to me."

"Of course. Is there anything else I can do for you?"

Victor opened his mouth to say, "no" but then immediately closed it. "Actually, there is. I was wondering if you could tell me where Iris is from."

"Iris? She is Chaonese."

Victor smiled and bobbed his head, gesturing a certain playfulness in the manner. "Of course. I knew that. I meant where in Chaon, though. I'm curious as to the city."

"She is from Faywynne, in the south of Chaon."

"Thank you."

"Why do you ask?"

Expecting this follow-up question, Victor had his answer prepared. "Well, since Kelis has been eliminated now, it is just her and I representing the great domain of Myoli. I hope to build some rapport with individuals from my own planet."

"That is wise and a quality of a good leader. I do wish you the best of luck in the rest of the Trials."

Victor nodded and left the room, making his way directly to Iris's room.

She opened the door with little hesitation at his knock. "So you came?"

"It was rather clear that you wanted me to."

"Come in, Victor." She flashed him a grin.

Victor entered. As he expected, the room was orderly and clean. Nothing was left out, and if it had been, like the dagger on the table, for example, it was to serve a purpose. Iris was far too sly to make mistakes, despite her coming in fifth, but what game was she playing with Victor? He was about to find out, and he, too, had a few tricks up his sleeve. She perched herself up on her wooden desk and slid the wooden chair out to him—another show of her fluidity. Was she doing it to intimidate him or to give him leverage over her? The Chaon women intrigued him more and more by the second. He took a seat.

"So?" He would let her open up first.

"Stop being careless."

Victor's eyes flashed open. "What?"

Iris leaned her neck to the side. "You heard me."

"What makes you think I am careless?"

"How you reacted with Kelis today at dinner. It is clear you feigned your condolences."

Victor's face grew taut now. Iris was even more perceptive than he would have thought possible. "And what does it really matter at the end of the day? She is gone. Her and that white-haired prince. Two less competitors. We are still in."

"Yes. We are, but I am not here to win."

Victor furrowed his eyes. "What do you mean?"

"I am here to make sure that you win."

CHAPTER 10

With a cocked head, Victor looked at her incredulously, but didn't speak. He let her words nestle into him for a moment while he took time to gather his thoughts. "What makes you think I need your help in winning?"

"Because you're already behind."

"The answers on that test don't matter. All that matters is who reaches the end."

"Yes. But do you think the Trials will get less difficult or more difficult?"

"More. Obviously."

"Then you are already on the chopping block." She grabbed her knife and spun it on her finger.

"I'm second."

She disrupted the knife from its spinning-state, snatching it and pointing it towards Victor. "And that isn't first."

"What's in it for you? And how can you help me?"

"We both know the main competition here. You saw him when he entered the lobby last night, same as me."

"Cyrus."

She nodded. Brushing a bang of brown hair out of her eye, she said, "Yes. The fireson."

"And how could you possibly help me with that?"

"Isn't it your family that says, Knowledge is Power?"

Victor sucked in a breath. He furrowed his brows. "Where are you from? How do you know my family?"

"I am from Chaon."

"Chaon isn't Empora."

"It's close enough that word travels, and you happen to be quite the prominent figure in Empora."

"What makes you say that?"

Iris tilted her head back and laughed. "You are the son of a lord, Victor. You are a prince. The eldest. And..." She bit her lip. "Never mind."

"And what?" Victor arched his eyebrows.

"And that kind of title means you are always in the spotlight."

Victor narrowed his vision on her. "You lie."

"You mean to tell me you're not always in the spotlight?"

Victor grunted. "No. Of course I am. But you were going to say something else. I know it."

Iris hummed and twisted her lips to one side. "Very well. You caught me. Yes, well, when you are the eldest prince of a current lord and when you can cast blue flames, word spreads fairly quickly about you."

Victor controlled his breathing and resisted bulging his eyes as much as he could. She knew. If she knew that, then she probably knew other things about his training. Did the others know? Maybe Kelis had known something, but Ka'Che was quite a distance from Empora, across the Krine Sea, so word traveling there would have taken a considerable deal more effort than simply being carried south on a wind and the whim of lips.

While he wanted to know how exactly she came to find out about him, he denied his curiosity for the moment. Instead, he needed to redirect the conversation and establish control again. "Where in Chaon are you from?" He studied her, wondering how she would respond.

"I grew up in Valbeach."

"I didn't ask where you grew up. I asked where you are from."

Iris smirked. "Clever catch. Faywynne, Victor. But you already knew that."

"I did. And you tried to mask it."

"I didn't try, I'm just making sure you are worth the investment I am offering."

"You have yet to make any such offering."

Iris pushed herself off the table. "I am willing to sacrifice my place in the Trials to further your own."

"I don't see how this handles Cyrus."

"It doesn't. Not directly, anyway. There is no way to do that here. Not while under surveillance and protection of the Guardian and his conseleigh. But I can do what I do best."

"And what is that?"

"Infiltrate people. Find out who they are. Their flaws. Their strengths. Their habits. Their ticks. Their idiosyncrasies. In essence, I've been trained to put myself in their skin."

"Like a skinchanger?" Victor guffawed.

"*Exactly* like a skinchanger." Iris looked at him with muddy, dead eyes. "Without the changing of skin, that is." The flat line on her lips curved into a smirk. She giggled to release the built-up tension.

"Is it part of your assassin's training?"

"Something like that."

"So you extract more information on Cyrus, hand it to me to use to my advantage later, and what do you get in return?"

"Verimas."

Victor coughed. "Excuse me. What did you say?"

"You heard me correctly, Victor. Verimas."

"I can't just give you a territory. That is part of Empora. That is my father's land."

"And when you win Guardianship, you will supersede your father, correct?"

"What purpose does Verimas hold for you?"

"None for me. But I am here representing some powerful entities in Chaon. Verimas is the perfect place."

Victor couldn't help raising an eyebrow. "For what?" He scoffed. "Nothing there but marshes and molehills to hide in."

Iris didn't take the bait. Instead, she kept quiet. Quiet enough that Victor reimagined the lay of the land in his mind, thinking of what value she, or anyone for that matter, would want with the city. It must have contained something, considering the fact she was going to throw away her shot at apprenticeship to obtain it for whoever she worked for.

Marshes and molehills aside, the city was close to the sea, so it could act as a port if ports were ever built, but it still wouldn't hold weight compared to that of Aeston a little further north. And no one would ever think to build a port because of the proximity to the Thieving Isles. While technically in Empora's control, the Isles were more autonomous than his father would have liked. People who lived there were rapscallions of the sea and vagabonds. But for all of its barbarity, it did have a rather unique, symbiotic relationship with Verimas. By taking Verimas, Chaon would also be taking the islands. That, he figured, must be what they want.

"Sure," Victor said nonchalantly, as if the promised exchange didn't matter.

Iris took the knife, threw it up in the air, hopped off the table and caught it with one hand, bringing it straight down to her extended, open palm. "Sure enough to make this a Blood Pact?"

The celerity and grace she had just demonstrated made Victor take a step back, eyeing the knife with reconsideration. She certainly would be an adversary in the ring. He looked from her dark green eyes, forests of mystery, to her knife which touched her exposed palm. Holding her position, she didn't tremble. She stood waiting for him to make his move.

Victor stood and looked into her eyes and then at her palm. Scars spoke of her previous contracts. "And what should happen if I lose?"

"As long as I do my part and help you advance, I've kept my part of the pact. It would be *unwise* of you to not keep yours, win or lose."

The way she said it caused Victor to push his brows together. He pushed his arm out, palm extended. With the other hand, he grabbed the knife. "To advancing." He drew the dagger down across his skin.

"To advancing." Iris swiped the knife from his hand and brought it down on hers.

They shook each other's hand with the bloodied ones, smearing the reds together while interlocking their other hands over top. While looking each other in the eyes, they said simultaneously, "May we bleed, may we bond, may we know each other's thoughts forward on. Pact intact, we shall act, or forever be in the Other's grasp."

Victor closed his eyes, expecting some kind of energy and Power. But he didn't feel anything. His shoulders slumped. Iris must have suspected this sort of thing happened a lot because the moment he slumped his shoulders, she entered his mind.

Victor.

Iris?

Yes. We are bonded now. We can feel each other and talk to each other through telepathy.

Victor took note of her glowing eyes, showing that she was using Telepathic Power. He had used this ability before, but only rarely with his brother and his father. *This is it? It feels only like Blood Bonding.*

Blood bonding stops at the first line. A Blood Pact holds us in the Other's grasp.

So I am now in debt to you? And you to me?

Something like that.

Victor cut the line of telepathy. He drew his hand back from Iris's, examining the smudge of red on his palm. He clenched his hand, feeling a slight twinge of pain at the open wound. "So, what's next?"

"What's next is making sure you stick around in these Trials until the end. I do believe it will be you and Cyrus in the finals, and I will have the information you need on him by then."

"What if you don't even make it past tomorrow?"

"Then I'll give you the information that I've collected up to that point before Guardian Crevon transports me back."

"One day's worth?"

"Don't underestimate what can be accomplished by the Bonded Guild."

"Bonded Guild? Does that mean—"

Iris already shook her head. "Do you see an animal with me?" She paused, letting her question be emphasized in the silence that followed. "Some in our ranks are bonded to animals, but not me. I bond with humans." She lifted her bloodied hand and waved it at him.

"And you seem to be quite proficient at it."

"I never fail my end of the bond. That is why my contractors put so much faith in me and why they sponsored my application to even be here in the first place."

"Who are your contractors?"

"The Sages of Gladonus."

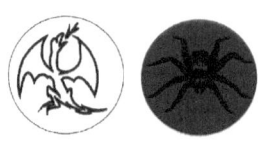

CHAPTER 11

E dwyrd, along with the five other remaining contestants, stood in the lobby just as they had when the Guardian first gathered them together. Above Edwyrd was a cupola of the Ancients, both holding their swords, tips pointed into the ground. They stood a body's length away from one another. He had only noticed it because Guardian Crevon had descended from his floor of the estate on a platform located in the middle of the lobby. Once the platform had fully retracted into the floor, clicking into place, the Guardian went to stand in front of his conseleigh, who waited perched on the large staircase that went up to the second floor.

Guardian Crevon smiled and extended his arms. "How are you remaining six doing?"

Mutters of *good* and *well* came forth from all the contestants' lips.

With pleasantries established, Guardian Crevon snapped his fingers, and the servants brought out four desks and placed them between the Guardian and the contestants. The conseleigh took a place behind each desk. Guardian Crevon stepped to the side of all of them, dragging the attention of the contestants with him. "Today, I will be testing your ability to cooperate with a partner. As Guardian, not only will you need good analytical skills, recognize others prejudices as well as your own, but you will also need to develop partnership and rapport. Not only during your one-year sabbatical in each nation, but throughout your Guardianship, you will have to coordinate with the families in power across the system.

"Before I put you into teams, though, it is essential that all of you receive some supplies for this task. From Conseleigh Shadir you will receive your map. From Conseleigh Ersa you will receive your tracking device. From Conseleigh Juniper you will receive your task. And from Conseleigh Barbeau you will receive a bag of supplies that you can choose to do with however you please. Some you may find necessary for completing the task, others may be included just for the illusion of being beneficial. It is up to you and your partner to sift through your sacks and try to comprehend what is essential and what isn't.

"With that being said, Caspian, come and receive your items."

One-by-one Guardian Crevon called the contestants to gather the items at the front of the lobby, just before the staircase. Edwyrd was called fourth, after Cyrus. The paper map in his hand felt oddly out of place with the electronic bracelet that Conseleigh Ersa gave him to strap around his ankle. Conseleigh Juniper had handed him another blue envelope, similar to that of Guardian Crevon's invitation letter, sealed in wax. He didn't open it. No one opened it. He assumed everyone, like him, waited to find out their partner before knowing what task they would have to complete.

After Victor finished getting his items, Guardian Crevon continued. "Now that each of you has your items, I will arrange you into teams. Speak your name one by one when I direct you to. You may feel a slight sensation, but it is nothing to be concerned about."

One-by-one each contestant spoke their name and a thread of green came out of their mouth. When it was Edwyrd's turn, he said, "Edwyrd Eska" and suddenly something caught in his throat. It tugged, almost making him want to gag, but soon it was over, and a strand of green data drifted into a green, holographic jeweled box that floated in front of him. After each contestant spoke his or her name, the box shook in spasms until eventually it exploded and in front of Edwyrd's eyes was a name.

Victor Zigarda.

Edwyrd Eska.

Victor looked at the name, not knowing what to think. Was he happy or sad that he hadn't been paired with Cyrus? He didn't really know. Edwyrd was just another contestant scraping by. He hadn't even gotten in the top half in the first trial. But if he remembered correctly, Edwyrd was from Pyre, so perhaps he knew a little about his main competition. Maybe even some of his mannerisms would give Victor a way to properly engage with Cyrus when the time came. It was an okay pairing, to say the least.

Edwyrd came to his side. Disinterested in his partner, Victor looked elsewhere. Who had Cyrus gotten as a teammate? He almost did a double-take when he saw how fortunate he had been. In what must have been a stroke of fate, Iris now stood aligned with the behemoth fireson.

Well, well... He wanted to smirk, but held himself back.

"Contestants, you have been paired as equally as possible. The strongest performer from yesterday's trial paired with the weakest. The second strongest with the second lowest performer. And finally, the middle two." Guardian Crevon pointed to Cordelia and Caspian's group.

So that is how...

"I wish you the best of luck in this pairing and in this trial. The team to complete the task last will be asked to leave tonight once dinner concludes. Is that understood?" No one nodded; all remained silent. They waited for the signal. "Very well. Let the second trial begin."

"Let's go." Victor wasted no time in hurrying up the stairs.

"Where are you going?" Edwyrd called back to him.

"The library. Knowledge is Power." Victor took the steps two at a time, and Edwyrd bounded to keep up with him. If the Pyrean had wanted to object to Victor's dominance, he didn't.

Together they strolled into the library and found a mahogany desk slightly hidden from view by the stacks of books. Victor dumped out his sack, letting the items slide out; Edwyrd did the same, but made sure to keep his separate. A smart thing, and something Victor took note of. The man was organized. Without Victor having to say anything else, Edwyrd began breaking the seal of his envelope same as Victor.

Strips of parchment fell to the table. Victor flicked a glance at his partner's envelope and noticed the same thing. Five strips of parchment had been inside each one. Victor grabbed one and read it.

"undone. By working together, another rung." Victor tossed it aside and grabbed another strip. "Showing off your partnership, and more of what you know." The next, "Woe to the team who is divided like foes." The last two made just as much sense.

"You only have five."

Only? Victor tore his gaze from his own lines of parchment and looked upon Edwyrd's. He had six. Victor furrowed his brows. "What do yours say?"

"Nothing. Nothing that I can make out right now. We need to work together to assemble the riddle." Edwyrd pushed his pieces of parchment towards Victor's and then came alongside him, eyes glancing over Victor's own words. "See here. These two." Edwyrd snatched two pieces of parchment from Victor's pile and put them together, one on top of the other. It read:

> "undone. By working together, another rung
> On the ladder you will climb. Putting them"

Victor saw how rung went with ladder logically compared to the other choices. Using this method, they assembled what they thought might come next logically.

"together, you will align with your goals."

"Woe to the team who is divided like foes." Edwyrd put the next line into place. "Here. This one, it rhymes."

"The first two didn't."

"Not directly, but here, look." Edwyrd pointed out the words *climb* and *align*, which were placed similarly in the length of the line. "We can use this to help us as well."

"Sure," Victor replied. He let the Pyrean take over the riddle's completion.

With new eyes, he observed Edwyrd, wondering if there was more to the man than met the eye. He was tall, yes, and had a solid frame that didn't allow much fat, if any. The somber man he had seen during the first night had vanished, though, and as he watched his teammate put the pieces of the puzzle together, he wondered if it was the Trials that brought out the change in his deportment or if he had only needed time to acclimate himself to the new environment.

"I think this is it."

Victor muttered the lines to himself.

> Two heads are often better than one, completing each other's
> sentences has never been more fun. Blindfolds off, covers
> undone. By working together, another rung
> on the ladder you will climb. Putting them
> together, you will align with your goals
> showing off your partnership. For the wise man knows
> Woe to the team who is divided like foes.
> knowledge requires you to sift
> under the dreaded sun, and above the shallow sea
> cupped in the hands of the Guardian's gift
> will be what you seek. Trust that the pack has everything you need.

"It doesn't feel right. Let's try this instead." Victor rearranged some lines in the middle, bringing one of them to the end and moving another up. He scanned over the final version with approval.

> Two heads are often better than one, completing each other's
> sentences has never been more fun. Blindfolds off, covers
> undone. By working together, another rung
> on the ladder you will climb. Putting them

together, you will align with your goals,
showing off your partnership. For the wise man knows
knowledge requires you to sift
under the dreaded sun, and above the shallow sea
cupped in the hands of the Guardian's gift
will be what you seek. Trust that the pack has everything you need.
Woe to the team who is divided like foes.

"Why'd you change it? Sift doesn't rhyme with knows."

"It doesn't need to. It already rhymes with goals, and wise men know knowledge."

"The ending then?"

"It is the only full-length sentence on one parchment. It belongs at the end. *Team* and *need* function like your rhyming idea, as well as *woe* and *foe*. It's a double rhyme."

"So then, this is it?"

"I believe so."

Victor studied the riddle for a long moment of silence with Edwyrd. "We need to focus here." His fingers went upon the lines that were above and below the word *Guardian*.

"Under the dreaded sun means that this gift is outside."

"I agree." Victor nodded. He undid the binding on his map and rolled out his map on the table behind him. He blinked. "It's missing things. Quick, bring your map over here."

Edwyrd spread out his map on the table. Sure enough, the areas of the map that were missing from Victor's appeared on Edwyrd's map. The sections of Edwyrd's map that were missing were filled out on Victor's.

"The Guardian really does expect us to work together," Victor scoffed.

"Ingenious." Edwyrd brushed each map, petting it almost as if to idolize it.

"You can drool over it later. Let's continue with the riddle."

"Right." Edwyrd nodded and came back alongside Victor, who continuously spewed the last few lines out on his lips. "Under the dreaded sun and above the shallow sea... under the shallow sea. Seas aren't shallow."

"How do you know?"

"Because I've seen one. I suppose there aren't many seas in Pyre."

"Only lakes of magma."

Victor's eyes widened. "A lake. That's it. How many lakes are there on your map?"

Edwyrd strolled to the next table. "Five lakes."

"Five?" Victor bit his lip. Was it really a lake? It would make sense. Lakes weren't as big as seas, yet still held water, so they would be, in fact, more shallow by comparison to a sea. "That won't do. What other topographical features are there?"

"Mountains, it looks like. On yours it looks like a valley of dunes next to a lake. Then there is—"

"Did you say dunes?"

"Yeah."

"As in sand dunes."

"What other types of dunes are there?"

"Snow dunes, but again, something you probably haven't read about. Where are they?"

Edwyrd pointed out the dunes on Victor's map. It was near a crossed-out section that had been filled in on Edwyrd's map. Lake Funghi.

"This is our best bet. Here!" Victor pointed to the lake and the small desert surrounding it.

"Why do you say that?"

"The word *sift*. It implies digging through sand."

"Good catch. We head there then. You're pretty smart."

"I've known some wise men my whole life."

Men that now wanted Victor to succeed so badly that they had sent another contestant here just to make sure he would. Truly, he wondered what purpose could he possibly serve to entities so great as the Sages. Moreover, he wondered how Iris fared with Cyrus. Being this intimate with him in the trial would prove useful to Victor later, and he wondered just how much information she could extract from him by seeing his thought process, skills, and everything else required of them while being partners. All Victor knew was that later tonight, he would be given the knowledge he needed to make this competition his own.

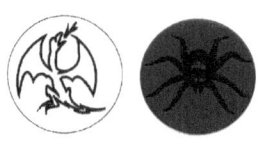

CHAPTER 12

B efore leaving the library, Edwyrd and Victor took a tally of everything in
their pack: a wire sieve, a pair of tweezers, a pen, a pad of parchment,
a small metal basin, two keys with the label *storage* on them, two canteens,
two small pill bottles, one half-filled with a gray substance and a black stone,
polished and smooth as if it was ready to be thrown over water, and the other
filled with a brittle, cerise-colored material that faintly resembled crumbled
leaves. The first looked like ash, so Edwyrd opened it up and smelled it. It
wasn't ash. He detected a faint scent of salt and sea for whatever reason. He
had smelled it before, while in training, but he couldn't place a name to the
element. Now he wished he had paid more attention to his mentor during the
potions part of training.

Victor was examining his own bottle when he asked. "What is it?"

"I don't know." Edwyrd handed over the bottle to Victor. "You recognize
this?"

Victor took a whiff from Edwyrd's pill bottle as well. "It smells surprisingly
fresh. Better than this one."

Edwyrd eyed Victor's pill bottle suspiciously. "Is that..." he muttered.

"You've seen it before?"

"Maybe. Give it here."

Victor rolled his eyes and handed it over.

When the scent hit Edwyrd's nose, he immediately understood what it was.
"Aahh. Great. It's crushed ard leaves."

"What is that?"

"Ash tasting leaves found on Pyre. Taste horrible, but they will rejuvenate us
to full strength."

Victor's eyes bulged at the comment. "Well, well, well. That is certainly a
surprise. Good observation, Pyrean."

"Edwyrd."

"Yeah. Right. Edwyrd, good job. What do you think the other is, then?"

"I don't know."

"It doesn't matter. Let's go to the storage unit." Victor held up one of the keys. "There should be something in there we can take before we go to the dunes."

"Okay. Gather the things together. I'm going to write down this riddle." Edwyrd grabbed the pen and the parchment pad from the farrago on the table. "This way we don't forget it."

"Good idea. It would be a pain assembling everything again," Victor said while packing up each sack.

"Do you think the others have the same riddle or something different?"

"Same," Edwyrd said while still writing. "Guardian Crevon designed this trial to be as equal as possible. That's why we are paired together. It would make sense he would make the riddle fair as well."

"That means we need to hurry. Who knows what extras could be in the storage unit. We don't even know where it is yet."

"Almost..." Edwyrd stopped writing. His eyes falling upon the second to last sentence. *Trust that the pack has everything that you need.* He straightened immediately from his bent over posture. "There is no storage unit."

"What?" Victor came over to him.

Edwyrd lowered his voice to a hushed whisper. "There is no storage unit. The keys are a trick."

"Why would he—"

Edwyrd was already one step ahead of him. He pointed to the line. "Trust that the pack has everything you need."

"And the keys are in the pack."

"But the storage unit, or whatever we would find in there, isn't."

"Why put it in there, then?"

"Why not? Lead us astray. Waste time. Another test of seeing which team is strongest."

Victor looked at him for a long while. Key still in his hand, he glanced at it. With a grunt, he shoved it in his pocket. "You better be right, Pyrean."

"I am. And for the last time, it's Edwyrd."

Even on his way out of the estate, Victor kept looking for any sign of the others. He couldn't find Cyrus and Iris, but he did notice that Cordelia and Caspian had the same plan as their team because they were stationed towards the front of the library. As Victor and Edwyrd walked out of the library, he caught their furtive looks, and afterwards they redoubled their efforts. He had also noticed them shuffle their body positions to cover the table, but Victor had already seen the large wire sieve and basin. This confirmed in his mind that Edwyrd was right about each team having the same riddle. The key, however, he wasn't sure about. The gambit could end up costing them the trial, or it could prove the key factor in helping them win. That was yet to be determined. All that Victor knew was that they were headed north, into the dunes of sand, towards the lake, and there they would find what they needed to find.

On the way, Victor studied Edwyrd more. If the two were successful, it meant that he would have to eventually destroy Edwyrd, and he wanted to make that as easy as possible for himself. No hard feelings towards his partner, of course. So far, he had proven himself worthy with minor observations, but there could only be one Guardian.

Not much to his surprise, Edwyrd didn't let the midday sun affect his progress. He trudged through the sand as if it were solid ground, most likely because of his upbringing in the environment such as Pyre. From what he had learned about the fiery planet, the conditions were harsh, and the men were born with fire in their veins. He wondered, then, if either he or Cyrus could cast a blue flame like Victor could. Did they even need to in order to be at the same level, or did their genetics allow them to have a stronger spell of fire Power without actually having the gift of blue flame? The thought intrigued Victor.

"What is your why?"

Edwyrd stopped. "My what?"

"Your why. Why are you competing in the Trials? I like to know everyone's why."

"It's not a why."

"No? Everyone has a why. It is what fuels us. Purpose drives us. Doesn't it drive you?"

Edwyrd chuckled and continued up another dune. "My why is a who."

Victor arched his eyebrows. "Oh? And *who* is that?"

"My sister and... Never mind."

"No, go on. Who else?"

"My mentor. They... They sacrificed a lot to make me who I am today."

"Is that why you were sad the night you arrived?"

Near the top of the dune, Edwyrd turned back around and looked at Victor. "Don't you miss the ones you left behind?"

Victor slapped the side of his thigh. "Not as much as I should."

"What do you mean?"

"It's nothing."

"I told you about my why."

Victor stopped and sighed. Arms akimbo, he said, "Very well then. My father is lord to Empora. Do you know of it?"

"I've studied."

"Yes, well, there you go," Victor said quickly, waving his hands.

"So, you don't want to take your father's place?"

"I want more than what my father's station can offer. Happy?" He kicked the sand and trudged off, regretting ever opening up to this stranger.

"So, you want Power?"

"I want what comes along with being Guardian."

Edwyrd caught up to him on top of the dune. "And what is that?"

"Do you ever stop asking questions?" Victor raised his voice, forcing Edwyrd back a step.

"Sorry." Edwyrd came to stand alongside Victor. "I tend to do that."

Victor sighed. "It's my fault for opening such a topic." He looked from Edwyrd's brown eyes to the lighter shade of brown sand that surrounded all. There on the horizon, though, was a speck of blue. "The lake. It's there!" Victor pointed.

"And it seems we aren't the only ones who have figured out the location."

"What do you—" Victor cut his sentence short as two figures came over one of the dunes behind them. Victor pulled Edwyrd downward, hopefully avoiding the gazes of whatever team was approaching them. "Let's go." Launching himself to his feet, Victor rushed downhill, keeping his back lowered. Edwyrd did the same, and conversation stopped as they traversed the dunes of sand as quickly as they could, hoping to avoid detection.

The plan failed.

CHAPTER 13

"**G**enius," Edwyrd murmured.

Cyrus and Iris rode atop the sand. Formed into the shape of a fist, it was punching its way through the desert. Iris waved at them as they rode past.

"Stop!" Victor yelled. "*Maa.*" Nothing. "*Maa,*" Victor commanded again. Still nothing. "What are you doing over there? Stop admiring them and help me overcome them! We have to work together."

Edwyrd shook himself free of his awe. "*Maa.*"

Nothing happened.

"What are you doing?" Victor spat.

"Trying to control the earth," Edwyrd said.

"That's what I'm doing. I'll focus on that. You focus on making us a vessel to travel." Victor clawed his hand in the air, pointing at the ground.

The two tried again. What looked like a large bird with a long neck formed underneath of them and rose out of the sand slightly. Slowly, it flapped its sandy wings and made its way through the desert. *Is that?* Edwyrd cocked his head at the shape the sand formed. *Vesel?*

Yes?

Startled by the sound of his dragon's voice in his mind, Edwyrd hopped away from Victor. When his partner gave him a curious look, he spun away. Fire burned inside of him, but it didn't overwhelm him. Not like before.

"Are you doing this? Or am I?" Edwyrd breathed.

"We are," Victor said. "But they're halting our advance."

Edwyrd blinked. He had thought to just voice the words to himself, never realizing how acute Victor's senses were.

I am part of your strength now. You only need to talk with me in your mind.

Edwyrd nodded. *That is good to know. Can you help us?*

I already am.

Why isn't it working?

We are not together. And it seems you are fighting for control with others.

You can sense that?

We are bonded now. I can feel your struggles.

"Can you even cast Power? Help us get moving again!" Victor barked.

Edwyrd refocused back on his surroundings. He tried pushing more Power into the sand dragon they rode upon, seeing it for what it really was now. But it didn't matter. Lowering his hand, their sand vessel disintegrated.

"What are you—"

"It'll be faster to run. We have the ard leaves for a reason." Edwyrd sprinted away, and Victor sprinted after him.

A half hour later, Edwyrd reached the lake. To his surprise, though, Cyrus and Iris were nowhere to be found. Nowhere. It is like they had merely vanished into thin air. *Perhaps they are traveling to a different spot? Does that make this one not the right choice?* He stood on the shores of the lake, tapping his foot in contemplation, battling his inner voice. *This has to be it.* He tried feeling for Vesel again but severed his connection prematurely as Victor showed up minutes later with beads of sweat on his face and an elevated breathing pattern.

"Where are the other two?"

"Gone."

"I can see that. But where? How?"

"I have no idea."

"Are we at the wrong location?"

"We won't know until we try. Maybe it is they who are wrong."

Victor said nothing. He looked over at Edwyrd, who was standing by a pedestal. It was the only other object in the area besides the lake and the grove of trees at its south-eastern point. The pedestal was shaped like arms forming out of the sand, brought together with the hands cupping the base of whatever it held. Upon closer inspection, he realized it was only a sundial.

"What's that over there?"

"Just a sundial." Edwyrd walked away from it, letting his fingers trail on the light coating of sand that lay on the granite dial.

"What did that riddle say again?"

Glad he had written it down, Edwyrd took the piece of parchment out of his pocket and read the riddle again aloud.

Two heads are often better than one, completing each other's
sentences has never been more fun. Blindfolds off, covers
undone. By working together, another rung
on the ladder you will climb. Putting them
together, you will align with your goals,
showing off your partnership. For the wise man knows
knowledge requires you to sift

> under the dreaded sun, and above the shallow sea
> cupped in the hands of the Guardian's gift
> will be what you seek. Trust that the pack has everything you need.
> Woe to the team who is divided like foes.

By the time he had finished reading, he came to stand alongside Victor. "Didn't you think it was in the lake?"

"The shallow sea. Yeah." Victor moved his way to the lake.

Edwyrd followed Victor to the lake's shore, and both men unstrapped the bags they carried. Victor grabbed the wire sieve from the pack and began fishing in the lake. After a few unsuccessful minutes, Victor grunted. He said something under his breath, and the lake started rippling. In a matter of moments, it was lifted up, a dense blue teardrop hanging in midair, exposing the ground beneath. Edwyrd's eyes widened. *The Power that takes... And the control.*

Victor marched into the basin where the lake had been. He turned back around. "Are you coming? We have to find it."

"I..." Edwyrd stammered. "Yes." Edwyrd caught up to Victor, and they walked under the giant blue teardrop. He couldn't produce words. He trailed Victor, eyeing the man with piqued interest, finally realizing what his mentor had meant when he had mentioned the people in these Trials were powerful enough to kill dragons.

"I'll look on the ground. You look into the lake."

"Why..." Edwyrd never finished his thought; he already knew the answer. The sun didn't affect him, and while this may have been true in normal conditions, in here, where the water above them was supposed to be shade, it acted nothing like shade. Instead, it acted like a magnifying glass, intensifying the suns' rays to a point where even Edwyrd had to shield his vision with his forearm as he scoured the depths of the lakes for something. After long enough of this futile strategy, Edwyrd put his arm down and stopped. "It's not here. This can't be it."

"It has to be. What else could the riddle be referring to?"

"The riddle said *above* the shallow sea. Not below it and not in it. That means it has to be on land. Maybe in the..." Edwyrd paused. An idea came to his mind. He spun back.

"What is it?"

"The sand. It has to be in the sand."

"But there is so much of—"

Edwyrd didn't wait for Victor to finish. Instead, he sprinted towards the sand outside of the lake. He took the wire sieve that Victor had deposited on the ground and began scooping up piles of sand around the lake.

In the midst of Edwyrd's excavation, Victor asked. "Your idea is this?" He crossed his arms and tapped his feet, searching around for something more.

"*A sea of sand*. Have you ever heard the expression?"

"No."

Edwyrd shook his head, never stopping sifting. "Maybe it's a Pyrean thing. In Nova, we have lots of sand. No water, though. Well... never mind. Anyway, we always call the sand sea because it stretches on for miles. Here it's the same thing. And it fits perfectly. You can't sink in it, so it's shallow."

"Maybe your idea is right, but we don't have time to sift through everything."

Edwyrd looked towards Victor from his hunched position. "And why is that?"

Victor pointed towards the south. "Because the other team is finally here."

Victor retracted his arm. Edwyrd stood alongside him now, the arm holding the wire sieve hanging limp at his side. "What else about that riddle? Give it here." Edwyrd dug into his pants and proffered the parchment. Victor snatched it out of Edwyrd's hand. "What is this referring to? This Guardian's gift?"

"Cupped in the hands of the Guardian's gift," Edwyrd repeated. "Hands..."

"Hands," Victor mumbled as well. He looked around, stopping on the pedestal. He cocked his head. "Why would—" He laughed. "It's in the sundial." He shook his partner's shoulders and sprinted towards the sundial.

When he started sprinting towards the sundial, the other two on the dune sprinted as well. "*Maa*." Victor raised his hands, creating a thick barrier of sand between him and the other team. While controlling the barrier, he continued running towards the sundial.

Edwyrd arrived at the same time, wire sieve in hand and the packs in the other. "Focus on the barrier. I'll get whatever it is we need."

Victor obliged, knowing that his Power was stronger than his partner's. In his peripheral vision, he noticed Edwyrd sweep off the sand from the top of the sundial with his hand, which was almost at three o'clock now, only for more to replace it, as if it sprung forth like a little spring of sand. It didn't function like a sundial, more like a fountain of sand, a continual well.

When Victor saw flames come up over his wall of sand, disintegrating it slowly through the hierarchy of Power, his eyes widened. "Use the sieve. You have to use the sieve."

"Right."

The next thing Victor knew, Edwyrd held the wire sieve out in front of him, a crystal orb the size of a fist securely inside.

In awe, Victor lost control of the spell. "We did it." He breathed.

Fire rushed towards them.

"*Vesi.*" Edwyrd pulled his hand across. The water from the lake knocked away the stream of flames that had been headed their direction.

For a tense moment, the two pairs looked at each other through the watery wall, the only barrier standing between them. Cordelia and Caspian nodded to one another. Edwyrd fell to his knees, the orb tumbling from the sieve to rest at Victor's feet.

"We... have... to... go," Edwyrd struggled. "Ard leaves."

Understanding his partner's advice, Victor took the orb and put it in the sack, exchanging it with the ard leaves. Strapping the sack to his back, and securing the orb, he ate the leaves. Instantaneously, Victor felt a gush of energy flood his body. All the energy that had been expended by the trial so far.

"*Maa.*" As Cyrus or Iris had done, so too did Victor shape the sand in the form of a fist, elevating his partner and himself up onto the hand.

The water barrier Edwyrd had raised collapsed and both Caspian and Cordelia went towards them. Victor directed the fist to cut right through them, causing both to dive and roll out of the way to avoid getting pummeled by the Power. Rejuvenated, Victor focused on nothing else but returning to the estate. He held such concentration that he didn't notice his partner had been bent over panting until Edwyrd finally said something when the estate was within distance.

"Where are the ard leaves?"

"I used them."

"All of them?"

Victor tossed him an empty sack. "You never told me not to."

"I..." Edwyrd bent over. "Have you never studied adored arts?" Edwyrd coughed.

"What is that supposed to mean?"

Victor knew exactly what it meant. It meant Edwyrd was calling him stupid, but it's not like he had access to whatever element that was. His family trained him in Power and hierarchy and observation and networking, not in adored arts. Those were best left to the individuals not meant to rule. But it also revealed Edwyrd's level of knowledge. The man *did* have knowledge of adored arts, and most likely more than just practical experience with the element. He wondered if that might help him later in the Trials after they won this one.

"Don't worry," Victor reassured. "We are almost there."

Edwyrd coughed. "Let me take over from here, then. You will need your strength."

"What do you mean?"

"Cordelia and Caspian are near the estate." He raised an arm and pointed.

Victor squinted but couldn't make out the individuals. *There is no way he can see so far.* "Impossible they are..." Victor didn't finish his sentence. Within seconds of drawing closer to the estate, he saw what Edwyrd had seen. "How is that..." Victor's voice tapered off.

"The spell."

Victor let the spell die slowly, transferring over the control of the earth to Edwyrd. No sooner than the time it took for Victor to draw the sword from his hip, did a watery serpent slither its way from the training courtyard. *A fist and then a bird and now a snake? Is all Power taking some elaborate form today?*

It arched its neck back. *"Maa."* It lurched forward, only to be met by a blockade of sand.

Victor frowned at the inanimate beast's futile attempt to break through the barrier. Because neither spell was better or worse than the other, it meant the success of the battle would only come from the user's strength of Power and the exertion of energy alone. Nothing else mattered.

Victor felt their earthen transport slow. He turned. Edwyrd's arm shook, and he was on one knee. "What are you doing? Focus. Carry us to the doorstep; I'll handle the rest." He knew his partner was tired, but orders were the best form of encouragement.

Edwyrd pointed and mouthed something.

Victor turned back around and saw a rush of flames crush the earthen barrier. The serpent lunged forward again. Victor tried the same tactic, but the earth he tried to command had resisted his authority. No time to think of anything else, Victor thrust his sword upward towards the impending serpent strike.

"Vesi!"

He knew it would be futile to draw upon the same water source as the serpent, so instead he had called upon the water dwelling in his body. The maneuver caused him to gasp in air as if he had been thrust out into space. His skin tightened. Varicose veins emerged on his body like an infantry of parasitic worms. Water laced his sword. With it in hand, he pushed upwards, ramming it through the serpent's skull as it crashed down on them.

The serpent disintegrated into a flood that brought Victor to his knees. Wetness clung to him, but whether it was from the watery serpent or his own sweat, he didn't know. He could only guess the latter as he sucked in air. Slowly, he turned to Edwyrd. His partner looked at him, eyes wide in awe.

"I can't do that again. Get us there."

"You have energy to run?"

Victor managed a nod.

"I'm going to do something else."

Victor would have retorted, but he didn't have the energy, nor the comprehension at that exact moment. The spell died, though, the earthen bird along with it. Up ahead, Victor saw a dome encompassing the other team.

"Run!" Edwyrd commanded.

Victor hit the ground running. Well, hobbling would have been a more accurate term. But he darted past the hollowed-out hut of earth as fast as he could, surprised a little at his partner's genius in the tactic.

When a loud burst erupted behind him, he didn't look back, focused on his goal. But when a large block of sandstone erected before him right before the steps of the estate, it caused Victor to stop dead in his tracks. He turned. Caspian and Edwyrd lay on the ground in the distance. Cordelia ran towards him, two lances at the ready.

Victor frowned as she stopped a few body lengths away from him. "Fancy trick you pulled there. Appearing here in no time. And the viper, I assume that was you."

Cordelia smirked. "Your guess is correct."

With his chin, he nodded to the barrier before the estate. "I could easily break this and win this contest."

"Then why don't you?" Cordelia arched an eyebrow.

"What makes you think I won't?"

"Because you would have done it already. You're taxed. And you have no energy left."

Her words sunk into his core. Yes, he had an elevated heart rate. Sweat slid over his brows. His breaths had become heavier. But who was she to tell him he had no energy left?

Puffing out his chest. "Would you like to see how much energy I have left?"

"I would like to see that very much."

Cordelia opened her mouth, exhaling, and then launched one of her spears at Victor. Victor side-stepped. At least, he tried. His feet were bound in place with sandy manacles. *That little...* Victor torqued to the left, barely managing to dodge her throw.

"*Vesi*." Victor drew upon the water of his body and broke the bonds free.

She was already at his person. She thrust one lance forward. Victor stepped backwards and to the side, sweeping it away. He flicked his sword towards her. She ducked. And then pounced on top of him, tackling Victor. She brought her spear down. He twisted his body. Spear struck skin and ripped open a gash along his ribcage. With a grunt, Victor dropped his sword and brought his right arm up, punching her in the face.

"*Voima*," he muttered upon contact.

The spell added force to his strike at the cost of his own energy. She flew sideways into one of the bottom pillars that held up the estate. The earthen barrier blocking the entrance collapsed. With another grunt, Victor picked himself up, putting one hand on his upper ribcage to staunch the bleeding. He then moved as fast as he could towards the lobby entrance, which was barely more than a hobble.

One step.

Two steps.

Three.

He climbed the staircase. No one else interrupted him. And in the lobby, he unstrapped the pack on his back. With both hands, he reached into the sack and withdrew the orb that his partner had retrieved from the sundial, bloodying it in the process. The blood mixed with the purity of the crystal amazed Victor as he held it up over his head. The conseleigh in the lobby observed him stoically. Cyrus and Iris were there, he supposed as well, but he didn't see them. With bated breaths, he focused on the Guardian, seeking his approval.

"Congratulations, Victor. You and your partner have won. You will advance."

Victor took in one more breath, smiling, and a tear of joy even flowed from his eye. "I won," he huffed. "I..." He never finished repeating the statement. He collapsed, seeing no more.

CHAPTER 14

W hen Edwyrd awoke, it was in a place he had never been before. The tonics and herbs reminded him of an apothecary, and sure enough, it was only moments after the fluttering of his eyes that a man dressed in blue and silver jackets—the colors of the Guardian—came over to him. Groggy, he blinked, making out the heart-shaped pocket on his breast where the lion of Guardian Crevon sat embroidered into the fabric. The tinnitus in his ears made his exhaustion worsen, but eventually, his body acclimated itself to the sights and sounds.

".... feeling now, Mr. Eska?"

Edwyrd put a hand to his head. He took a quick surveillance of the room, asking a question he already knew the answer to. "Why am I here?"

The adored laughed. "Why you should already know. Your body exhausted itself. How you are here should be your real question."

Edwyrd groaned. "Then how?"

"Conseleigh Pax and Conseleigh Barbeau lugged you up here. You and the others." He flicked his eyes to his right.

Edwyrd followed the man's gesture, shocked to see Victor alongside him and Cordelia across the room. Caspian still lay asleep in his bed, an adored waited on him to make the first sign of movement.

"My name is Adored Warren." The adored brought Edwyrd's attention back to him. "I'm the personal adored assigned to you until your recovery is complete. How does your body feel?"

"Tired."

"Yes, beyond that. Do you have bones that need mending or wounds that need closing? We couldn't find any on you when examining you earlier."

Edwyrd moved his body, flexing each joint to test it. He then rolled his ankles and rotated his neck. "I'm fine."

"Then I will be back with some ard leaves for you." The man set down the clipboard on the machine that calculated Edwyrd's vitals and retreated into another part of the apothecary.

As soon as the man left, Edwyrd twisted towards his partner.

"Victor, what happened? Did we—"

"Yes. We won. No worries."

He sat propped up against his own stroller as well, arms crossed. His fingers tapped against his flexed forearms.

Edwyrd relaxed and sunk back into the cushion he had been propped up against. *That means...* His vision drifted over to Cordelia, who twirled the blue-barbed feather necklace in her fingertips while answering the adored assigned to him. She must have felt Edwyrd gazing at her because she looked up, gave him a half-hearted smile and returned her concentration to her feather.

"Here you go."

The adored came alongside Edwyrd and put a plastic petri dish with a dose of crushed ard leaves on the table next to him. He poured some water into a glass. "Take this, Mister Eska, and you are cleared to leave. Your body will be as good as new." He smiled at Edwyrd and left.

"Mr. Zigarda, are you ready for your stitches now?" Another adored stopped at Victor's feet, carrying a tray full of sutures and scissors and other small utensils.

Eyes wide, he turned to his partner. "Stitches?"

Victor grunted. "Her." He pointed to her with his chin and made no effort in concealing his voice.

Still too entranced by her feather, Cordelia didn't notice.

With sliding curtains, the adored closed off Victor's area. "Take off your shirt."

"Aaahhh."

Another groan in the room distracted Edwyrd from whatever procedure Victor was now undergoing.

"Here, sir. I am ready for you."

Caspian had woken up, and the female adored assigned to him moved in like a hawk, ready to do her duty. She took his blood pressure, temperature, and checked his lungs.

"Take this, Miss Morgan, and you are cleared to leave. Your body will be healed in no time."

The adored's words pulled Cordelia from her fascination with the feather necklace. She smiled and said her thanks, but didn't take the ard leaves placed on her bedside stand right away. Sighing, she looked at the cerise ard leaves for a moment. Then her eyes locked with Edwyrd's, noticing him noticing her.

She mouthed something to him and then pinched the leaves and put them in her mouth, swallowing them with the water on her bedstand.

Quickly, Edwyrd did the same. The reaction caused Cordelia to giggle slightly. She nodded her head towards the exit, and Edwyrd smiled. Together, they left the apothecary.

Outside of the apothecary, they passed a wall that featured two portraits. One was the first Guardian, Jorey Raule, and the second one was Matthau Crevon. Cordelia stopped at the portraits and Edwyrd stopped alongside her.

"I saw these when I went exploring after we were taken to our rooms the first night."

Edwyrd just listened, a part of him hoping she would continue, but never expecting her to.

Cordelia let a slight chuckle escape her lips. "This was one of the reasons I wanted to become Guardian." Edwyrd turned to her, and she turned back to him. "Because women also are powerful. We also can protect, defend, and safeguard a nation. So far it has only been males."

Edwyrd didn't have anything to say, so he remained silent, still looking at her until she returned her gaze to the portrait. She lingered for a moment and then continued walking; Edwyrd kept with her stride.

"If I were to say the name *Thalassa* to you, would you know who I am talking about?"

"No. I'm sorry." Edwyrd shook his head.

"Don't be. She is a Creature of Legend from Acquava. A giant sea serpent that lives around Leviathan Bay. She protects, defends, and safeguards Acquava when she needs to. I've always felt drawn to her, as if her purpose were also my own. Becoming Guardian would allow me to do that on a grander scale."

Edwyrd nodded. "On Pyre, there is a legend of a fiery serpent named Chantico. She hasn't been seen since shortly after the Great War. Many in Nova think she no longer exists."

"A fiery serpent and a watery one. We do truly come from different worlds, don't we, Edwyrd?" Cordelia paused at the top of the steps to the lobby, turned and smiled at him.

Edwyrd blushed. His heart pounded as fireflies crept into his stomach. "It seems so."

Cordelia took her first few steps down the staircase. "And soon we will be worlds apart yet again. Tell me, why is it that you wanted to become Guardian?"

"Why?" His voice cracked. This was the second person that day to ask him his why, as if it were the only question that ever mattered. Wasn't it obvious why anyone wanted to become Guardian?

"Yes." Cordelia chuckled. "Why? I told you my reason. Challenging the status quo, furthering the role women can play in society. And I would have succeeded too, but..." She stopped at the bottom step. She sighed. "Never mind. I am happy that you advanced. You seem good-hearted. I suppose if I hadn't purposely gotten some questions wrong, perhaps it would have been you and I as partners in that second trial." She walked towards the wing where she, Edwyrd, and Cyrus slept, but then went towards the lobby doors. "Would you care to take a walk with me outside?"

Edwyrd's heart fluttered. He wasn't exactly sure what he was feeling, but it felt right. "Sure."

Outside, Cordelia and Edwyrd walked around the perimeter of the estate. Both were silent for a while, simply enjoying the presence of one another and the coolness that only night could provide. Eventually, Cordelia talked again. "You never answered my question. Why is it you want to be Guardian?"

Edwyrd looked to the nighttime sky, admiring the stars. "My sister."

"You have a sister?"

"Had," Edwyrd corrected. He sighed and tore his gaze away, knowing that she wasn't among the stars anymore.

"Oh. I'm sorry. What happened?"

Memories of Vesel barreling through Alicia's earthen barrier and pinning her underneath his talons seized Edwyrd's mind. He didn't answer.

"I shouldn't have asked." Cordelia blushed.

"She sacrificed herself so that I could be here."

"Sacrificed herself? What do you mean?"

Edwyrd shook his head. "It's nothing. Never mind. I'm here for her, and to make sure she is remembered. To make sure her sacrifice doesn't amount to nothing."

Cordelia examined him for a long moment. Then she turned her gaze to the nighttime sky. "And so you look to the stars for that?"

Hands in his pockets, walking alongside her, Edwyrd also glanced upwards. "No. I look at the stars, seeing just how many people I can save from the same sort of fate." Cordelia didn't answer. "My mentor told me that we all have stars. And that, if we are diligent enough, and lucky enough, we could find our star and wish for something."

"I've heard the same thing. Do you believe it?"

"It's a nice thought, but how someone would actually go about doing it seems hard to imagine. There are so many."

Cordelia smiled. "That's true. What would you wish for if you found it?"

"I don't know. Probably for my sister to come back."

"She died recently, then?"

Edwyrd gulped. "Right before the Trials."

"I'm sorry... Wow... That's... that's devastating. I do hope you win, for your sister's sake. Victor will be your main competition."

"Not Cyrus?"

"Cyrus is from Pyre. Same as you. He represents a threat you know. Victor is a threat you don't know."

"What do you mean?"

"He's powerful. Very powerful. I haven't ever felt anything like it before."

"What do you mean?"

"The way he slew my water serpent spell."

Edwyrd recalled the way Victor had laced his sword with water and then struck it up and through the serpent's head as it lashed out at them.

"It would have taken an extraordinary amount of energy to do that," Cordelia continued.

"It was the ard leaves. It wasn't him."

"Ard leaves?"

"That was the cerise substance found in the sack. It's an element on Pyre. It's how he regained his strength. I don't know what the other one was." The comment made Cordelia chuckle. "Why do you laugh?"

"The other one was an element from Acquava. Vanishing sand, found on the southern island of Talyn."

"Vanishing sand?"

"You use it and draw a perimeter and it transfers whoever is in the perimeter to a destination they have already been before within a certain radius."

"That is... well, that is certainly something. But, still, how does that tell you Victor is powerful?"

"The ard leaves explain some of it, but to use that kind of water, water powerful enough to ward off my own, he drew from his own reservoir of strength inside of him. He could have dehydrated himself, but he didn't."

"Speaking of that spell..." Edwyrd looked at the stream that cut through the stone training courtyard they were now walking alongside. "How did you do it? Are you..." Edwyrd struggled for the right word. He wanted to ask the question inconspicuously, but after failing in his attempt to be nonchalant, he just asked it directly. "Are you bonded?"

"Bonded?" Cordelia laughed. When Edwyrd didn't, her smile flattened. "You're serious, aren't you?"

"Well, it was interesting that you could make your water into a serpent."

Cordelia shook her head. "No. No. No. I'm not bonded. To be honest, it just felt right. I'm Acquavan; I've always had a strong affinity with water, and I've always felt a stronger connection to Thalassa than most."

"Are you going to seek her out?"

Cordelia guffawed. "No. Never. To do that would be suicide. But my father told me he saw her once."

"Really?"

"When he was in Talyn on a business with the lord. My mother had fallen into the water, and he dove down to save her. That is how they met, actually. I told you before. While underneath the water, he saw her." Cordelia flashed a grin at Edwyrd. "After rescuing her, he learned she was an adored, and she taught him all sorts of things, including about the vanishing sand exclusive to their island. It truly is funny how fate works."

"You have no idea," Edwyrd muttered.

"What was that?"

"Uuhh... Nothing. Go on."

"Well, you can be bemused by fate or angered by it. I try and stay the former."

"What do you mean?"

"I mean if I would have not missed a few answers purposely on that first trial, I may have been your partner. Then I would have known about the vanishing sand and you the... the... what was it again?"

"Ard leaves."

"The ard leaves, right. We may have even gotten first place. Instead, I got led around on a wild goose chase looking for the storage unit."

"Victor wanted to look for that as well, but I told him not to."

"You're smart, Edwyrd. I should have listened to my gut and not held back."

"Why did you?"

"Because you never want to reveal your full hand all at once. It ruins the intrigue, doesn't it?"

"I suppose. But do you think the others are holding back as well?" Edwyrd asked half out of curiosity, and half out of wondering if she suspected him of holding back at all. In truth, he hadn't been, but he also knew he hadn't felt as strong as he had when he was with Vesel. He wondered what it would take for him to regain that strength.

"After what I felt from Victor, I can say most likely Cyrus or Iris are just as lethal."

"And you're judging Victor's strength just because of the water spell he cast? I already told you—"

"The ard leaves explain some of it. Yes, it shows he is resourceful. But he has strength, too. After you passed out, he and I dueled. I was trying to steal your orb so that my team could continue. He's good with a sword. Good enough anyway, but when I missed a strike, he punched me and that is when I felt his Power."

They were back around the front part of the estate again. "What did it feel like?"

"A tsunami crashing into me. I couldn't stand to his force. He used a spell to increase his strength on contact; that much I am certain of. It flung me back like I was a cat."

"Cat?"

"It's an animal that overruns our city. They're cute when they want to be."

Edwyrd wondered if dragons could ever be cute. They overran Nova. He doubted it.

"Anyway, he's powerful, so watch out."

"A punch told you that? What makes you so certain?"

"Because, Edwyrd, I can cast blue flames." Cordelia looked at the estate. Lamps hanging on the outside pillars by the staircase had been lit since they first stepped outside. Cordelia put some space between herself and Edwyrd and brought her palms out. *"Palo."*

Blue fire engulfed her hand, devouring Edwyrd's attention. Those remaining were certainly in a league of their own, and if he wanted to compete, he would need to find a way to enlist Vesel's help or see his wishes and dreams go up in flames.

CHAPTER 15

Victor sat through dinner preoccupied. It was painfully slow. And he understood why, as another two contestants were leaving. To stay on the Core as long as possible, they ate slow or hardly touched their food at all, preferring to talk more than eat, as if that would buy them time from returning to the monotony of the mundane. Edwyrd had sat in between Cordelia and Cyrus, and Victor happened to be placed between Iris and Caspian. Each teammate sat across from one another. Cordelia shared words with Edwyrd, and in the same vein, Caspian talked with Victor, something that he wished he could have avoided. He only wanted to talk to Iris, but that would come after.

"I messed it up for our team." Caspian looked at his plate of food, knife in one hand, fork in the other, and a frown across his face. It was as if he was a prisoner in his father's dungeon, looking at his last meal.

Would Victor have felt the same way if he had to go back home without anything to show? The statement roused Victor enough to arch his eyebrows. "What do you mean?" Victor cut into a steak covered in mushroom and peppercorn.

"The riddle. I..." Rejecting his food, Caspian put down his fork and knife. He folded his hands together. "Did you go searching for the storage unit?"

Before Victor could respond, Iris laughed. "Isn't that what you fishermen would call a red herring?"

Victor's eyes widened. He felt his face grow hotter. He corrected the slight slouch in his shoulders and laughed it off as well. "That nearly got me, too," he lied. He cut into another piece of his steak and put it in his mouth.

"Be I the only one?"

"Makes you feel better, Caspian, Cyrus would have done the same thing had I not corrected him." Iris popped a grape into her mouth.

That certainly made Victor feel better, but at the same time, he expected it. They had both answered the pen and parchment question wrong on the first trial, showcasing their tendency to oversimplify a complex problem. That meant one other thing to Victor—Cyrus was brash. Perhaps in the final Victor could use that to his advantage.

"We be spending an hour looking for that storage unit." He took up his fork again and stabbed at a filet of fish and reluctantly put it in his mouth.

"That reminds me." Victor turned to Caspian. "How did you get back to the estate before us?"

"That be Cordelia. One of the—"

"Vanishing sand," Iris interrupted. "That is how we got back, as well. Don't you know it?" Her eyes gleamed and twinkled.

If ever Victor had felt more inadequate, he couldn't place a time. He shook his head. He glanced at Cordelia for a second, who was eating her cream soup. What other kind of mysteries did these other planets hold? In fact, what mysteries did Victor's planet hold that he hadn't been made privy to, even though he was a lord? Iris's voice pulled him back from his thoughts.

"You should really come to Chaon sometime. We have even better sand."

Caspian leaned forward so that he could see Iris. "Better than sand that be vanishing you?"

"Sand that eats you instead." She giggled.

Victor had no idea to tell if she was serious or not. The more time he spent with her, the more he realized how much of a vixen the woman was. Who had he exactly done a deal with? And would it all be worth it in the end?

Caspian shook himself free of an invisible net. "I never want to be visiting Chaon. Sereya be bad enough as it be."

"What do you do there?"

Victor exhaled. Why was Iris trying to make small talk? It was only delaying the inevitable. And would it really matter in the end? He was going home. How would they ever hear from each other again?

"Fisherman. For the north. We catch the big fish and send them up to the frozen parts. They don't get much up there."

"Frozen parts?" Victor played along, feigning intrigue.

"Where Christian be from. They be ruling us."

"Northerners always feel as though they control the south. Isn't that right, Victor?" A wry smile spread across her face.

His face grew hot. "When it is a part of the south that is rightfully ours."

"But what if it belonged in the south more than the north?"

"Then maybe..." Victor turned to face Iris directly now. "Some sort of deal could be made." He flashed a forced smile.

"Fabulous news. It brings me hope for the future."

Victor sighed and turned back to his food. In this way, the dinner continued until eventually Guardian Crevon stood and made his closing remarks.

"Tonight marks another night finished. And it pleases me to see that all of you have been making such close connections, even though time has been quite limited. Cordelia and Caspian, while you cannot stay, I do not want to send you away empty-handed either. As contestants who have bypassed the first round, you will be rewarded for your efforts, and it seems only right to give all of you these now." Guardian Crevon snapped his fingers.

The personal servants for each of the contestants came out with a small white box wrapped in a blue bow.

"Contestants, open up what you have been handed."

Victor lazily picked apart the bow. Caspian opened his first, revealing a watch. Iris held up an identical one as well. His box held the same and a series of eight numbers reading: "Telecommunication number 12765893

"Telecommunication," Victor muttered.

"Contestants, what you see before you are brand new. They are not available for sale yet, but as there have been some recent advancements in technology, I present to you what is known as a telecommunicator." Guardian Crevon held up his wrist and exposed his own telecommunicator by pulling on the blue silk of his shirt. "I use these to communicate with my Hown instantaneously should there be a need. You may use it to keep in touch with anyone who has one. All of you have an eight-digit telecommunication number. Simply upload the number into the watch's mainframe, and once the data is stored, you can call that individual at your leisure. This helps ensure that the bonds forged here have a chance of never breaking."

"So it's similar to Blood Bonding?" Cordelia asked, turning over the watch in her hands.

Guardian Crevon beamed and snapped his fingers. "It is exactly like Blood Bonding, but it uses technological advances instead of relying on Power and kinship."

If only these were presented to us the night before, then I wouldn't had to have... Victor shot a furtive glance over his right. Iris played with her watch, scrolling through whatever data was appearing to her. Victor looked back at his own.

"What be your telecommunicator number?"

He glanced at Caspian. He was reluctant to give it to him at first, but realized that everyone on the other side was exchanging numbers. Victor pulled out the sheet of paper in the box and handed it to him. "Here. Let's keep in touch." His words were empty, but would Caspian really have the sense to pick up on it?

Most likely not. He really wanted to connect with Cordelia. There was more to her than he originally thought, just like Iris. But Cordelia, well, Victor wouldn't have another shot at obtaining her number, so he made it a point of excusing himself after Caspian finished logging in his number and maneuvering to the other side.

"Edwyrd, we made a strong team." He extended his hand, holding his telecommunicator card between his index and middle finger. "Let's connect?"

Edwyrd hesitated. Had he come off as insincere? No. Impossible. Sure, the man would be eliminated in the next trial, but that didn't mean it wasn't useful to connect. They had been partners, after all. And Edwyrd, whether Victor liked it or not, had saved them time in figuring out the riddle. That, in and of itself, called for some form of propriety in exchanging numbers.

"Sure." Edwyrd smiled and picked the card from between Victor's fingers.

While Edwyrd plugged in the numbers, he turned to Cordelia. "May I get yours as well? It is quite a treat meeting someone from a different planet. You fought well."

"I'd be delighted," she said with a smile. She batted her eyelids.

Was she being sarcastic, or was Victor overthinking? "Thank you." Then Victor turned his attention to Cyrus. "And you, Cyrus?"

"Of course." The man bobbed his head.

Once he had received the numbers from the other contestants, he turned his attention to Guardian Crevon. "My Guardian, if I may be excused, I am still feeling a little drowsy after the apothecary today."

"There is no need to explain yourself, Victor. Rest up. Continue to heal. The day after tomorrow, the next trial will begin. You'll need your strength."

Victor nodded his head and bowed. "If it is anything like the last trial, my Guardian, it will require more than just my strength."

Guardian Crevon didn't respond. He merely beamed and nodded. Victor returned the gesture. Once turned, he furrowed his brows. *What did that mean?* Pushing open the double-doors of the dining hall, he walked out alone. In the hallway, he felt for Iris's presence.

Meet me in my room. We have much to talk about.

We certainly do, Victor. We certainly do.

CHAPTER 16

That night in Victor's room, he saw a depth to Iris that hitched his breath multiple times. The cunning and scheming in this woman chilled him. Not because it was something he didn't think he could replicate, but it showed him how much he truly lacked. When the Sages had mentioned to him that there was only one other like him, he now understood that Cyrus wasn't that individual. It was this woman.

"... and that is how you will win." Throughout her explanation, she had been leaning back in the wooden chair, tossing her knife casually up in the air, counting its revolutions while never losing track of her thoughts, catching it and repeating it. As she said those words, she caught it and pointed the knife at him. "Do you understand?"

Victor glanced from the knife to her eyes. He had been trained under the supervision of royalty his entire life; he had been granted every single whim of his desire; his father had put him with the best tutors, the best trainers, and had sacrificed a portion of his time and health in cultivating an upbringing that would make Victor like his namesake. And yet, here, under the intense gaze of those forest-green eyes, he felt inferior.

Trying to find some flaw in her plan, if only to wipe the smug assurance off her face and replace it with at least a spatter of contemplation, Victor asked, "How do you know everything will go according to your plan?"

"Because I've learned that the Guardian for all his Power and prowess is utterly predictable. The Trials now are the same Trials as before. You know that, right?"

Victor nodded, hoping she wouldn't see past his false bravado.

"This next trial will test Power. Edwyrd will be an easy win for anyone. I will give you the win should you face me, and you have the strategy now to beat Cyrus, should you need it. The man toys with his inferiors. A fatal flaw if you ask me. I can never understand why so many individuals beat around the bush instead of going straight for the jugular." She glanced up from her knife, which she had been using to trim her nails. "Do you know what I mean?"

"But you don't think I will face Cyrus this round?"

"No. You'll face me in the third trial."

"And you know this because of his *predictability?*" Victor's voice cracked with interest. Had she seen something he hadn't?

"Yes. If you paid closer attention, you would know that as well. All contestants took the first trial at the same time and in the same conditions. The second trial aimed to equalize the playing field as well by pairing the weak with the strong. Do you think it was an accident that I got partnered with Cyrus?"

Victor did his best to continue his breathing normally. But it got caught in a few places. What she had just admitted to him was a level of prescience he didn't think possible. The knowing unnerved him and he wondered just how much the Sages influenced her life. Were they merely sponsors like they were to Victor, or had they trained her themselves? And, if the latter was true, then why did the Sages need him to win instead of her?

"No. Of course not." Victor corrected his slouched shoulders. "The Sages trained you well."

"They had no part in my training. They only told me what to look for."

Victor resisted the urge to cluck his tongue. She hadn't fallen for his bait, but she did provide him valuable insight, nonetheless. "And that is how you know for certain the third trial will be you and I?"

"Yes. Keeping things equal, Victor, Guardian Crevon will not put you against Edwyrd. You were just partners, after all. He will put those two from Pyre against one another and put us Myolians against one another. And Edwyrd and Cyrus will go first because their names come first in the alphabet."

"Seems rather obvious." Victor chuckled.

"It is painfully obvious when you know what to look for. People are predictable. We are *creatures of habit,* as the saying goes." She giggled. "Edwyrd will lose. So will I. And then you are here to take on the big bad Cyrus by yourself."

Victor leaned back against the headrest of his bed, arms folded across his chest, fingers kneading into his forearms. Ahead of him lay the same downward flaming spiral he had seen in Iris's room. He looked at it now with intensity, unsure of what to say. Her words brought him out of his slight trance.

"You will learn that the best element isn't fire or earth or lightning or water. It isn't ard leaves or vanishing sand or maro nector. It's surprise. And everything I told you about Cyrus, and what you will see the day after tomorrow during his duel with Edwyrd, will keep you from being surprised in the final bout with him. Understood?"

He ignored her question. "Why didn't the Sages just send you here to win? Why me?"

"Because I cannot stay here on the Core."

"You make it seem like a death sentence."

"Far from it. Being Guardian grants you longevity, Power, and the freedom of traveling anywhere you desire with that little reimaje on his head, but I am not interested in any of those things."

Victor cocked his head towards her. He raised an eyebrow. "And what are you interested in?"

Her eyes gleamed and sparkled. She stood up from her chair, sheathed her throwing knife, and walked towards the door. Her left fingers tapped the painting Victor had been staring into, and her right hand opened the door. "Revenge and rebirth," she said without looking back.

She closed the door silently behind her, leaving Victor floundering in a sea of confusion.

CHAPTER 17

Perhaps it was being in the open air instead of the lobby, or perhaps it was because there were only four contestants remaining, but everything felt empty. While he hadn't interacted with Caspian much, save for offering him his telecommunicator number when the man asked for it, Edwyrd had communicated with Cordelia quite a bit and a part of him missed her standing beside him. Now, he stood shoulder-to-shoulder with the final four. In front of all of them stood Guardian Crevon, blue and silver cape blowing in the slight breeze of the afternoon, and his conseleigh.

"I have tested you for your intelligence. I have tested your partnership ability. Now in the final two trials I will test more practical abilities that you will need to have as Guardian. Today's trial will be a trial with Power."

Edwyrd's eyes brightened.

"It is a fairly straightforward trial. You will be paired against another contestant. You will be given an element to cast, and whoever of you can hold the spell the longest will be the winner. The trial concludes when one contestant can no longer hold the spell or merely forfeits. Is this understood?" Guardian Crevon took a few seconds to examine each of them. All of the remaining contestants nodded their head in turn. "Excellent. Just like before, you will speak your name and Power will do its job in assigning your opponent randomly."

Each contestant spoke their name. Perhaps it was his nerves, but Edwyrd seemed quieter than the others. It may have just been the expectant tugging in his throat, which he braced for this time, but which still never got easier. The green holographic box with all four names shook in spasms, eventually exploding. In front of Edwyrd was the name of his opponent. Hair stood up on his arms. Hesitantly, he turned to his left, meeting Cyrus's orange eyes. Not blinking. Not wavering. The harshness of their land made them like that.

"You have received your contestants. It seems fate wants to pit you against each other on your own planet. How interesting." Guardian Crevon chuckled.

"We will begin with Edwyrd Eska and Cyrus Oraine. Victor and Iris, please take a seat on the bench while the other two take over the arena."

The two stayed in the center of the stone courtyard. The Guardian of the Core turned to face them once Victor and Iris removed themselves from the area. At each of the four posts around the arena, shaped into the likeness of swords thrust into the earth, stood the conseleigh.

"Conseleigh Shadir, which spell should these two contestants cast?" Guardian Crevon swept his blue eyes over both Edywrd and Cyrus to his left where the conseleigh stood.

"They are fireborn, so why not test them with water instead?" Conseleigh Shadir raised an eyebrow and offered a slight chuckle.

"That seems very fitting," Guardian Crevon laughed alongside his conseleigh.

Water? Edwyrd closed his eyes. He breathed in and out, assuaging his nerves.

Vesel...

Yes, Edwyrd.

Do I have your Power?

You've always had my Power. Ever since we've bonded.

Edwyrd bit his lower lip. *But why don't I feel like I did when we bonded?*

Because we are not close by. My strength is your strength. But your true strength comes from within...

What do you—

"Edwyrd? Are you ready?"

Edwyrd's eyes blinked open again. He lost connection with his dragon. Blushing, he nodded. "Sorry, my Guardian. I was merely centering myself."

"Very well. Are you centered now?"

"Yes, my Guardian."

"Good. The trial ends when one of you forfeits or can no longer cast. Is this understood?" Guardian Crevon cast a lingering gaze on each of them.

Edwyrd nodded. Cyrus did the same.

"Then please come together to the center of the court and face the stream. Each of you should have equal distance to the source."

Edwyrd approached the middle of the courtyard. Cyrus met him, hand open, arm extended. After a moment of hesitation at the sportsmanship, Edwyrd accepted. Cyrus's grip was stronger than most, but he made sure to keep his expression neutral. It was time to dance with the fireson, and he couldn't afford to let any trepidation or intimidation show.

"Die by fire, die with honor. Living in Pyre, nothing is higher," Cyrus said.

"Nothing is higher," Edwyrd repeated. He mimicked Cyrus's nod.

"Are you both ready?"

Edwyrd stood alongside Cyrus. Both looked at the water. "I am," they said simultaneously.

"On the count of three, cast your spell. One."

Edwyrd inhaled, breathing in the serenity of the moment that still lingered. "Two."

He closed his eyes.

"Three."

Edwyrd opened his eyes. "*Vesi.*"

Two pillars of water sprouted up before them. Each barely reached waist level at first. And like a levy, Edwyrd engaged in a Power tug-of-war with his adversary, the spells of water vacillating between high and low in constant flux.

Sharp jolts entered his mind whenever Cyrus would put more Power into his spell. Edwyrd, in turn, would increase his Power to combat the threat. This cycling was similar to those fishermen of other planets he had read about, those who would loosen the slack on their line, letting their fish expend their energy, only to reel them in afterwards once all of that energy had been depleted. Was this the tactic Cyrus was using? Was Edwyrd only a fish on the line to him? Or was he overcompensating his own energy expenditure?

Cautiously, Edwyrd flicked a glance towards Cyrus, seeing his state. He stood, arms outstretched, focused on the water before him. Even if he felt Edwyrd's eyes upon him, he didn't turn to acknowledge his opponent. He kept focused on the task ahead of him. He didn't show any signs of fatigue. No sweat on his brow. His arm didn't fidget or tremble. Edwyrd turned back to the water, wondering how long he would be able to maintain the same composure.

It took longer than he imagined it would have before his bonding with Vesel, but in time, sweat spotted his forehead. It slipped into his eyes. Dripped onto the noon ground around him. From everything he had witnessed so far about Cyrus, his demeanor and confidence, the way he plowed through the desert with a fist, how he brought no weapons with him to the Trials, he knew Cyrus to be more than capable. If Edwyrd truly was a fish on Cyrus's hook, he would need to think of a plan to turn the tides of Power.

He couldn't close his eyes—for that would ruin his control on the spell—so he hyper-focused on the water before him. The others around him disappeared. The humming of the rippling water became white noise to Edwyrd, the sweat on his face a familiarity he welcomed. It cooled his naturally warm body.

His shoulder ached, but he had experienced worse cramps. Edwyrd merely enjoyed the tug-of-war he was experiencing with Cyrus, each taking turns to overpower the other, like waves rushing the shore only to retreat a moment later. It was the natural ebb and flow of things, and Edwyrd was in such a state of serenity and focus that he was present. Present. Living only now. In this moment. Truly feeling everything going on around him. Noticing his breath. Feeling the sweat running down his neck and darting behind the collar of his clothing. The light breeze on his face. He connected with himself, and he no longer needed to see Cyrus to know the man was far from fatiguing. He could feel that through the Power, and Edwyrd thought that this was how Cordelia must have felt when she felt Victor's Power.

In that moment, he appreciated Cyrus. No matter the outcome, he appreciated the man who pushed him to his limits. And Edwyrd was sure the man would continue to push Edwyrd past his limits, forcing him to adapt, and so when Edwyrd's fingers began trembling and a spasm rippled through his body, he knew the conclusion to this trial was near.

It also meant one other thing—it was now or never. Edwyrd pushed back on Cyrus's influence, stretching his fingertips and focusing on controlling the water in front of him, growing it to a level higher than that of his opponent. A slight shift of movement and sudden shuffle of stones alerted Edwyrd to Cyrus's changed posture. The behemoth was showing his weakness. Edwyrd pushed more. He tightened his neck and his face, transferring that energy into the spell. With all of his intent, he focused on raising the level of water. And slowly the vicious vacillation of Power began to ebb, siding more with Edwyrd. He felt Cyrus slipping, his Power diminishing. Wide-eyed, Edwyrd focused and continued his stream of intent on water ahead of him. He knew somewhere far away Vesel was with him, granting him strength, for surely that was the only reason he was ahead.

Edwyrd tightened his control of the spell before looking over to Cyrus, whose posture had slumped. The man's tree-trunk arms were folding under their own weight and the strength necessary to maintain the composure of the spell. Eyes wide, Cyrus looked at him. Edwyrd tried understanding the quick glance, but he couldn't tell what he had seen. Was it admiration? Acknowledgement? Desperation?

Then a wave of Power deluged Edwyrd. It pushed his spell of Power down, capsizing him. He went to one knee, but still he held onto the Power by a thread.

What is...

He glanced at Cyrus and noticed something peculiar. His sweat had dissipated. Edwyrd's eyes widened. *No!* He returned his gaze to the Power in front of him, only just a pool of water now. He wouldn't be able to do it for long, but he knew what he needed to do to win.

"*Vesi.*" He muttered once more underneath his breath, and this time he split his spell in two. He fought Cyrus on the two fronts he was raging war on, internally and externally. In a moment of quick decision and thinking, Edwyrd drew from the natural sources of water present outside and the water that comprised his body. A dangerous tactic, but the one that Cyrus was surely using now to give him the edge, and as the saying went on Pyre: one must fight fire with fire. Or, in this case, water with water.

Diving into both sets of spells, he pushed back on Cyrus and once again brought him back to a stalemate, which also brought the goliath to one knee. Hunched and hobbled, they stayed there, merely looking at one another, knowing that the spell they were truly controlling was their own and now, more than ever, needing to know the others' condition. Edwyrd wanted to cry, but couldn't. The tears in his eyes had dried up like the plains of Dragon's Ruin. His throat was bare and rough. His cheeks gaunt. He tried salivating, but only felt the dry taste of ard leaves without any of the rejuvenation properties. His eyelids spasmed. Fingers twitched uncontrollably. Coughs cut his throat like swords to his skin. Still, he held his spell and maintained his gaze on Cyrus. He was faltering as well, his own arm lowering and his hand shaking. His eyes burned as bright as ever, with an orange intensity that meant he was prepared to go all the way.

Only pillared on one arm, Edwyrd held up one hand, focusing on still controlling the water in front of him. Neither's spell was little more than a pool. When swallowing hurt more than breathing, and when he could barely hold open his eyes, he thought about Alicia. He thought about her sacrifice. And he thought about Vesel. *True strength... within...* They weren't solid thoughts, just mere apparitions, ghosts that vacillated in and out of his mind at the state of his pounding heart that was on the verge of near collapse. But he pieced them together.

His opened his eyes, staring down his opponent. "From within," Edwyrd grunted. With one final tithing of energy, he pushed his outstretched arm further.

Cyrus's eyes widened. His body shook, and he fell face down on the stone floor. Edwyrd grinned. He had done it. He had won. Immediately, he let his spell die. He turned over onto his back, resting, looking up at the sky that seemed a shade of silver that he had never seen in his life. Footsteps rushed alongside him. A figure he couldn't quite make out took him underneath his shoulders.

"Edwyrd, are you okay?"

The C on his vest told Edwyrd he was one of the conseleigh, but his face was shadowed.

He didn't have the water left to speak, so he merely nodded his head. With one weak arm, he pointed. The conseleigh must have known exactly what he needed, for in a matter of seconds water from the stream came in the form of Power to his mouth. It flowed seamlessly into his lips, rejuvenating the parched and cracked countenance he had maintained during the duel.

As Edwyrd slowly regained the strength necessary to sit up, he noticed the swarm of conseleigh around Cyrus. The Guardian of the Core himself, bent down on one knee, cradling Cyrus in one arm and holding his hand over his forehead with another. The Guardian moved his finger underneath the chin of the man.

"... pulse ... adored ... now."

Edwyrd couldn't quite understand the order being barked; his brain was still too foggy, but he could see what had happened. He didn't need any words to tell him that Cyrus didn't move. Couldn't move. He didn't need an adored to tell him what he already knew to be true from the lack of breaths arising from Cyrus, from how his body was limp in the Guardian's arms.

Cyrus had pushed himself to the end.

Edwyrd had killed Cyrus.

Cyrus was dead.

CHAPTER 18

V ictor sat on the bench, carefully observing all the things Iris told him to take notice of. He watched how Cyrus controlled his Power, letting him be subdued in some moments, only to come back stronger in others. The Powers vacillated, and it all worked in fatiguing Edwyrd. At least, according to Iris's information, that was a tactic he was prone to use. Victor saw the necessity in that. No person ever showed all their cards at once. To do so would be foolish. He had already shown too much to Edwyrd during the second trial while overcoming Cordelia's water serpent. Thinking about that, Victor was quite pleased she had been eliminated as she would have given him trouble; he had sensed her Power when they dueled, and she had given him the wounds on his ribs that ached in his hunched position. To alleviate this, he straightened his posture. He shot a furtive glance at Iris, who only continued watching the duel in front of her.

Edwyrd seemed to adapt well to Cyrus's strategy, and he was lasting longer than Victor had imagined possible, but also, this trial was different than he imagined. He thought that they would have needed to duel with Power. Run a gauntlet of Power obstacles at the very least. But a contest of mere endurance? A tug-of-war with Power? This was another way the Guardian of the Core was chosen? Where was the danger? The excitement? The prowess that the Guardian of the Core had become synonymous with during the legends of each Guardian warding the system from the Curse of Pirini Lilapa?

It was when Cyrus shifted his weight that Victor became intrigued. *Fatigue?* He switched his gaze to Edwyrd. The man sweated too. His arm wavered. Edwyrd had noticed Cyrus's shift as well, and he aimed to capitalize on it. Edwyrd focused even more intently on the water. But then something happened that Victor didn't imagine—Cyrus fought back. His own puddle of water became a pillar that towered over Edwyrd's own. Now it was Edwyrd on the verge of defeat. He had turned it around in a matter of seconds.

Well, that is no...

Victor stopped. He realized why that sudden shift had occurred. Both men no longer sweated. Their skin was slowly shriveling. *They're drawing from inside...* Victor had a mental relapse to how he had used his own strength to combat Cordelia's watery serpent. He didn't know how many others knew to be so resourceful when needing an extra source for such a spell, but these two were. Cyrus by himself. But had Victor's display given Edwyrd this same knowledge?

Once again, the two were in a stalemate, falling to their knees. Cyrus dropped first, pillaring himself with one arm. Iris came and sat alongside Victor.

"Well, this is something, is it not?"

"What is happening?" Victor muttered.

Cyrus collapsed on the stone court. Edwyrd faltered shortly after him, stopping his spell. The conseleigh rushed in from the corners. Even Guardian Crevon stepped forward, quickly inspecting Edwyrd but then turning his attention to Cyrus. He put a gloved hand to his head, and then fingers to the man's throat. Afterwards, one of the conseleigh scurried away.

"A surprise," Iris mumbled.

Trying to get a better view, Victor stood up on the bench. Iris joined him. From his position, Victor couldn't hear anything. From his peripherals, a man in a blue and white lab coat ran out to the courtyard, carrying a stretcher. The two male conseleigh laid Cyrus on it and carried him off, the adored alongside them. Before joining them, Guardian Crevon gave an order to Conseleigh Ersa. The conseleigh nodded and helped Edwyrd back to his feet. Conseleigh Juniper tried to help, but Guardian Crevon held her back. All watched as Edwyrd left the premises.

Hands behind his back, Guardian Crevon turned to them. No emotion betrayed him. "It is your turn."

"My Guardian, you can't be serious in continuing the trial right now. Cyrus—"

Guardian Crevon held up a fist. Conseleigh Juniper silenced herself. "As Guardian you may encounter unfortunate circumstances that you feel will require time to heal from, but what if time is not available to you? You see a loved one perish in a battle, yet can you stop and mourn, or do you continue fighting?" He arched an eyebrow. "Both of you will continue fighting today. Come."

Victor gave a furtive glance to Iris. Cautiously, he stepped down off of the bench and walked towards Guardian Crevon.

The Guardian turned "Now Conseleigh Juniper which spell shall these two cast?"

Conseleigh Juniper gasped, stumbling over her words.

"I forfeit."

Guardian Crevon whipped his neck to the side. Victor spun around. Iris hopped off the bench and strolled forward.

"You what?"

"I forfeit. I can do that, can't I?" Iris arched an eyebrow and crossed her arms over her breasts.

Guardian Crevon turned toward her. "Forfeit? Now?" Try as he might to hide his composure, the faintest trace of choler still showed in his blue eyes and the sharpness of his voice.

"Yes."

Conseleigh Juniper put a hand on his shoulder and put herself in front of him. "My Guardian you cannot force her to continue against her will."

"I am not willing to throw my life away like Cyrus for Guardianship."

Guardian Crevon inhaled deeply, closing his eyes. When he opened them again, placidness had overtaken any of the anger that Victor had thought he'd seen. "If that is your decision, then perhaps you are not the best candidate for this position." With laser-like intensity, Guardian Crevon focused on Victor. "Congratulations, Victor. You will be advancing to the finals. Miss Cike, pack your things. I'll be taking you home personally tonight. With this trial settled, I best go check on Cyrus." He stalked off, calling out to Conseleigh Juniper to follow him.

The conseleigh, who had appeared to want to say something after being left alone with both of them, shut her mouth and hurried after the Guardian.

Victor meandered to the spot where Cyrus fell. How had Edwyrd won? Had Cyrus merely been careless? Or what had led to Cyrus's downfall?

To his dismay, the stone court awarded him no answers. There was no blood. There wasn't even any water, and that had been the spell the two had cast. Arms crossed over his chest, looking down, he tapped his foot while biting his lower lip.

"Well, that certainly worked out better than we had anticipated."

Iris's shadow merged with his. He looked up from the stone court. "Yes, but how did it happen?"

"Does how really matter?"

"Maybe not to you, but I have to face him in the final trial."

"You gave me information on Cyrus not on Edwyrd."

"And were you not just his partner in the second? Shouldn't you have dissected his ability already?" Iris raised one eyebrow.

Victor chastised himself for not opening up more to the man in hopes of gleaning more of Edwyrd. He knew the man to be intelligent, but he had never shown a prowess for Power. In fact, he had shown the exact opposite. When Cyrus had carried Iris and her on his sand fist through the desert, Edwyrd had been struck in awe. When Victor lifted the entirety of the lake, he had seemed captivated that such a thing could even be done. And when he had slain Cordelia's serpent, the same intrigued look had shown on his partner's face. If anything, the man had shown a fascination with Power as if he had never truly understood all of its capabilities. How, then, could he have won such a trial? And against such an adversary?

"What does that make of our contract, then?" Victor ignored the temptation to look at his palm.

"It does nothing. We still have a deal. I helped you advance. The fact that you can no longer use the information I gave you is another thing."

When Victor stayed silent, Iris continued. "Regardless if you win or lose the next trial, my part of the bargain has been upheld. It will be your turn to do the same in time."

"Verimas will go to Chaon. Don't worry."

"Oh, I'm not." Iris smirked. "But I would be worried if I was you should that not happen." She turned and started walking away. Then she stopped and looked over her shoulder. "Apprentice or not, I would be worried."

She walked away again, leaving Victor in solitude on the stone court, wondering who he had struck a deal with and to what extent it would be paid.

CHAPTER 19

E dwyrd paced in his room. He walked towards the painting and away from it until finally he couldn't handle looking at it because it reminded him of his first conversation with Cyrus, so he flipped it over. That was when Conseleigh Shadir entered. Edwyrd thought he was to be taken to the apothecary, but he wasn't. Instead, it seemed that the conseleigh had come to talk with Edwyrd in hopes of busying him so that his mind didn't drift off into the abyss of worry. But did the conseleigh know he was already past that? Could he understand how he felt? Could he see it in the way Edwyrd continued pacing, rubbing his hands together, or his unusually heavy breaths? Or was he merely focused on providing a soliloquy meant to assuage Edwyrd's own guilt? Was he told as a conseleigh not to consult Edwyrd's feelings, or had being raised on Pyre made him immune to empathy like most on the planet?

"...strong. He's a fireson, after all. He will be fine. Trust me."

"How can he be fine if he's dead? I killed him."

The conseleigh coughed into his fist. "I should have known better than to lie to you. You're much too astute for that." His orange eyes flared for a moment. He stopped mid-stride. They remained aglow for a matter of moments. When the flare subsided, he turned to Edwyrd.

Edwyrd's eyebrows arched. "Who was that?"

"Guardian Crevon. He is coming in to talk with you. The trial is finished."

"He still held it after what happened?"

"Life goes on. Mustn't it?"

Edwyrd opened his mouth in response, but knew it was stupid for him to contend with that. What the conseleigh said was true. Life did go on. As it had continued after Alicia's death. And it would now continue after Cyrus's.

"You'll realize that as Guardian of the Core should you become his apprentice. Death comes for any man. You will have to replace your conseleigh when age or battle takes us."

"But those deaths are natural. I killed Cyrus. Me." Edwyrd stopped his pacing and turned to the conseleigh, pointing at himself.

Arms crossed over his chest, Conseleigh Shadir shook his head. "You didn't kill him, Edwyrd. Not you." He took a hand out from under his elbow and waved it at Edwyrd. "Cyrus could have ended the spell whenever he wanted to, but he chose to stick it out to the end."

"So did I. I could have stopped and then he wouldn't have died." Edwyrd collapsed onto his bed.

"But then you would not advance to the finals."

Edwyrd shot up. "What does any of that mean when I have a death on my conscience?"

"For a fireson, this is a worthy death. Die by fire, die with honor. Living on Pyre, nothing is higher."

Edwyrd pushed his breath upwards and folded his arms over his chest. He collapsed once more on the bed, disgusted that the conseleigh would try to justify the death with the Pyrean mantra. *He didn't even die of fire, though. He died from water. Possibly the worst way to go.* He stayed silent, staring up at his ceiling until a knock came at his door. Edwyrd turned his head. The conseleigh went over to open it.

"Guardian Crevon, would you like me to stay or leave?"

"You can leave us. I think it's best if Edwyrd and I had a talk alone."

Edwyrd hoisted himself up into a sitting position once more.

"As you wish, my Guardian."

"Thank you for keeping him company for a time, Pax."

"My duty." The man bowed and turned to Edwyrd. "Edwyrd, take care of yourself."

Edwyrd frowned. Was this part of the strategy to free him from his guilt? First, send in someone who should be able to connect with him, but who had only succeeded in annoying him with an archaic axiom, and then send in the Guardian of the Core himself to tidy up the remaining bits and pieces? Who next would console him should the Guardian fail as well? A member of the Twelve?

Suspiciously, he eyed Guardian Crevon as the Guardian entered. Hands behind his silver and blue cape, the Guardian looked out the window first briefly, and then leaned against the desk in Edwyrd's room, hands on his thighs. Both men stared at one another. What could the Guardian possibly say that would make this situation better? He had killed a man. And not just any man, a kin of his, a fellow Pyrean.

"I assume you are astute enough to know what has happened."

Edwyrd remained silent.

Guardian Crevon nodded. "I figured as much. Was he your first?"

Edwyrd nodded. But then he thought about that statement and opened his mouth. Alicia had died by his intervention as well. A pang of fire cut through his gut. He closed his mouth and nodded again. This time he added a soft, "Yeah."

Guardian Crevon watched him, as if he understood Edwyrd was hiding something. He didn't pry further, merely saying, "That explains some of it then."

"Explains what?"

"Your demeanor."

"Someone just died."

Guardian Crevon closed his eyes and nodded. "I understand that, Edwyrd." He opened his eyes and smiled. With a soft voice, he said, "I was once in your shoes as well, having killed my first. But the more we are exposed to something, the less it affects us. As Guardian of the Core, you live a life longer than most others due to the Power you receive from the Twelve. You see nations rise and fall. You see lords come and go. You change the cabinet of your conseleigh time and time again."

"But you never actually killed any of them."

"And did you *actually* kill Cyrus?" Edwyrd stayed silent. "Or was it his own drive to beat you that killed him?"

"I pushed him to his limits. If I had not copied his tactic, he would have won."

"And then you would be leaving the Core shortly."

"But at least he would be alive."

"Tell me something, Edwyrd. Do you believe Cyrus thought you an adversary?"

Edwyrd furrowed his brows at the question. He didn't respond right away. After a little pondering, he shook his head, although he was reluctant to do so. In all honesty, Cyrus probably didn't imagine anyone here to be much of a threat, save Victor, perhaps. And he remembered that Cordelia seemed to stand out to him, but he couldn't consider her an adversary because she was a woman.

"Perhaps then Cyrus made a grave error in underestimating the situation again."

"Again?"

Guardian Crevon tilted his head to the side and bit his lower lip. "I suppose it doesn't matter now that he is dead, but Cyrus got the pen and parchment question wrong."

Edwyrd searched his mind for the specific question. "That is the one asking how much it costs, correct?"

"Correct."

"It was one-hundred-and-five copper cures, correct?"

"That's correct."

"What does that have to do with—"

"That question is only difficult because some individuals do not give it the full attention it deserves. They look at the question, initially see it as inferior, and take as little time in solving it as possible to conserve their mental energy for the larger tasks at hand. It shows a carelessness that I think Cyrus wouldn't like to admit. You gave it the same amount of attention as the other questions."

"How do you know?"

"Because you got it right, and you recalled it right now."

"I only remembered it because you mentioned it."

"Regardless, you went into the trial ready to face your adversary. Cyrus went into the trial, I'm assuming, ready to be declared victor. So when you put up resistance, he resorted to last-ditch efforts, and it was his own desire to advance that caused him to die. You merely adapted to the situation and used the resources you could to stave off his Power. You were resourceful, Cyrus was reckless."

Edwyrd took a moment to digest Guardian Crevon's words. While still in the process of filtering through them, the Guardian continued.

"During my time as Guardian I've learned many things from each nation. There is a saying that the southerners of Sereya have that I think you'll find particularly interesting right now. Do you want to hear it?"

"Sure." Edwyrd nodded.

"Walk the path. Climb the cliff. Conquer the mountain. But do not die for the crown." Guardian Crevon waited a moment for Edwyrd to process it. "Do you know what it means?"

"Know when enough is enough?"

Another smile came to the Guardian's lips. "You certainly are bright, Edwyrd. It surprises me you didn't get more answers correct during the first trial. Were you holding back at all?"

"Holding back?" His face flushed. He hadn't held back anything in any of his trials.

"I take that as a no then." Guardian Crevon laughed. "Don't feel ashamed. Some did. I could tell by their answer patterns. Iris and Cordelia did. And, for them, that is fair enough. They wanted to use the element of surprise for later. Although what good that did them now, I don't know." Guardian Crevon sat and bit his lip. "Anyway, I digress. Where was I? The crown. You're right. Cyrus should have given up, but he wanted to win. It was the fireson nature in him to be better than the rest, but someone so smart should have realized there was something different about you."

Edwyrd gulped. "Different?"

"Certainly. To be honest, I didn't expect you to hold your own against Cyrus, seeing what he was capable of in the first two trials, but you outdid him. It makes me think you are hiding something."

Edwyrd coughed. "Is that... uhmm... is that wrong?"

Guardian Crevon shook his head. "Not at all. And I won't ask you to divulge what it is, but I do sense something. I could tell ever since I asked you the first question."

Edwyrd sighed. "It's my sister."

"What?"

"That is what I've been hiding. Before the trials, my Guardian, she died."

"I'm sorry. How did it happen?"

He didn't really want to respond, but he was talking to the Guardian of the Core after all, so Edwyrd gave him as brief an answer as he could. "A dragon killed her."

"There are many of them in Nova."

Edwyrd wanted to ask how he knew, but he remembered part of the role of apprenticeship was spending years on planets at a time to learn the ways of nations, their customs, interacting and building rapport.

He sighed. "I watched her die. I was powerless to stop it."

"So that is who you fight for?"

"Who I fight for?" Edwyrd repeated the words to himself silently under his breath. "Yes. I suppose it is."

"Good. Use that strength to your advantage. When we fight for something, we are often stronger than if we had no motivation at all, or merely selfish motivations." Guardian Crevon pushed himself off the desk and sat on the chair in front of Edwyrd's bed, so that he was eye-level with him. "But do not think that either of those deaths are on your hands, Edwyrd. Cyrus chose his own path. Your sister was a byproduct of fate and misfortune."

"And is that all I'm meant for, fate and misfortune?"

Guardian Crevon studied Edwyrd. He forced a laugh and stood straight. "Who is it for us to know what we are meant for? Only the Ancients can guide us in that. Tell me something, do you believe in them?"

Edwyrd nodded. "I studied under Garrett Omyon. He's told me many things about them."

"Really? Like what?" Guardian Crevon raised an eyebrow.

"Ancient Lyoen is a woman."

Guardian Crevon bobbed his head. "Yes. Not many know. What else?"

The sapphire eyes searched Edwyrd. Edwyrd studied them. Should I? He bit his lower lip. "Well," Edwyrd started, trying to keep his voice casual. "He told me about Ether Weapons."

Guardian Crevon opened his mouth. "Is that so? What did he say?"

"That the Ether Weapons were created by them," Edwyrd said the most plausible thing he could think of, but in reality, his mentor told him nothing of the great weapons, besides the fact that he had once had one.

Guardian Crevon laughed. "No. I'm afraid that one isn't true. The Smiths created the Ether Weapons."

"Smiths?" Edwyrd muttered.

"Forget I said anything." Guardian Crevon cleared his throat. "Anyway, I am suspending the final trial for a few days. It wouldn't be fair of me to pit you against Victor after such an arduous trial for you and such a..." the Guardian paused. "such a failure in the other one."

"Failure? What do you mean?"

"Iris forfeited her match with Victor." He sighed and stared at Edwyrd. "That is something you must come to anticipate. If you do happen to become the Guardian of the Core, Edwyrd, things happen without you planning them. Almost as if fate wants to simply mock you and all of your meticulousness." He shook his head and waved his hand. "Anyway, it will be you and Victor in the final."

"What is the final trial, my Guardian?" Edwyrd hoped the Guardian would divulge something.

Guardian Crevon smirked. "If you are smart enough, you will have already figured it out. But I cannot tell you directly. You will only have to wait and see. Is there anything else?"

Edwyrd was in the process of shaking his head no when he paused. He cocked his head, raising his chin slightly. "Could you tell me more about bonding?"

Guardian Crevon furrowed his brows. "Garrett Omyon didn't mention anything to you?"

"He talked about it in passing, but when Conseleigh Shadir was here earlier something happened."

"His eyes glowed?"

"Isn't that a show of Blood Bonding?"

"It is." Guardian Crevon nodded his head.

"So then you two are?"

He laughed. "No, we are not related. My conseleigh and I perform a ceremony monthly to keep us bonded together. You will learn about it in time should you become Guardian."

"What other types are there?" He asked the question, already knowing the answer, but he hoped his feigned ignorance could lead him to figure out how to leverage his bond with Vesel to his advantage.

"Well, the second most common type is bonding with an animal."

Second most common? Is there more than just two? Edwyrd thought about that as Guardian Crevon continued.

"...said we are all meant to bond with some animal."

I know that better than most.

"Maybe even multiple," Guardian Crevon continued. "I'm not entirely sure, but I do know it's nearly impossible, for the probability of running into your animal out of the billions that roam each planet would be an act of fate. Like finding your star."

"But what would happen if you did do it?"

Guardian Crevon took his hand out of his crossed arms. "What? Find your star or find your animal?"

"Animal."

"Well, then you would receive its Power and ability."

"And would you always have access to it?"

"You never always have access to any bond."

"Never? But you mentioned Blood Bonding with—"

"Unless you are directly related by kinship, you do not have constant access to a Blood Bond."

"So what about bonding with an animal?"

"I am no expert in this, and the reimaje I wear can only tell me so much. The previous Guardian would have been much more of an expert on this, but from what I know there is a ceremony in the bonding process itself, and after that the continued strength of that bond only depends on proximity and emotion."

"Emotion?" Edwyrd muttered under his breath. He looked up. "Why?"

"I'm afraid I cannot tell you that. You will learn when—"

"Because we're made from emotions."

Guardian Crevon studied Edwyrd long and with deeply furrowed brows.

"Lord Omyon told me during my training."

The Guardian released a breath. "You certainly were fortunate for such a mentor. I'm surprised Garrett would offer such information freely."

"He didn't. It was an accident."

"Accident?" Guardian Crevon arched an eyebrow.

Edwyrd retold the day when he thought Lord Omyon would dismiss him but instead came over to his house to offer him the mentorship.

"A fortunate slip of the tongue then for you."

Edwyrd forced a smile on his lips.

"Yes. Just as each object is composed of elements, this chair here primarily wood, for example, humans and animals were formed
through some sort of combination of emotions."

"So the more passion we have, the better that connection would be?"

"In a sense, yes. But bonded animals also feed off of your emotions just as one would feed off of their strength."

"What do you mean?"

"The more dire the situation, the more emotion one would tend to show. Cyrus, for example, displayed a greater amount of passion at the end of his spell than in the beginning. That is because he was close to death, and so his survival instincts took over and he gave it everything he had. His emotion caused his Power to surge at the end of his life."

Edwyrd didn't speak. He didn't want to talk about that topic. "And the third type?"

"What makes you think there is a third?"

"Because you said second most common last time. It implies one, two or even several more."

A smirk crossed the Guardian's face. "Good. Yes, there is one more. You can bond something to something else."

"Like object to object?"

Guardian Crevon shook his head. "Not exactly. It's worse than that. This is where you lock someone's physical body and their soul inside some sort of object. Usually this is reserved for the worst type of grievances."

"Do you know of anyone who has received that?"

"I do."

"Who?"

"That is a story for a different day, and perhaps one told by a different person. Garrett Omyon can tell you more about that than I can."

"Why him?"

"Because it happened during his time on Gladima. To someone close to him. And it was one of the acts that started the Great War. Only after that War, Edwyrd, did the position of the Guardian of the Core come to exist. Now, is there anything else?" When Edwyrd remained silent, Guardian Crevon stood and walked away, pausing at the threshold. He looked back at Edwyrd. "You turned the painting around."

"I..." Edwyrd blushed. "It reminded me of Cyrus. We spoke about it after the first trial."

Guardian Crevon took it off its hook and examined it. "Oh? And? Interpretations?" He turned his head toward Edwyrd.

"I thought it was a hypnosis spiral. Cyrus saw it as how we achieve victory."

"Interesting thoughts." He put it back on the hook. "Which way do you want it?"

"Facing me is fine. What do you think it means?"

"I've already told you." Guardian Crevon smirked and exited the room.

CHAPTER 20

A fter his conversation with Guardian Crevon, Edwyrd had examined the painting and ruminated about the Guardian's meaning. Not thinking of anything, he plopped down on his bed. "He didn't tell me anything," he had muttered. But that wasn't true. The Guardian actually had said quite a bit to him, just nothing about the painting. The Guardian's mention of *Smiths*, who- ever they were, had spurred him into action to examine the library. However, as he was walking up the steps to the second floor, the conseleigh and the Guardian were coming down, carrying an air-compressed black bag, which could only hold Cyrus's dead body.

Conseleigh Ersa had taken him to the apothecary after he retched onto the staircase. The adored had advised him to take some sedatives to calm himself, which he had obliged. And while they made him sleepy and lethargic, they did little to quell the nightmares that plagued Edwyrd that night. If anything, Edwyrd was sure that they only induced them. Nightmares of seeing Cyrus's face grow taut and gaunt, his body shriveling, collapsing and breaking into tiny pieces on the stone floor.

The second day Edwyrd had better success, but food still didn't sit well in his system. He had excused himself from lunch early, feeling oddly uncomfort- able about it being just Victor and himself at the dinner table along with the Guardian and his conseleigh. Of course, it was obvious that just he and Victor would be at the table, Iris being taken home sometime later the earlier day, but as he began eating, his mind began racing and eventually he once again thought of Cyrus and upheaved his stomach into his wing's bathroom. Sitting in his room that day, he decided to turn the painting back around, knowing he wasn't ready to face it yet. And maybe he never would be. Why did such trivial things hold so much meaning?

To placate his mind slightly, he maneuvered, successfully this time, to the second floor and into the library. He wandered its stacks, trying to figure out some sort of order in the assortment of texts that seemed random. They were random; the servant assigned to the library eventually told him, after letting him wander aimlessly for at least thirty minutes.

"No way to catalog everything here. We have texts going back to even the Great War. We use this now." She showed Edwyrd the electronic tracking system at the front of the library and gave him a quick tutorial on its use.

He pecked the keyboard like a rooster pecking seeds off the ground. S-M-I-T-H-S. The search resulted in more than two-hundred texts, but as he clicked on each title randomly, checking to see a little more information, he noticed many were just referencing the word blacksmith, instead of only smith. *Hmmmm...*

He opened his mouth to call over the woman to help him filter his search but decided against it. What if word got back to the Guardian about his search? Even now, while searching, did this system have some sort of history to see what had all been looked for? Before going further, Edwyrd played with the device a little, finding a settings tool under an icon of a cog. From there, he could select history, and just to be sure that it worked, he decided to test it out by clearing his previous search request.

It didn't work. Well, it would have worked had he had the appropriate passcode to enter to clear the search history, but he didn't. That meant that whatever he searched for could be traced by the Guardian and, most likely, his conseleigh as well. Did that even matter? He decided that it did.

Hovering over the keyboard, shoulder hunched, Edwyrd had stood there in the same position for such a long time that the servant woman came over and had asked if he needed anything else. After hiding the screen with his back and blushing and laughing, he had responded 'no' and quickly turned around and pretended to be busy, typing in an innocuous search term N-O-V-A. Over one-hundred more texts appeared on the screen afterwards. He sighed. Then an idea came to him. Pecking the keyboard once more, he typed, R-E-C-L-U-S-E. While the man wasn't related to what the Guardian told him, he figured that this library might hold more answers than what his mentor was willing to give him on Nova.

The results showed nothing.

Damn. Edwyrd slapped his leg. He breathed through his nose. *Figured as much. Probably not even his real name. Of course, it isn't. That's just what we call him. Oh well.*

Trying to still make this day as productive as possible, Edwyrd reverted to manually checking the library for the S-M-I-T-H texts he had searched for earlier but quickly lost hope. There were just too many. Did he need this information so badly? On that day, the answer was a *no.* Defeated, he returned to meandering the halls, hoping that his aimless walking would provide him some spark of epiphany. None ever came.

When the third day arrived, Edwyrd was surprised by how refreshed he felt after the lack of nightmares. He supposed it was because he had yet to view the painting again. However, even though he was refreshed, to acknowledge that he felt better meant the Trials would continue. He couldn't have that. Not yet. This might be his only opportunity to use the Guardian's extensive library to his advantage. He couldn't imagine the Guardian waiting too much longer for him to 'find himself' before just awarding the Guardianship to Victor due to Edwyrd's incompetence to handle loss. While this wouldn't be the best way to handle the situation if he were Guardian, Edwyrd wouldn't put it past Guardian Crevon to do such a thing, after learning how the man tried to still continue the third trial in spite of Cyrus's death.

Due to this belief, Edwyrd feigned fatigue and sickness while at breakfast, hardly touching his food, despite his ravenous hunger.

"Would you like to go to the apothecary today, Edwyrd?"

Edwyrd blushed. "I... I don't think it's that serious..." Edwyrd blinked. Correcting himself, he said, "I mean that serious to bother the adored. Maybe just another day." He grimaced in pain. "I just need some time to lie down."

"Another day it is then. We shall conclude the Trials tomorrow." Guardian Crevon raised his glass.

Truly sick this time, Edwyrd raised his glass as well and looked across the table to Victor, who narrowed his focus on him. Edwyrd took a sip from his glass, keeping his eyes on Victor all the while, seeing his final opponent do the same. Calculation cold in his eyes, he looked at Edwyrd as wounded prey. And partially, he was right.

Edwyrd excused himself from the table. His stomach suddenly felt sick again.

In his room, Edwyrd did lie down on his bed, but he chastised himself for his blunder in the dining room and pondered more on how to search for a text to give him answers. Mind wandering, his vision did as well, and it eventually landed on the turned-over painting. *The damned painting.* Edwyrd grunted and walked to it. Combating his fears, he flipped it over and faced whatever the hypnotic fire spiral was meant to represent. If Cyrus were here, how would he have faced Victor in the finals? His first conversation with Cyrus, the man admitted he carried no weapons, just gauntlets. How then would he have ever succeeded in facing anyone in an actual battle? He would have been without an actual weapon.

Edwyrd looked at his hands as if they would provide him answers. Surprisingly, they did. An idea popped into his mind. *Without weapons...* Eyes alit with revelation, he rushed out of the room and went up to the second floor. He asked the female servant for a pen and a piece of paper to write on, and she obliged.

With these two items, he once again searched for Smiths, coming up with the same results as yesterday, most of them in reference to blacksmiths. Clearing his search, he typed in blacksmiths, results populating one-hundred-and-fifty now. Tediously, he went back and forth, seeing which texts had been canceled out by his refined search. Fifty was still too large of a number to deal with, though, so he used one more tactic. He searched for the term *Ether Weapon*. This resulted in a list of results as well, more than seventy-five, but he didn't care about all the titles, only the ones that also had matched his narrowed down smith result. There were only four. His eyes lit up and quickly jotted them down.

He typed in the first title into the search function and then followed a holographic green line to where the book was located in the library. Plucking it out and putting it at the back table for later inspection, he then repeated the process with the other three.

This should do. He thought as he sat down at the table.

He spent the next hours scanning through the texts. The first book had merely listed out the Ether Weapons that the Smiths created. There were four swords, three staffs, one lance, one axe, one hammer, and one shield. The second text he examined went on to list the names of each of the Ether Weapons, but only noted the location of Adonis, the Guardian's blade. The others, it seemed, were lost to time.

Except they aren't lost to time, Edwyrd thought. *Lord Omyon had one, and he gave it away.* It was the third book, though, where Edwyrd found more information than he could have asked for, but it came from a place he didn't expect. The title of the book had been called *A Bard's Tales* and inside was just an anthology of stories. After skimming the stories, he eventually stumbled upon the words he had put in the search.

"...With the Smiths created, they set about the task set before them by their creator, Ancient Lyoen. The Sages had helped Ancient Bane in creating Power, and wanting to outdo him, Ancient Lyoen tasked them to make weapons out of the ether of the universe, which she gave them. They bickered over how they should be designed, but eventually the Smiths created eleven Ether Weapons.

One Smith created the swords. Another the staffs and lance. Another the axe and hammer. But it was the last one who had made the shield.

They brought their weapons before Ancient Lyoen, displaying them at her feet. She was pleased until she saw the shield.

She looked at the man. 'Why did you make a shield? I asked for a weapon.'

'And the best weapon is a good defense, is it not?' The Smith raised an eyebrow. 'This shield can stop and reflect any attack. You can test it out yourself, my Ancient.'

She did. She drew her copper sword and struck down on the shield. The shield didn't break. It didn't budge. Instead, the shield repelled the weapon, pushing the Ancient back a step. Her eyes widened in marvel. 'This is truly magnificent.'

Edwyrd skipped a bit of the story. The other Smiths were caught up in a combat with words, claiming how their weapon could do this or that. Eventually, the Ancient stopped this and told them that they could each keep one of their items, but the others were to be given to her and she would give them away as she pleased.

He went on to read how Ancient Lyoen gave a staff to Garrett Omyon, and a sword to a man named Zas Banegul, of the other tribe, the Evolics. The story concluded on a positive note, showing how this simple act of giving bridged tensions and brought the two tribes closer together.

After finishing the story, he flipped back to the beginning to see the title: *Forged.* It was a simple title, and if it hadn't been for the fact that some pictures were within the story, pictures of the supposed Ether Weapons, Edwyrd assumed, then he probably wouldn't have stopped on it at all. But he had. He looked at the rough sketches of the Ether Weapons, noting all of them, seeing how large the shield was. It looked like a heater shield from the picture. Then he reread the part where an Ether Weapon was given to Garrett Omyon. His thoughts returned to the last conversation he had had with his mentor. He had given his Ether Weapon away to a friend of his who had needed it more.

Edwyrd closed his eyes, trying to remember as much of that conversation as possible. He had accused his mentor of lying about the Recluse being his friend, of handing over his Ether Weapon to him. But as he thought about it more now, he came to realizations. *Even if the Recluse has the staff that Lord Omyon gave him, it is only good for attacking. Dragons can breathe fire. They could attack him from a distance. An Ether Weapon might be able to stave off a few of them, but a thunder of them like Alicia had been up against? Impossible. Someone defending themselves against that would need Power. Or...*

Edwyrd bit his lips and opened his eyes. He flipped again to the image of the shield and fingered it. *What if...* His mind sprinted ahead of itself, too fast to process the thoughts entering it. *Is the Recluse of First Blood like Lord Omyon? It would make sense as to why they're friends. Does that mean he is as powerful, too? Can the shield he carries reflect attacks? Along with the Ether Weapon, it would make sense that dragons wouldn't attack him. But what does that mean?*

His breath hitched. Mouth slightly agape, Edwyrd leaned back in his chair. Two thoughts penetrated his mind. *Is the Recluse a Smith? What does that mean if he is?*

CHAPTER 21

"It has been a week and a half. The eight that began here were meant to be here, some failing to showcase their talent. Others never getting the chance to show it at all. But that is to end with this final trial. You have shown me your intelligence. You have shown me that you both can work together in teams. I have seen your Power. Well, yours, anyway, Edwyrd." Guardian Crevon flicked a smile. "But now it is time you show me everything. For the fourth and final trial, you both will duel against each other. No limitations."

Edwyrd gulped. "No limits. What exactly does that mean?"

"It means exactly as it sounds. You will use everything at your disposal. The last contestant left standing will be deemed my apprentice. Is that understood?"

Finally, a trial that matters. A sly smile spread apart his lips, and he narrowed his vision on Edwyrd. "Perfectly." Victor held his gaze with Edwyrd until the Pyrean looked away. The man shifted in his chair.

The only thing that mattered was how Victor chose to spend his time until the afternoon when the trial would take place. He had already continued practicing during the days of intermission. He'd also meditated about Edwyrd's strength, because surely the man was more formidable than he first thought if he had been able to beat Cyrus.

It had come to him yesterday in a moment of enlightenment as he had reexamined the stone court. Cyrus's hamartia was overconfidence. The fatal flaw of many in stories Victor read during his tutelage. It was the undoing of a fool who toyed with his opponent instead of dominating him from the beginning. Would Cyrus choose to do that? Who knew? Dead men didn't tell tales, but Victor assumed it was perhaps the *honor* of fighting someone from the same planet. *Honor* never sat well with Victor. Results are what really mattered, and if one achieved them through dishonorable means, did it make a difference? Was it really about journey instead of the destination? Victor didn't think so.

And that led Victor to formulate his strategy: pure obliteration. It wasn't any real strategy, but dragging out the inevitable defeat would give Edwyrd time to think and respond, and Victor knew that the man could certainly do that. While he hadn't shown any signs of physical prowess to the extent of Victor's own, he did exhibit a celerity of mind. While painfully nascent in Power, having been in awe of Cyrus's show of Power in the second trial and Victor's own use of water against Cordelia, he had successfully used those techniques himself.

It wasn't just that, though, that Victor had been ruminating about for the last few days. He had also reexamined every single encounter with Edwyrd, from the initial meeting of the distant man in the lobby to their time together in the dunes. And during this thorough examination of Edwyrd, it became poignantly clear to Victor that Edwyrd had drive.

Drive equaled strength. And his strength was a who. Not a why. While he had been too focused on the trial at hand to understand it then, he understood now, especially when he recalled Edwyrd saying his sister had sacrificed so much. His sister had died. And it must have been in some way that forced Edwyrd to feel like he had to compete.

Knowing that, Victor better understood why it had seemed that a light had flipped on in Edwyrd and how he managed to outperform expectations. The strength, he was sure, came from coming to grips with whatever had plagued him at the beginning. And even though he said he was okay, was he really? How could he be in just a handful of days? Victor's brother still felt guilty for the death of their own mother ## years ago, so what little hope did Edwyrd have?

None.

Not if he couldn't bypass his past. As the Epochian proverb went, 'a guilty man is his own executioner.' And judging by the look on his face when Guardian Crevon had told them that the fourth trial would be an all-out duel, Victor knew Edwyrd wasn't truly over his past. It wasn't in his nature to kill again, and that made him weak. It certainly seemed the Sages, once again, were prescient to what no one else could have known, for both individuals they had chosen would need to get their hands dirty. Iris by sacrificing herself to move Victor forward, and Victor for making good on that sacrifice.

Victor casually looked down at the scar on his palm. A smirk came to his lips. *Your debt will be repaid soon enough. It is only a matter of time.* With his scarred hand, he took his cup and sipped more wine from it, feeling the bitterness hit his tongue. Fate was certainly cruel and bitter, and Edwyrd was in its grasp—a lamb being led to the slaughter.

Edwyrd finished lunch and walked away as silently as Victor had. Was there a point in trying to sway his mind? Defeated, Edwyrd stalked back to his room and slunk into his bed. He closed his eyes, trying to find the peace and calm that he needed. Even this little activity didn't go undisturbed. Five minutes into closing his eyes, the telecommunicator on his wrist vibrated.

Edwyrd blinked, not realizing what it was at first, and then held the screen of the advanced watch up to his face. *Cordelia?*

He fumbled around with the buttons until he stumbled upon accepting the call by pushing the crown on the top of the device. Out in front of him, a green, holographic image of Cordelia showed. Edwyrd blinked again. *What kind of...*

"Edwyrd," Cordelia's holograph said. "What happened? Did you win?"

Edwyrd righted himself in his bed. "What do you mean?"

"You're still on the Core. I can see the room behind you. Are you in bed?"

Edwyrd blushed and whipped the covers off of himself, feeling ashamed for trying to relax into his depression. "No," he lied.

"I can see the bedrest behind you." Cordelia laughed. "So you won? You're apprentice!"

Edwyrd shook his head. "Why would you think that?"

"Because it's been four days and you are still at the Core?"

"The last trial got postponed to this evening."

"Postponed? What happened?"

Edwyrd gulped. Of course, she didn't know. She had been taken from the premises almost a week ago. For the next half an hour, Edwyrd recapped the events of the third trial and the aftermath of it, leading up to the announcement that morning about the last trial.

"Cyrus died?" She blinked.

Edwyrd nodded.

"You beat Cyrus? How?"

The fact that she would ask him annoyed Edwyrd. Had no one thought him a threat in this competition? Did Cyrus really carry that much weight and respect?

"I am not as weak as I look."

"What color is your flame?"

"Orange," Edwyrd admitted.

"Cyrus was blue. I could feel that about him; the same way I felt Victor as a blue. I knew you weren't just from conversing with you. So then..."

"It's my sister."

"Your sister."

"Yeah," Edwyrd conceded. "She..." Edwyrd wanted to open up about everything, but would she understand? No. She had already cast him off as hopeless in his fight against Cyrus. "Never mind," Edwyrd pushed out.

"Never mind what? What is it?" Cordelia pried.

"She gave me strength."

"What does that mean? I thought she was dead."

"She is." Edwyrd thrummed the side of his leg with his other hand, wondering how much to divulge. "But it's her memory that made me fight on."

"And that helped you beat Cyrus?" Skepticism was thick in her inflection.

After an intense moment of glaring, Edwyrd buckled under the weight of her suspicion. For the first time, he opened up about that day with his sister and his run-in with Vesel. He explained to Cordelia how he and the dragon bonded and how he had given Edwyrd increased strength and stamina. By the end of it, Cordelia's mouth hung slack.

"You're telling me you bonded with a dragon? And on accident?"

"It was fate..." Edwyrd pushed out. "Fate. It seems that's all my life is made for."

"Sure. Does anyone else know?"

"I think Guardian Crevon suspects something. Victor probably notices something as well. He is too astute not to, but I don't think either knows the full reality of it. You didn't even until I told you."

"Cyrus aside, that..." She took a moment. "That certainly explains a lot of things."

"It does?"

"Your comment about how fate works. I understand it now. And I understand your interest in my water spell, too."

"But you aren't bonded to Thalassa."

"No. I'm not, but..."

"But what?"

"It's nothing. You've given me something to think about, that's all. So what are you going to do?"

"I'm still deciding. I was going to meditate on it but then you called."

"Well, meditate with me. The answer is obvious, you have to do it."

"It isn't your life on the line."

"And neither is it yours."

"What do you mean?"

"Think about everyone you would be failing should you not even attempt the fourth trial. Look past your sister. Look past Cyrus. Think about everyone. Not only that, but think about what you could do if you were Guardian. The changes you could make."

Edwyrd didn't want to hear any more of her advice. She was becoming pushy and not helpful. "Thank you." Edwyrd stayed courteous, but short. "I will think about that. I hope you give some thought to whatever you're going through as well."

"I will. It sounds like you need some space, but Edwyrd..."

"Yeah?"

"If you win, you get that fancy reimaje to wear. You know what that means, right?"

"I have a personal wormhole."

"And then?"

"I could have unlimited Power."

"And then?"

"Uhmm...," Edwyrd rolled his eyes upward and thought about the question.

"You could visit me in Acquava."

Edwyrd's eyes lit up. *That's right. I could visit anyone.* Edwyrd smiled. "And then?" he teased.

"Maybe I could take you to go see Thalassa."

"That would certainly be something."

"It certainly would. Bye, Edwyrd. Good luck. Keep moving. Don't stand still."

"What?"

"It's a saying on the Hart Isles."

"What is it?"

"Those still standing, don't stand still."

"Thank you for the advice."

The connection cut and Edwyrd put his hands behind his head. Back against the headrest, he stared off into the painting that hung on the wall opposite him. It wasn't spectacular by any means. It was simply a crimson red line that circled itself like a whirlpool of lava painted against a golden backdrop. Edwyrd stared at it again, trying to see what Cyrus had seen.

What did the artist have in mind for the spiral? Did it show an upward spiral? Or a downward descent? Still not in the right frame of mind to appreciate the painting, Edwyrd entertained different thoughts between the painting's interpretation and his conversation with Cordelia.

In the midst of his pondering, he realized one thing—Cordelia was right—he had to continue. Not just for Alicia. That was an obvious reason. And not even just for Cyrus as well. Both of those sacrifices and unfortunate twists of fate told Edwyrd that he had to go on, but what really spoke to him was when he remembered her encouraging him to think about everyone. What had that meant? He hadn't given it much consideration in the conversation, but now he knew what she meant. Literally, it meant everyone. Everyone in this system.

If he forfeited, he realized that the Guardian of the Core would have been chosen by a test, a simple paper test, designed to only test a certain type of intelligence, nothing else. It had been Edwyrd who had helped secure the win for their team during the second trial, and while Victor was certainly part of that victory as well, Edwyrd had steered him away from the wrong answer, and at the end of the day, had produced the actual result. It made Edwyrd realize that if he were to forfeit, then the system would be in the hands of a brash Guardian. And while that trait may certainly become corrected through training and the apprenticeship that followed, he knew he would feel awful if it led to an unfit ruler, one that he could have outperformed if only he had shown up.

Also, by becoming Guardian, he had the Power to change things. He could rewrite the next Trials as Guardian to be better, to protect individuals like Cyrus from being killed. He could prevent a trial like the one he was about to face from ever happening again. He could test contestants in his own way. He could break the wheel, not simply continue running the same one, and if he did that, he could only imagine how far the system could advance.

He stood up from the bed and walked over to the painting. Almost instinctually, Edwyrd put his finger in the middle of the fiery spiral, and then traced the line upwards until it reached the painting's border. As he studied it closer, he saw the blends of colors used in creating the fire: the orange, the yellow, and the red. Why hadn't he noticed them earlier? Upon seeing those slight nuances, he understood what the painting meant. Cyrus had been close. The artist had wanted to symbolize progress with the gold. And how that progress sometimes took blood, but it wasn't only blood. It was fire. It was passion. More importantly, it was what he had been told all along. Emotion. True power came from within. Why had he only pieced it together now despite it being so obvious? And it was the culminating emotion cultivated by those three entities that would lead upwards towards a golden era, a halcyon.

Which of those traits had Cyrus lacked?

It didn't take him long to realize the answer to that: passion. Compared to Edwyrd, the man didn't have an adequate why. And Edwyrd now realized how that why would fuel him in the end; he fought for more than just himself and his reputation. He fought for the entire system.

He closed his fist as he closed his eyes. Reaching within himself, he recalled times with Alicia. Soon after, Vesel's memory came back to him as well. It didn't haunt him like it usually did. This time it soothed him, warmed him, and he embraced Vesel's presence wholeheartedly, finally understanding his bond with the dragon.

Edwyrd?

Are you with me, Vesel?

I've already told you. I'm always with you.
All of you?
Not all of me. I am here.
What happens if I need all of you to help me?
Then call on me with all of your heart.
You will come?
I will do whatever I can.
That is all I can ask for, my friend.

The dragon roared in his mind at the sentiment. Edwyrd smiled, hearing his bonded animal's cry. He reopened his eyes and looked at the painting in front of him once more. If he let the fireblood in his body take control of him, he would ascend to victory. He could feel it.

Chapter 22

Victor stood inside an arena with checkered tiles of blue and gray. Some of them were worn and chipped, revealing pieces of cracked earth underneath. *We're someplace under the estate.* Around him were bleachers made of stone and granite. The Guardian sat on a throne of polished mahogany, his conseleigh sitting around him. Nearest to the arena were two adored who sat next to two wooden chests which, Victor assumed, had to be healing kits to patch up the winner of the match. And the loser, if he survived.

Before coming here, he had been blindfolded same as Edwyrd, who stood opposite him in the arena. He, too, took in his surroundings as if he was trying to find some secret advantage for what was to come. But there was nothing here for their advantage. Well, perhaps that wasn't entirely true. Around the arena, there were four lamps. That, in and of itself, wasn't peculiar, but the lamps rotated in color, one blue and one red, then blue and then red again. The glow seemed to be off, and so Victor knew that two of the lamps were using fire and the other two were electricity. *Earth. Fire. Electricity.* Searching for a source of water, Victor found nothing, meaning the only way to cast the element was to draw upon their own body's supply. Something that, given the last trial, could result in fatal consequences.

Victor kept his face straight, not wanting to give too much away, but inside he was thrilled with his quick surveillance. It meant that fire would be the most powerful spell in this duel because to cancel it out easily, one would have to take from their own reserves and syphon their own strength. It could be done once or twice, maybe even three times from what Victor saw of Edwyrd's last performance, but if his opponent wanted a safer approach to facing him, which Victor suspected he might, then to truly face him he would have to either cast fire and vie for Victor's control or cast electricity. Either way, Power itself, and the amount of it one had, would be the determining factor in victory, not the hierarchy of Power.

Unless Edwyrd had special skills he didn't realize, or the man was superior to him in battling with a sword, it meant that this trial was already over. There wouldn't be any opposition... there would only be an obliteration.

Victor turned his head towards Guardian Crevon, waiting for the trial to begin.

Edwyrd had taken note of the surroundings, just as he had always been taught to do. He didn't let those observations distract him, though, as he would have in the past. There was too much at stake in this trial, and he would see it through to its end, whatever end that would be. From his observations, it fared well. All but water could be cast, meaning fire was the strongest element as there was nothing in the natural hierarchy of Power that could subdue it without causing a serious toll on the individual.

That posed an interesting dilemma. He had never actually seen Victor's Power; he had only heard about it from Cordelia, who said he could cast blue flames because she felt his energy when she had dueled him. This blindness to his opponent would have worried him if he was anything other than a fireblood. Still, even if he didn't want to contend with Victor directly via Power spells of fire, he could always cast electricity and battle him that way. Assuming what Cordelia said was true, he wouldn't hold on long much past a few initial bouts of Powercasting, which meant he had to close the gap and see how Victor fared in his sword play. Strategy in mind, he turned his head towards Guardian Crevon's voice as the man spoke.

"Contestants, you stand in the middle of the arena. An arena very much similar to the ones they used in Gladima, which this Core presides over. It was in those arenas that the Twelve—the gods whose Power you will be granted when you become Guardian—came to be known for their prowess. There is no better arena, then, to test you for your own prowess and capability.

"When the Curse of Pirini Lilapa comes, and you have to answer, how will you respond? You will have to be resourceful, surely, so make use of your resources around you. You will have to be brave and look death in the eyes, and you are already here doing that in front of me and my conseleigh. Most importantly, you will have to be strong." Guardian Crevon exchanged a long glance with each of them. "And so Victor Zigarda and Edwyrd Eska, may the best man win. You may begin."

Before the man had even finished his sentence, Edwyrd had his sword unsheathed. He leaped forward into action, not standing still because those who did no longer stood.

The initial attack on Edwyrd's part threw Victor off-balanced. He didn't suspect someone with such grief and agony to be so bold and decisive, but perhaps the man had done it to stave off Victor's want to just quickly end this thing with Power. For that, Victor applauded Edwyrd, silently in his mind, of course, for he was too busy dodging and parrying the man's offensive to actually clap for him. The intensity of the attack forced Victor back and didn't allow him to think or to engage with his surroundings. Lucky for Edwyrd. The strikes were strong, but nothing Victor hadn't experienced before.

Victor held up his defenses, knowing that Edwyrd would most likely tire before him. After all, he didn't have the regal training that Victor had, and he certainly wasn't as genetically capable. He would allow this to continue for a little while yet, using the time to gauge the true strength of his opponent. He needed to make an accurate assessment of Edwyrd's Power before beginning his assault.

This wish was granted to Victor sooner than expected. After a barrage of stabs and slices, all of which Victor parried, Edwyrd lashed out downward with his sword. Victor blocked, but it brought him to his knees. Edwyrd's eyes flashed. This brief distraction allowed for a foot to come slamming into Victor's face, sending him rolling backwards. He landed on his back, a confident Edwyrd over him. One elbow propped on the floor, he wiped his lower lip with his thumb and noticed a line of blood. *So it begins.* He smirked. *He must have used Power with that combo.* Cautiously, he got to his feet, keeping his eye on Edwyrd. His opponent made no move to strike him while he was down.

Stupid. Victor laughed. "Is that all you have? I thought this was meant to be a duel."

"It seems I've drawn first blood."

"Only because I've allowed you to."

"And you're only standing now because I've allowed you to." Edwyrd pointed his sword at Victor.

Victor's brows furrowed. "Your benevolence will be your downfall."

"And carelessness will be yours."

Victor took a quick observation of his surroundings. "You have no idea what you're talking about." He walked around in a circle, forcing Edwyrd to do the same. Victor stopped when Edwyrd faced an electric lamp and was standing on a cracked tile that showed the earth underneath. "*Maa.*"

Victor charged. Tendrils of earth shackled Edwyrd to the floor. Victor lunged, sword out in front, but Edwyrd batted it away. Victor went overhead. Edwyrd brought up his sword.

Victor threw a fist into his opponent's exposed ribcage. "*Voima.*"

The spell sapped Victor of some of his own strength but added to the intensity of his punch. With Edwyrd's ankles locked in place, the spell only sent him backwards, crashing into the tiles with a hard thud. His head bounced off the tiled pavement. Victor pounced on him, sword raised, ready to force Edwyrd into concession. Edwyrd twisted his torso, making Victor's pounce sloppy. His opponent dropped his sword and punched Victor in his ribcage. It must have been laced with Power because it sent Victor sliding over the tiles, back to the middle of the arena. Victor grabbed his sword that had fallen out of his grasp. He spat. *He certainly learns quick.*

"*Palo,*" Edwyrd said. Orange fire wiped the earthen shackles clean. Edwyrd got to his feet, and, keeping his eyes on Victor, he grabbed his sword.

Orange. That's what I thought. Knuckles to the ground, he pushed himself to his feet. "That tickled." Laughing, he rubbed his side. His laugh turned into a guffaw.

"Why are you laughing?"

"Because this duel is over, orange flame." Victor waved his hands together, but before he could speak, an earthen tomb encompassed him, blacking out his vision, allowing him to see no more.

Edwyrd blinked at the earthen tomb he had just created. *That should hold him for—* Edwyrd winced and twisted back his head and neck. Already Victor was prying apart his earthen spell with his own vie for the Power. The man was certainly powerful and sly. He had never expected Victor to shackle him in Power, but if he could do that, then what stopped Edwyrd from entombing him? Nothing. It had worked for a little while during the second trial, so why wouldn't it work here?

He didn't need it to last long. Just long enough to put Edwyrd into position exactly behind where Victor was. Using his time wisely, Edwyrd darted behind Victor's location, poised and ready to force the man into withdrawal from this contest without any further injury. Saving his Power reserves, Edwyrd let the spell die and waited for Victor's back to face him.

The earthen tomb crumbled.

Victor faced him, grinning wide. "Hello, Edwyrd." He jabbed his sword forward. "Nice try."

In shock at Victor's prescience, Edwyrd didn't realize what happened next. He should have a sword in his stomach, but his reflexes must have taken over because he was only bleeding from his side. Then Edwyrd lurched forward. The grip on his sword failed, and the blade clanged to the ground. The intensified kick sent him careening back into the wall, hitting it with such force that the fire lamp above rattled in its sconce. The shockwave bounced his head off the wall behind him, blurring Edwyrd's vision.

Tinnitus didn't allow Edwyrd to think clearly, nor could he hear. Vertigo didn't allow him to properly see and react. But he didn't need any of his senses to feel his predicament worsen. The room grew inexplicably hot, and a mountain of blue swelled in front of him. It rained down upon him, drenching him in raw, blue fire.

Victor crowed. That had gone better than he had expected. The earthen tomb was certainly a clever idea, not allowing him to see what was occurring outside. Too bad Victor had already seen that technique. It was only natural, then, that Edwyrd should want to approach him from behind, so he had turned his body around while inside and waited for either his Power to overpower Edwyrd's or for Edwyrd to collapse the spell himself. And now his opponent slumped against the wall. No sword in his hand. Nothing to defend himself. This match was over, and he would make sure of it right here. *I learn just as fast.* Victor smirked, satisfied with his performance.

"Edwyrd, do you forfeit?"

The man said nothing.

"Do. You. Forfeit?" Victor repeated, louder this time.

The man only groaned.

"Very well, then." Victor huffed. *"Palo."* He drew upon the essence of the flame inside the lantern above. To gather more energy, he turned his body slightly and called out to the other lantern on the opposite side. Together they produced a massive swelling of raw, blue Power that circled in front of Victor like a sweltering cloud of fire. Victor gave one glance to Guardian Crevon, who said nothing. And he took that as his cue to continue. Victor closed his eyes. *Goodbye, Edwyrd.* He unleashed the bulging cloud, letting it rain down upon Edwyrd in a deluge of blue.

Victor held the fire for a few seconds, inundating his opponent. Obliterating him. Not wanting to see what remained of the body, he was beginning to turn around when shock held him still. Disbelief pried open his jaw.

"How..." Victor's mouth went dry. The fire that had passed over him had seemingly no effect. Edwyrd groaned and got to his feet. "What did you do?"

"Nothing," he replied.

Victor gasped. "You have the gall to tell me nothing? Nothing?" His voice escalated. "*Palo*!" He said it with more vigor this time. Blue tendrils of flames circled Victor's hands and shot towards Edwyrd.

"*Palo*!" Edwyrd retorted.

Orange flames darted out of Edwyrd's hand. But those orange flames weren't just flames. If Victor hadn't known better, he would have thought the fire had shaped itself to the likeness of a dragon's head. The mouth opened, swallowing Victor's blue flames. The orange and blue flames met with a dynamic clash, and for the first time in his life, Victor felt a strength he had never encountered before. It brought him to his knees. Sweat palpitated his skin as he tried to fight against the dragon flames, flames that were swallowing his own and making the dragon's head grow larger. Soon, he realized there was nothing more to be done. *This can't be...* On his knees, a victim to his fate, the flames of the orange dragon swallowed him whole.

CHAPTER 23

E dwyrd couldn't bring himself to look at the crumpled body that lay on the floor before him. Victor Zigarda had been stripped completely naked, his armor and clothing burned off by the flames. A slight sound, like a cough, tugged Edwyrd's attention.

"He's alive!" Edwyrd shouted towards Guardian Crevon.

The adored on standby rushed to the arena floor as well as the conseleigh and the Guardian of the Core himself. All of them stood around Victor and the two adored who worked frantically to save his life. Edwyrd couldn't watch any of it, though, so he turned around and focused on the flame behind him. Then he looked down at his hand.

Vesel was that... Edwyrd gulped. *Was that you?*

You called out to me, and I came to you.

He wanted to continue the discussion with his bonded animal more, but a hand clasped him on the shoulder. "Edwyrd."

He spun around to see the Guardian of the Core. "My Guardian." Edwyrd blushed. "I'm sorry about..." Edwyrd let his eyes drift to the gurney that now wheeled away Victor Zigarda's body, marred and ruined beyond comprehension. "I'm sorry. I didn't mean to."

"You didn't mean to?"

Edwyrd shook his head.

"I am wondering *how* that happened. There is only one explanation." Guardian Crevon furrowed his brows. "Edwyrd, are you bonded?"

Edwyrd gulped. "I am."

"You are bonded to a dragon?"

Edwyrd nodded his head. "It happened before I came to the Trials. Immediately before. I..."

"Say no more. What is done is done." Guardian Crevon waved a hand. "I knew there was something different about you, but this, well, this is a first for me. Follow me to my chamber. We should have a discussion about everything that has happened and that will happen."

"Everything that will happen?"

"Now that you're my apprentice."

"Apprentice..." The words fell out of Edwyrd's lips before he could realize what he was saying. "I'm apprentice... Me." He pointed to himself.

"You are. Shall we go?"

Edwyrd shook his head in disbelief. He beamed and nodded. After taking a few steps, he asked. "Shouldn't you blindfold me?"

"No. Not anymore. You will learn more about me, my secrets, and the secrets of the Core in time."

Guardian Crevon led Edwyrd down a hallway lit by fire and electronic sconces. Eventually, the tunnel ended, and they climbed a circular staircase that fed them out to the area behind the lobby staircase. Servants were in the lobby, all poignantly aware that something had happened, for they had their noses upturned and a few of them still loitered about, talking to one another in hushed whispers. Guardian Crevon gave them all a nod, and they returned to their work of polishing and cleaning. He proffered his hand to Edwyrd while standing in the middle of the lobby. Edwyrd took it and stepped onto a platform that was raised to the third floor.

On the third floor, he saw portraits of twelve individuals hung throughout the circular vestibule. Almost as if reading his mind, Guardian Crevon stepped off the platform and waved his hand around, showcasing them. "Take a stroll around here and meet all of these people."

Edwyrd obliged. *Pearl. Crestal. Theothe. These are the Twelve! But why do they look...* He didn't finish his thought, walking forward until a portrait of a broad-chested man with a chubby face and cropped orange hair like flames gave him pause. His eyes were a deep shade of brown. "Fueoco," Edwyrd breathed.

"I take it you understand who you see?"

Edwyrd looked at the Guardian, who still stood waiting for him to complete his lap. "These are the Twelve? The gods?"

"The same."

"They are... us." Edwyrd examined each remaining portrait as he moseyed back to the Guardian.

Guardian Crevon chuckled a little to himself. "Something like that. Did you expect them to be something different?"

"I..." Edwyrd finished his lap, stopping beside the Guardian. "I guess I had never actually considered the possibility of meeting one of them."

"Well, you will have to eventually during the annual Meeting of the Twelve."

"Where is it?"

"On the planet Onkh, in the southern part of Sereya. On the top of the planet's highest mountain, Mount Volan."

Edwyrd brightened. *That means I could see Cordelia at that time as well.* He thought about the possibilities of connecting with her again. He didn't really know much about her, but she seemed genuine and true and loyal, and those were all qualities that Edwyrd gravitated towards. Probably why he couldn't stop thinking about her now. *She will be impressed to hear that I won.*

"Come inside." Guardian Crevon led Edwyrd through two golden doors, into a large chamber compartmentalized into three or four separate areas. In the center of the room, facing away from the veranda behind it, was a throne made of gold and plush velvet cushions. Off to the side was a desk and to the left of the desk lay a golden bowl that stood upon a silver pillar. The other doors were closed, so he couldn't see anything else, but the amount of space in this apex dwelling made just him and Guardian Crevon seem small.

"This is where you will live once you are Guardian. You will have the entire space to yourself. It'll be good for meditative—"

"You have this entire place for yourself?" Edwyrd butted in. He covered his mouth. "Oops. I'm sorry."

Guardian Crevon chuckled. "It's okay. Yes. To yourself. This whole place and the view are all yours."

"But what about your..." Edwyrd stopped. While in school and even under the guidance of Lord Omyon, he had learned about the Guardian's vows, so he already knew love was prohibited. And for him, that had been okay. He had never known it before; he had never connected with anyone before. But Cordelia had shown him more warmth than a fireblood woman would ever show. And it had stirred something inside of him. Opposites attract. Isn't that what they said?

"What is it?"

"Nothing, my Guardian." Edwyrd kept his head lower.

"Edwyrd, come now. You are my apprentice. You can ask me any question you want now."

Edwyrd frowned. *Should I ask? Will it be disrespectful? Of course not. He just asked me for questions. This is my chance.* Obliging the voice in his head, Edwyrd asked, "Why can't we love?"

"When you love somebody, you will want to create families with them, and those children can receive the Power—"

Edwyrd shook his head. "No. I understand why I cannot have heirs. But why can't I love or marry someone?"

"Why is it important to marry someone, Edwyrd?"

"It isn't. I haven't thought of it before, to be honest, but my parents married, and they had me and my sister."

"And that is what married couples usually do. They love one another so intensely and so passionately that they have intercourse, resulting in children. Children who may or may not have those same abilities and genetics as their parents."

"I know that. But what if I were to love or marry someone, but not have offspring?"

"Would you truly be happy then?"

"Perhaps." Edwyrd had never thought about why someone would marry and not have children, but he assumed there were individuals out there who did such a thing.

"I see the point you are trying to make, Edwyrd. But here is a question I pose to you. What is a marriage between one individual and another?"

"Well, it's an oath to one another."

"A bond." Guardian Crevon bobbed his head. "Good. Kind of like the oath or bond you are about to take at Coronation." Guardian Crevon paused and then smiled. "Very similar to the bond you have with your dragon."

"Vesel?"

"Yes." Guardian Crevon's eyes lit up, and he snapped his fingers, as if an idea had just come to him. "What were to happen if Vesel were to die? Do you know, Edwyrd?"

Edwyrd shook his head.

"You would die. Well, perhaps. Most likely. Only the strongest of individuals can survive the severing of a bond. And this is why bonding with an animal can be one of the most foolish things an individual can do, for while you do have an increased strength and ability, you also have each other's weaknesses as well."

"Ability?" Edwyrd thought back to his conversation with Vesel when they had first bonded. *I bond with the person, not their greed.* Edwyrd focused on finding Vesel's pulse and the dragon came easily into his mind.

Yes, Edwyrd?

What ability did you give me? Are you the reason my flames turned to a dragon? Is that it?

I manifested myself within your Power. I told you I would burn for you, but that is not the ability I have given you.

Then... Edwyrd blinked his eyes. *The fire. It doesn't burn me. That's why...* He thought back to his own encounter with Vesel, remembering how the silver flames had enveloped him, same as Victor's blue flames, but how he had felt nothing. It made sense to him then. *I am immune to fire.*

Yes. You have some of my blood in you now. Dragon's blood and fireblood.

You saved my life.

And I will save your life time and time again. I will be your shield and your strength, Edwyrd. Until you forgive me for what I've done.

At the mention of the last item, Edwyrd cut connection with Vesel. He didn't want to remember that scene. Not right now.

"You just reached out to him, didn't you?"

"How could you—" Edwyrd closed his mouth. *Of course, he knows. He is the Guardian of the Core.*

"The eyes."

"They glow when I communicate with him?"

"It is how Telepathic Power works."

"I thought that was only in human bonds."

Guardian Crevon shook his head. "It is for all bonds, Edwyrd. What did your dragon tell you?"

"I'm immune to fire. That is his ability he bestowed upon me."

Guardian Crevon chuckled. He bobbed his head, brows furrowed in thought. "It certainly seemed like fate has won you that victory, then. You should have died with Victor's flame, do you realize that?"

Edwyrd blushed. He nodded. "He's very strong."

"One of the reasons why the Sages chose him to be their sponsor for the Trials, I am certain. They will certainly be stupefied when they come to the Core to teach you instead of him after Coronation." Guardian Crevon laughed again. "But you played even better. You never revealed all the cards in your hand. Even I didn't know. And sometimes that is the greatest lesson someone can know: Only when we are not seen do we show who we truly are. Do you know what I mean?"

Edwyrd shook his head. "I don't, my Guardian. Sorry."

"I mean to say that the person who you truly are." Guardian Crevon came closer. "The person here." He put a finger on Edwyrd's chest, right above where his heart would be. "Who you are at your core, the true nature of someone's core is only seen when that individual doesn't know he is being watched. As my mentor, Guardian Jorey Raule taught me, ethics isn't what we do when someone is watching, ethics is what we do behind closed doors when no one is watching. Do you understand now, Edwyrd?"

"Yes, my Guardian."

"Good. Now, to finish up our topic of bonding. Edwyrd, if you were to marry someone, you would create a bond with them. Emotionally, physically, spiritually, mentally. They would become part of your identity. When they die, a part of you would become lost."

"That is just life."

"For most people, that *is* just life. And people accept this part of life, preferring the brief bliss to the heartache a loss of a loved one brings after. But not for the Guardian of the Core. Because of the Power imbued in us by the Twelve, once the Passing occurs fifteen years from now, you will no longer age until you fulfill your own Passing. That is why I look the way I look, even though I am two-hundred-and-twenty-eight years old."

Edwyrd quickly calculated the math in his head. "So, I will never look older than thirty-five?"

"Yes. That is correct. And while you may not age, the others around you will, Edwyrd, and losing someone close to you once is already pain enough. What if you married multiple times after each one died, only to see the next one die at the end of their life? What if you did give birth to offspring, only to see them die before you? Consider how unbearable that would be as a parent. Replacing a conseleigh is one of the hardest things I ever have to do as a Guardian because my four aides are my family. You will be immune to the ravishes of time, but those around you will not be, and that is why it is forbidden for Guardians to love and to be intimate and to marry. If your significant other were to die, then you would be pained for the rest of your life. Does that answer your question?"

Edwyrd nodded.

"Curiosity is a good trait, regardless of how many cats it has killed." When Edwyrd didn't respond, Guardian Crevon frowned. "Do you not get the joke?"

"I do not."

"That's right... no cats on Pyre. Well, maybe someday you'll come to appreciate it." Guardian Crevon chuckled to himself. "Now there are more important things to worry about, such as your Coronation."

"What do I have to do?"

"Through my reimaje, I will be transferring all ten of the current lords or ladies here once the stage is set. They will ask you a question. Something to gauge the type of individual you are to make sure you are fit for defending this system. If you achieve a majority of their votes, you will be my apprentice."

"And if I don't?"

"With doubts like that, perhaps you aren't the kind of apprentice I would have hoped you to be." Guardian Crevon winked. "My conseleigh and I will be busy preparing the stage for the event." His eyes glowed momentarily. "I should go check on Victor. He has finally awoken. To be honest, I am surprised he is still breathing as well. It is a testament of his strength."

"What should I do?"

"I would spend time in the library. Go over the current encyclopedias of the families in power and make sure you get a sense of who they are. It will be your job to woo them and to gain their favor come the end of the week. You will also need an outfit for coronation. I will have your personal attendant arrange a fitting for you sometime between now and then."

"Will my family be allowed to attend the event?"

"I'm afraid I will be only taking the families in power. The strain traveling through space puts on the body is something only those with Power can handle, and if I am not mistaken, your parents cannot cast, correct?"

"That is right, my Guardian."

"Don't worry. I will take you to see them after Coronation. And you will see them again during your apprenticeship."

"The reimaje. What kind of Power is that? I have never seen anything like it before in my life."

"And you will never see anything like it again. It is Ancient Power, Edwyrd. Taken from Gladima in the moments before the Great War sealed up the planet to be what it is now, this Central Core. It is one of a kind. It allows me to travel through space as I please, as long as I have been to that area before. It blocks my thoughts from others should I wish it. And it also acts as a map of the sky."

"Ancient Power? As in Ancients Lyoen and Bane?"

"Yes." Guardian Crevon opened his mouth and then closed it. A gleam in his eye, he looked at Edwyrd. "Speaking of the Ancients, did you find the text you were looking for?"

Edwyrd's neck tightened. "Text?" He produced a nervous laugh.

"Lydia mentioned you had spent most of your time in the library before the fourth trial. I saw the search history, Edwyrd. Researching Smiths and Ether Weapons, were you? Why those?"

Edwyrd gulped. "I... I just wanted to use the full extent of my resources here before I went back to Nova should I have lost."

Guardian Crevon bobbed his head. "That is smart thinking, I suppose. Why the sudden interest?"

"Lord Omyon used to have an Ether Weapon. I just wanted to find out more about it."

"Did he now? That is something even I didn't know. I only know of the location of four others."

"Really?" Edwyrd's eyes lit up.

"The Sage Cronos, who you'll meet after Coronation, he has one. A staff. The Paen household on Acquava carries one. Myethos and Luenar carry one and then there is mine." He shrugged his shoulders, gesturing to the longsword that had always been draped over his back. "But Lord Omyon had one? Hmmm... What happened to it?"

"He gave it away."

"Interesting." If Guardian Crevon was more shocked by Lord Omyon's act of charity, he didn't show it; instead, he studied Edwyrd intently and asked. "To whom?"

This was his chance. Edwyrd's heart pounded. "The Recluse!"

"The Recluse?" Guardian Crevon arched an eyebrow. "Is that name supposed to mean anything?"

"I mean. That is what we call him on Nova, but I don't know his real name. I think he gave it to him."

"Hmmm... Never heard of the... Is he the hermit?"

Edwyrd blanched. "The hermit?"

"When I spent my year on Nova, I saw a man very occasionally wander into town. Never really paid much attention to him. At that time, everyone called him—"

"Yes. That must be him! Who is he?"

"I don't know..." Guardian Crevon pondered deeply. After coming to no conclusion, he focused again on Edwyrd. "Surely Lord Omyon has his reasons for doing what he did. Now—"

"That's it! Just brush it off?"

Guardian Crevon furrowed his brow. His aloof nature suddenly stark. "No. But there is nothing we can do now about it." His features softened. "We will have a talk with your mentor after Coronation and try to get some answers then. For now, focus on the task that lies ahead of you. Focus on passing Coronation."

CHAPTER 24

Victor woke. In truth, he wished that he had stayed in the state of darkness that had overtaken him.

With his sudden jolt of activity, the Guardian's conseleigh and the adored crowded around him. Their attention caused Victor unease. He tried moving, but couldn't, realizing his arms hung in straps suspended from the ceiling. Across his chest and waist, a fastened belt prohibited his movement. He was clothed, but not in anything familiar. His skin was nothing but light blue-and-white bandages; they covered every inch of him, even the finger-width spread of skin between his upper lip and his nostrils. The only thing that the bandages weren't wrapped around was his eyes, mouth, and nostrils.

He heard murmurs of "contact the Guardian" and "he's awake" but shock paralyzed him from processing the owners of the voices. It was only when the head adored, the one who had sewn him up after he and Cordelia's fight, pushed his face in front of Victor's that he understood who was talking to him.

"How do you feel?"

Was that a serious question? Victor couldn't tell. Moreover, he didn't exactly know how to respond, for he couldn't feel anything.

"Nothing," he replied, not knowing what other answer he could give. "I feel nothing." This problem intensified as realized he hadn't even felt his mouth move. Why was that?

"Perfect."

Victor blinked, but he felt no twitch, no moisture to ease his burning eyes. They were so dry now. What was happening? "Why can't I blink?"

"Your eyelids have been burned off."

Victor gasped. "Burned. Off?"

"All of your skin has been burned off. You are lucky to be alive."

Phantom impulses caused him to try to blink again, only to fail.

"You mustn't do that. Here." The adored bent over and tipped Victor's head back and squeezed liquid eyedrops into his eyes.

He felt the splash and cooling relief of the eyedrops. His vision became blurry, but he was glad to have some feeling. It meant he hadn't completely lost of all his senses.

"Now just another moment." A hand ruffled the back of his head, and another sensation came to his eyes. When the sensation stopped, Victor saw the adored putting a handkerchief to the side of Victor's bed. "It will take some getting used to, but you won't need eyedrops forever. Just until your eyes get acclimated to not being able to close again."

"Will I be able to sleep?"

"Yes. There are others like you."

"What do you mean, like me?"

"Those who suffer from *veilless eyes.*"

His brows furrowed. "Veilless eyes?" he repeated, coughing into his fist as he did so.

"It's an adored term for those people who cannot close their eyes. About twenty percent of people in the system have some form of this condition."

"Twenty percent of people don't have eyelids?"

"No. Twenty percent of people cannot close their eyes properly. Less than one in one million is born without eyelids."

"Is there anything that can be done?"

"In your condition, no."

"What do you mean by *my condition?*" Victor writhed in place, held down by his straps.

The adored took a deep breath. "Usually, those who are born veilless are babies born without eyelids. Genetically unlucky in that part of their development. We can usually culture skin flaps to attach to their eyes to help their ability to close the eyelid and thus improve their vision. We cannot do the same to you."

"And why not?"

"Because all of your skin has been burned off. We are in the process of culturing it and regrowing it as best as we can now, as you can see from the bandages about your body. Eyedrops and sunglasses when you sleep are what we can prescribe to you now. This will help to maintain as much of your vision as possible. I hope—"

Victor righted himself in his bed. "Wait. So my vision will be gone?"

"Not gone. Just altered."

"Why?"

"Because they will be under constant fatigue without eyelids. You will get used to this in time, but it may result in what you see being not as clear due to the fact they cannot rest and renew their strength. Like I said before, we can prescribe for you eyedrops and sunglasses to help you with the transition phase of this process. I hope you understand."

Victor said nothing.

"Do you feel cold at all?"

"I already told you I feel nothing," Victor spat.

"Aahh, yes, that's right. I suppose that means it's phase two of the process, then."

"Phase two?"

"The first phase was to put your body into a complete state of coldness and numbness, and now the skin underneath the bandages is being cultured and cured as best as it can." When Victor looked at him with the same slack mouth and blank stare, the adored elaborated, "The bandages are regrowing your skin as best as they can. This is usually a pretty painful experience, which is why we completely numb the body beforehand. You should consider yourself lucky you are not feeling anything.

"And that is also why you can't move. You have to stay stationary for the cells to spread, coagulate, and form at their own pace."

"You can regrow my skin, but you can't do anything for my eyes?"

"Eyes are delicate things. And as I said before, we could if you would have had any part of your eyelids left, but there was nothing salvageable."

"What do I do now?"

"You wait. I believe we'll be able to remove the bandages by tomorrow, but I wouldn't expect getting much sleep for the remainder of your time here."

"Because of my eyelids?"

The adored flashed a faint smile. "If only that, Victor. No. Because of the amount of pain you'll be in once the anesthesia fades and the feeling *does* return to your body."

Victor tried shifting, but he couldn't.

"I've notified Guardian Crevon of your condition, Victor," Conseleigh Juniper said. "He will be here shortly. He is still talking with his apprentice."

Apprentice. The word cut through Victor's heart more than it ought to. After all, his body was numbed, yet he could feel that. And he felt the disappointment that went along with it. The shame. How had things gone so wrong? Victor was winning throughout the whole duel. He hadn't given Edwyrd a chance to recover. He hadn't ever showed weakness to his opponent and let the man take advantage of that moment; he had been ruthless, yet it was all for nothing. It was

Edwyrd who was Guardian Crevon's apprentice and here Victor lay strapped in, tied up, in bandages that were constructing his skin.

For one of the first times in his life, he didn't have anything to say. The conseleigh offered him vacant condolences before dismissing themselves to other tasks that needed tending to before Coronation, eventually leaving him alone with Conseleigh Juniper. Why she stayed, he wasn't exactly sure, but she stood, arms crossed, looking down at him with an authority that made Victor uncomfortable. The adored came to check on him occasionally, which saved him from her intensity momentarily, but she turned back into the same staunch figure when he departed. After a few of these exchanges, Victor tilted his head back to the side facing her.

"Is there something I can help you with?"

"Yes. There is."

Victor groaned. A slight sensation was coming over his body now. "What is that?"

"Do not forget who you are, Victor Zigarda."

"And who is that? A loser? Someone who lost to a nobody?"

Bending closer, she spoke in a hushed whisper. "No. The son of Lord Hayden Zigarda. The heir to his family's throne, and the man who should have won these Trials. Fate interceded on Edwyrd's behalf, but you should have won."

"Thanks," Victor pushed out. He wanted to move away from her, the intensity in her scaring him a little more than it should.

"There will be times when you don't feel that you know who you are, but I know you do. Deep down in here, you know who you are." She poked his chest, but he couldn't feel it. "You are the ones who the Sages chose to be Guardian of the Core."

"They also chose Iris."

"Yes. I know that, too."

Victor was shocked momentarily, before her next words left him speechless.

"The Sages chose me, too, when Guardian Crevon was looking for his newest conseleigh. If I had been younger, I would have been chosen to participate in these Trials, but as it were, the conseleigh had Trials of their own. I was chosen, and I won, as I knew I would have because of their wisdom. Sages know all, don't they? And as your family's motto goes: Knowledge is Power."

Victor let her words wash over him. "Why you?"

"Because I know what it is like to be unique. To not fit in. You noticed that about me from the very first moment you saw me, did you not?" Her gaze pivoted between both of his eyes now. She was so close to him, he could smell the foreign flowers of her perfume. "When you go back, you will know that as well. But know that there are others who have never fit in before. Who were persecuted. And you will do your part in making sure they get back home."

"Where is that?"

"Here." Conseleigh Juniper eyebrows arched, and she flipped around. "Guardian Crevon, you are finished with your apprentice?"

"We had many things to talk about."

"As did we. I was just keeping Victor some company."

"And how are you feeling, Victor?"

"Nothing. Still, nothing."

"Adored Jayr tells me you are lucky to be alive. Do you feel lucky?"

"I cannot blink. I cannot feel. I cannot move. And I lost a trial that I should have won. Lucky is the furthest thing I feel. I feel cheated, if I am being honest, my Guardian." Victor felt Conseleigh Juniper studying him, but he kept his focus on the Guardian instead.

"Will you give us some time alone, Yun?"

"Of course, my Guardian. He is all yours." She smiled, bowed, and left.

Hands folded behind his back, Guardian Crevon looked down at him. "You fought bravely and excellently, Victor. I want you to know that."

Victor didn't say anything. He already knew that he had. "Why did I lose then? What in Abaddon's name happened? Why wasn't he burned, but I was?"

Guardian Crevon's chest expanded and sunk again as he took in a deep breath. "After my discussion with Edwyrd, I've found out that he is bonded to a dragon."

Victor coughed. He tried blinking but couldn't. This irritated his eyes, and he called the adored over to administer eyedrops. While the adored dabbed his eyes with the handkerchief, he said, "Did you say dragon?"

"I did."

"But... where? How?"

"Edwyrd's bond happened before the Trials began and he kept it in Nova. It seems the bond was so strong that it reached across space to give him the strength that he needed in the end."

"But what about my flame?"

"When you bond with a creature, you inherit an ability from that animal. No animal will ever tell you what it is that you will be gaining, mostly because they want to make sure the person is bonding with them for the right reasons, not the wrong ones, but I've come to find out that Edwyrd is immune to fire now since being bonded with a dragon. That is why it didn't affect him."

"But..."

"Do not feel bad. That is what I came to tell you. It truly was an act of fate that put Edwyrd into victory. I saw your skills on the arena floor, and I do believe you will be a great lord someday."

"But... That isn't fair..."

"Is it fair that Edwyrd was never brought up under the training and supervision of a family in power like yourself? Is it fair that Edwyrd's natural ability is only to cast an orange flame instead of a blue flame? Is it fair that for him to bond with his dragon, he had to witness his sister being killed?"

Victor had no answer.

"Life isn't fair, Victor. Sometimes that is just how it goes, but feel blessed that you, too, have another chance. You should have died in Edwyrd's flames, but you didn't. That is a testament to your willpower, strength, and resolve. I hope that you use those things to your advantage in the future. They would be a shame to waste."

The adored came back. "Anything yet?"

"Nothing. When will I begin to feel something?"

"The longer you don't, the better. Trust me."

"I understand there will be discomfort, but how long until I feel it?"

"It won't just be discomfort, Victor. It will be pain. Pain is a constant in the healing process. Without it, we wouldn't know good from bad."

"I don't care about your philosophical—"

Guardian Crevon chuckled and turned to the adored. "Have you been reading more philosophy books, Galen?"

"I want to keep my mind sharp as my profession, my Guardian."

Victor huffed. Loud enough that both turned their attention to him. "Pain. Discomfort. Whatever. When will I feel it? I want to feel something."

"Soon. We will give you sedatives to keep your pain as manageable as possible for the time you are here."

"And how long will that be?" Victor tried shifting.

"It will be at least a week."

"A week?"

"Yes, my Guardian. Burns like this usually take even three weeks or longer to heal, but Victor is strong. And our supplies here are of the finest quality. One week. Maybe one week and a half. Two at most. We will see."

Guardian Crevon turned back to Victor. "When I gather the lords and ladies for Coronation, I will make sure to bring your family here to see you. They will want to see what has happened. But I will send a message to them now."

"What are you going to say?" Victor widened his eyes. And then coughed.

The adored dripped drops in his eyes.

"That you were strong. That you fought brilliantly. That you live now to live another day."

"But you will tell them I was defeated."

"I cannot lie, Victor. They will know. What else can I say?"

Victor had no answer for that either. After Victor's prolonged silence, Guardian Crevon smiled towards Victor and nodded. He walked away, as did the adored, leaving him in silence and stillness. *What will Father think? Brother? Will Renaul see me like this?* His breathing intensified as his mind raced through the scenarios. He flashed back to the dragon, eating him whole. Swallowing him in orange flames. His heartbeat intensified, bleeps on the monitor next to him ushering the adored back into the room.

"Calm. Calm. Calm, Victor. Here." Adored Jayr brought a cup of some white liquid to his mouth and tilted the contents into his mouth.

Victor swallowed. "What is it?"

"Poppy milk. Drink. Drink." The adored tilted the cup back more.

The monitors bleeps next to him slowed as his heart rate did. His eyes became heavy. The adored grabbed a pair of sunglasses and set them gingerly on his face. The room blackened. And there in the darkness, he succumbed to nothingness.

CHAPTER 25

Victor didn't know what was worse. The interminable pain his body experienced or how alone he felt. Days had passed. He had no idea how many. The adored came to check on him off and on, but for all day every day his body lay limp and strung up, contorted in such a way that made it nearly impossible to move while his skin regrew itself underneath the bandages.

When his discomfort became unbearable, he screamed. His screams were sirens to the adored in the apothecary, who came to give him another dose of white poppy milk mixed with icy, blue petals plucked from what he had come to learn were Katarh flowers. The flower's petals acted as a cooling agent, regulating his internal body temperature and alleviating discomfort from the heat his body produced in sewing itself back together. The milk poppy induced lethargy and drowsiness. It numbed his senses back to a mild discomfort as best as any medicine could. Discomfort that had abated enough to allow him to sleep.

This he did over and over again. A perpetual state of Elysium, the halfway grounds between life and death. Stories growing up told him how that place was paradise, a magical place where people waited to ascend into Axiumé or down into Abaddon. It was anything but.

Everything in this world was anything but what it was supposed to be. His victory. The Trials. His condition. His life. Iris. The Sages. Edwyrd! Had that Pyrean even bothered showing up to see the mess he had made Victor? Probably not. Victor only hoped that his discomfort paled in comparison to Edwyrd's. Sure, the man might have become Guardian Crevon's apprentice, but the price he had to pay for it was high. Cyrus's death. Victor's maiming. Could Edwyrd even sleep at night, knowing all the pain he had brought to people of this world?

It was supposed to be my victory! "AAHHH!" Victor struggled in his bonds.

"More poppy!"

Someone shouted. A cup was brought to his lips and the sappy white liquid forced down his throat. His heart rate lowered. His writhing ceased. Pain left his body. Sunglasses came over his face, leaving him in nothingness and darkness once more.

"...your son, Hayden."

"Victor?"

Darkness. "Father? Father, is that..." Sunglasses were taken away from his face.

His father stepped back a pace, his mouth slack. To his father's side, his brother looked on just as shocked.

Guardian Crevon stood to the right of his father. "He is still healing."

"When will the bandages come off?"

An adored came into view. "He still needs a few days yet."

"Is that so? How long since this..." His father coughed. "This happened?"

"It's been a week now."

His father's eyes lingered on Victor. What hid behind those stalwart charcoal eyes he had inherited? His state of anesthesia mitigated his ability to read people. His heartbeat slow, he watched on as his father studied him like a spider might do to something that had just landed in its web.

"I will give you some alone time with your son. Coronation begins in a few hours. Be in the lobby by then."

Victor's father nodded and Guardian Crevon left. The adored did as well, but not before directing Victor's father to the vase of poppy milk on the counter and the bowl of blue petals. "Those are for if your son begins to feel pain. Administer them to lessen it." The adored left.

Like a cornered cat, Victor's eyes darted between his father and his brother. Both towered over him. When had Renaul gotten so tall? It hadn't even been a month. What was wrong with him? Had he no sense of anything any longer?

His father ran a finger over Victor's bandages, but Victor felt nothing. "How did this happen?"

"I should have won!"

His father shot his attention from Victor's left arm to his son's lidless eyes. "That isn't what I asked. How did this happen?"

"Flames. Didn't the Guardian tell you?"

"He told me you were defeated by a man named Edwyrd Eska. What color were his flames?"

"Orange."

"Orange?" His father's voice cracked. "You lost to someone with—"

"I shouldn't have lost."

"Yet, you did."

"The orange flame was bonded with a dragon. I... I never knew. Fire was completely useless against him." Victor looked directly up at his father now, who stared down at him. Bags underneath his eyes spoke of his exhaustion. His project was wearing him down fast. "Father, are you okay?"

His father frowned. "I am better than you, Son."

Victor's heart swelled.

"I can see that now."

"What is going on back home? Is the Web completed yet?"

"The Web proceeds. But slowly. And it will be even slower now that this has happened."

"What do you mean?"

"This setback. You were supposed to win, Victor. Then the fame you would have brought our house would have sped up construction. Everyone would have wanted to lend a hand to build it to gain favor with me, the father of the next Guardian. Now, I'll have to continue doing it myself. And Renaul."

Renaul proudly stepped closer to his father's side. "It'd be my pleasure to help."

Victor's eyes widened. "I can help too."

"Can you? You're in bandages."

"But not for long. I will be back in a few days."

"And am I to believe that you will have the same strength in you as earlier? The same drive?"

"Father, I will. I won't let our house down."

"But you already have. By losing."

"I didn't lose!" Victor fumed. He struggled against his bonds. His father retreated a step; his brother only looked on in sick amusement. "I didn't lose." Wetness formed in Victor's eyes. They slid into his bandages.

Victor's father came in close to him. Hot breath pounded Victor's face. "Everything was laid out for you to win. Everything. And you didn't."

"He was bonded to a dragon."

"So, flames didn't affect him. Is that all? Did you only have one plan? Smart men have contingency plans." His father thumbed the tear swelling in Victor's eye. "And get rid of those. They're useless." He stood up straight again and brushed out the wrinkles that had creased the bottom of his black tunic. "When you come back to the Web, feel free to rest and recovery as you need." His father nodded and smiled. "Your brother and I will finish the Web."

"But I can help as well."

"You can help by remaining..." His father searched for a term, finally finishing his sentence with "hidden. Your brother will be the face of the Zigarda name now."

"Fa..." Victor couldn't finish his thoughts.

"It is nothing personal, Son. Sacrifices have to be made."

"I... I don't understand." Victor shook his head.

"I am afraid that your presence might... hmmm... how to put it... distract people from their jobs. Rumors may spread. And nothing gets accomplished when rumors spread. Other families may see us as weak, perhaps challenge us. I would rather not have that. Do you understand?"

"So you wish me to be a stowaway? Some shadow in the corner?"

"Do not be so dramatic, Victor. You are still my son, just..."

"Just not the one you want to be seen in public?"

"Well, you put it rather bluntly, but yes. A family must make a name for itself. All great families do. The Evbers on Epoch I've learned have been ruling a little over four-hundred years now. Isn't that impressive?"

"We will too, Father. The Web will be the finest achievement Empora has ever seen."

Victor's stomach churned as his brother cajoled his father.

"It will be, Renaul. But it takes work and sacrifice."

"Of course." Renaul bowed.

"Do not worry, Victor. I will not lend this Edwyrd a vote. How can I after what he's done to you?"

The words were empty. Marred or not, how could the apprentice assume the vote of a man whose son he just beat? It would be utter stupidity to vote for the man. Victor never looked back at his father.

"Son, did you hear me?"

"I heard, Father."

Victor shot a glance at his father and then looked away, back to the poppy milk on the table and the blue leaves.

"Very well, then. I am off. Do you need anything else?"

Feeling began to crawl back into his body. All over and all at once. The last round of sedatives was fading, and soon pain would replace the numbness he felt. He thought about asking his father to administer some poppy milk and Katarh petals to make sure the sensation never advanced that far, but he merely shook his head and sent his father and brother away.

He didn't want to feel numb anymore. He wanted the numbness to leave him, even if it was pain that replaced it. Feeling something for once was better than feeling nothing at all.

CHAPTER 26

E dwyrd stood in the middle of a decagon. At each vertices of the decagon an erected pillar stood bearing the crest of each nation's lord or lady that had come to test him. Besides Lord Garett Omyon and Lord Asher Haco, Edwyrd had no idea who these individuals were, save for the brief scanning of them that he did while studying in the library the days before this event. He knew he would receive his mentor's vote, that wasn't a question, and most likely he wouldn't receive the vote of Victor's father. He had noted Victor's father and Victor's younger brother, Renaul, but Victor, Edwyrd knew, still was healing in the apothecary. Under the instruction of the Guardian, Edwyrd was told not to visit Victor until he had time to heal. Edwyrd had obeyed, knowing that time, if anything, was the greatest healer. And while Victor may not be able to forgive Edwyrd right now, hopefully, in time, the two would be able to make amends.

He had no idea what to expect in regards to the other votes. During the week before Coronation occurred, he had studied until his eyes drooped at any literature related to the current lords and ladies of the nations. He hoped to find some individual nugget of commonality amongst them, so that he could build rapport with them and secure their vote. Hopefully, it would pay off.

Conseleigh Shadir was finishing up a speech about the significance of the event and how the lords and ladies gathered today were the foundation for the next two-hundred years of the system. If they saw fit to move Edwyrd forward to being an apprentice, and thus Guardian of the Core in fifteen years, then they would be also responsible for how the rest of the system would develop for two centuries.

What weight, Edwyrd thought, and he considered how much more would be on his shoulders when he succeeded Guardian Crevon.

"With that, let this Coronation begin. I will be calling you forward in alphabetical order of your nation. We will start with Acquava. Please, Lord Calder Paen come and cast the first vote."

Edwyrd readied himself. He turned towards the man in his forties. Shaggy black hair matted his head, making it look more like a mop head. It was longer than normal men's hair, coming down to below his ear. "I stand before you today with the voice of my own, but I believe I speak for many in this audience in saying that this experience is an absolute treat. I hardly ever meet with any other lords besides those on my own planet, and even then, the communication is arduous. The Power that Guardian Crevon showed me firsthand, showed all of us firsthand, is tantalizing. The idea of interconnectedness has always been something the Paen family has strived for since my grandfather, Lyonell Paen."

Where is the question? Edwyrd tapped his foot, trying to keep track of everything the man said before he finally came out with his point.

"What will you do to bring the interconnectedness to this system?"

Edwyrd didn't respond right away. Was such a thing even possible? He assumed it could be. After all, Guardian Crevon had given him and the final six telecommunication devices, and that had worked for him across planets with Cordelia. And even Vesel was able to reach him across planets as well. He had an idea then for striking a good compromise of both and hitting home for the Paen ruler.

"Your grandfather was bonded to a dolphin, if I am correct."

Lord Paen's eyes gleamed. "Yes, that is true."

"Well, I will tell you a little about myself. Shortly before my own Trials, I bonded to a dragon."

Susurrus rushed out from behind him, hushing him. He ignored the temptation to look back. *Should I have done that?* Edwyrd pushed his lips to a side. *Doesn't matter now. Everyone knows. They would have found out in time.* Edwyrd patted his legs, waiting for the whispers to die down. When they did, he continued.

"My bond with my dragon has saved me countless times during this competition, and that is the strength of bonds. It is the strength of relationships we forge with one another. I believe to be a better system, we need to have better bonds and better communication, so I will make it an initiative of mine to increase technological advances so that the families in power of each domain can stay connected."

"That is a very wise agenda. Edwyrd Eska, you have Acquava's vote."

The Acquavan lord pushed a button on his pillar and a blue light shot out from it, stopping right above Edwyrd. *Well, that's one. Nine more to go.* He didn't have to get all nine, nor would he. He knew that. But from what Guardian

Crevon had told him, he needed to get at least a majority of their votes, which meant he needed five more.

"Lord Senlin Khan of Chaon, please proceed forward."

Edwyrd scanned for Chaon's sigil on the pillars in front of him. He shifted his posture accordingly and saw a man with even longer black hair than that of the Paen lord, braided and extending behind his back. His face was sharp, and his eyes narrowed in on Edwyrd as he took his position at the podium.

"Tell me, Edwyrd, what are your plans for infrastructure regarding private academies?"

"Do you mean like adored academies and weapons academies, my lord?"

The lord merely grunted and nodded.

"I believe they need to be developed further. If there is something that I have learned here is that not every planet is home to the same materials as the others. I learned this especially during my second trial. Therefore, not only do I plan on bringing together the nations in a bond of interconnectedness, but I hope to establish an adored academy and a weapons academy on every planet, and the curriculums which are linked together to help seekers of the knowledge gain a holistic understanding instead of merely fragmented parts."

"That is certainly an ambitious goal. But will it happen?"

"In my year-long sabbaticals on every nation, I plan on gathering the knowledge needed to have a rudimentary understanding of where each Academy lies and then bring them together in a holistic manner. I hope you see that I have thought this through, my lord."

"And I hope you see it through. Here in Chaon, we have a saying similar to the Acquavans: words are sand, but fake words are devilssand." The hard man leered at Edwyrd. "Still, you are wise and ambitious, and I think you will make a good apprentice. Chaon gives you its vote."

Edwyrd breathed. *That's two. But what is devilssand? I'll have to research that later.* Cresica was called next where his fortune continued, but afterwards came Empora. And with conscious dread, he knew his streak would end.

He breathed in and exhaled. Whatever he said, he assumed, wouldn't matter here, but it would matter to the other lords. He didn't want to say anything to make himself seem incompetent. With dead-set eyes the same charcoal gray as his son's, Victor's father leered at Edwyrd from the pillar directly in front of him.

"If there was one thing about the Trials that you would change, what would it be?"

There are many things I will change in these Trials. Edwyrd clenched his fist together, not knowing quite how to respond. Was this a trick question? Or did the father actually care about what had happened to Victor?

"There would be safety boundaries to prevent..." Edwyrd selected his next word carefully. "... *mishaps* from happening."

"Are you referring to what happened with my son?"

"That was a most unfortunate mishap."

"Even more unfortunate than what happened with a contestant named Cyrus?"

Edwyrd blinked. He put his hands behind his back, so that the lord wouldn't be able to see him pop his knuckles in agitation. "Both of those situations didn't need to happen, and will not happen when I am Guardian."

"I disagree."

Edwyrd's jaw dropped. He shook himself out of the shock just a moment after, but what had Victor's father just said?

"I believe contestants need to be pushed to their limits. They have to want to give it their all if they are to represent our ideas in this system. You will ruin the Trials by changing them, just like you ruined these with a lack of integrity. Empora cannot give you its vote; not to someone who is bent on changing tradition."

What. Was. That? Edwyrd didn't even hear the next name of the person after Victor's father. Had his father condoned Edwyrd's actions, yet thought he cheated at the same time? What was wrong with the lord, or did he merely seek out any opportunity to prove him wrong?

Next thing he knew, he was being asked a question by the lord of Epoch, Lord Sylvain Evber. The man was of average height, with brown hair and spectacles that covered plump and speckled cheeks. "This notion of the Trials changing is quite interesting, but I am more interested in knowing how this system is going to change under your supervision as Guardian of the Core. As the longest reigning family in Power here in this system, we have seen many changes, and the Evbers of Epoch want to know what more we can expect."

What were Edwyrd's goals? He had already mentioned some to Lord Paen of Acquava, and to Lord Kahn of Chaon. And, of course, he would change the Trials. But what others did he have in mind? Once again, he didn't respond right away. This agenda would be his to carry out throughout his term, and all the leaders here would know of it.

After some time, Edwyrd began, "As I mentioned to Lord Paen, I want to improve communication through technology and I want to make the Trials safer, as I mentioned to Lord Zigarda. But I want to go a step beyond that. I want to make planets safer to visit. My own planet is dangerous, and if you are not born with fire in your blood, walking upon it is certain suicide. Be that as it may, I want to make that an opportunity for people to experience. Right now, the interplanetary travel is a waiting line of the affluent. Those individuals who have enough money to afford a voyage to another domain, and to also stay there for a handful of weeks while they wait to return home. Surely, there are things lost in the ways of old that can point us in the direction of how these individuals are able to transverse space and time. It will be my agenda to make visiting other planets feasible for everyone and to make sure that travelers to those planets are safe beyond measure. This way we all may truly experience what this grand system of Gladonus has to offer us."

"Beautiful words for a beautiful time. I do hope you bring about this halcyon age, Edwyrd. You have Epoch's vote."

Another beam shot overhead. There were four now, all coruscating together in a sphere of Power, above him. What type of Power, he didn't know. There were many things he didn't know, Edwyrd was beginning to discover.

To Edwyrd's delight answers came to him easily, and by the time that his mentor Garrett Omyon was called up to the decagon dais, he had already secured the six votes he needed to be the apprentice to the Guardian of the Core. There was no longer any pressure, but that didn't mean Edwyrd would just give up. He still wanted to impress his mentor, whose vote meant more to him than anything else, and he knew that his mentor would be objective, not just giving him the vote because he had been tutored privately by him. His mentor was strange like that, but it was a strangeness he respected in the man, and the wisdom he had provided Edwyrd had led him here, to apprenticeship.

"Edwyrd, you have great dreams and visions for the future. It is nice to see, but what if the best days were already in the past? Is there a way that we can return to the days of old, before the Great War?"

An interesting question. Edwyrd bit his lower lip. He had only heard his mentor speak of Gladima, the planet of origin, a few times. There all elements existed. Harmony had been established. But it had been ruined seemingly over the escalation and corruption of Power. Was Power to blame then or ambition? Was his mentor trying to subtly tell him that he was being too ambitious in his dreams and that to do less was to actually to do more? If any man spoke in riddles, it was this man.

Edwyrd would match him with an indirect answer of his own then. "I believe fate is already working to take us back to the days of old. We can try to steer our own destiny as we might, but it is truly fate that has dominion over the horse we ride or the dragon we fly. I know fate has steered me here before you today, and I believe it will continue steering me, and so if the best days are in the past, then it will be. And if the best days are in the future to come, it will be. Everything that will be, will be."

Lord Omyon smirked. "Spoken like a sage. Fate has certainly played its hand in your life. And I believe you are right. Let us see what else it continues to do during your time as Guardian. Edwyrd, you have Nova's vote."

Edwyrd mouthed the words, "Thank you," to his mentor, who gave an appreciative nod back. That made seven. The next man to come to the stage was the lord of Sereya, who gave Edwyrd approval as well, making his vote eight. For the first time, Edwyrd's eyes bulged. Could he achieve all votes, save Victor's father?

"Lord Asher Haco, please come to the stage and cast the last vote."

If his blood hadn't been fire and warm from the votes of others, it would have gone cold. Edwyrd gulped and turned to the sigil of a cluster of volcanoes in the colors of reddish brown and orange. Dark-skinned and stern, Lord Haco looked down at him from his pillar. His hair was cropped like Edwyrd's, showing stark eyes, deepset and black like charcoals that were primed for ignition.

"While my vote doesn't necessarily matter in this Coronation, my question is this: When is enough enough?"

The man had been the one to nominate Cyrus. His question forced him to reconsider that day. It also forced him to think about the time with Guardian Crevon again, and the discussion that occurred afterwards, and it was in this nostalgia that he found his answer.

"I do not think I cannot supply you with an answer that will be sufficient for you, my lord, but here is what I have, honest and true. Cyrus was the first person I killed. And for nearly a week it tore me inside to the point that the Trials stalled for my recovery. I couldn't sleep straight knowing that he had pushed himself to the extremes, likewise pushing me to the extremes as well. So when is enough enough? That is something each individual has to come to on their own, but I heard a saying that they mention in the south of Sereya, that has stuck with me. It goes: 'Walk the path. Climb the cliff. Conquer the mountain. But do not die for the crown.' There is no prize we can accept in this system that is worth death, so enough is enough when you say it is."

The man fidgeted. It was as if he was contemplating whether he wanted to accept Edwyrd's answer or not. He appeared as though he wanted to, as if Edwyrd had stirred something in him, but in the end, the man chose not to support him. It didn't matter, but Edwyrd could tell that grudges were particularly dangerous and harmful and some people had no way of letting them go. He wondered if Victor would hold a grudge, or if time would eventually absolve him of any animosity towards him.

Edwyrd hung his head as the man left the pillar. He turned and watched the man flow back to his seat. As he took his spot, Guardian Crevon, who had been out of sight this whole time, appeared at the back of the cliff where the Coronation was being held, where all the lords and ladies had filtered in hours before. He strolled down the blue and silver carpet, approaching Edwyrd with a smile on his face. As he came down the aisle, all the lords and ladies turned and kept their attention on him, and when one stood to show their respect to the Guardian, the others did as well, until everyone was standing by the time he had proceeded halfway down the aisle.

With calculated steps, Guardian Crevon stepped up from the dais and walked around Edwyrd, circling him once, before standing alongside him. He put his hands in the air, gesturing for the families in power to take their seats. Guardian Crevon waited until all of them were sitting down. When they had taken their seats, the Guardian turned towards Edwyrd, looking him directly in the eyes.

"You have gained enough votes to become my apprentice, Edwyrd. It is a good thing to see. But now before I deem you my apprentice, you must take your oaths in front of all the individuals here. Are you ready?"

Edwyrd nodded.

Guardian Crevon turned his attention to the audience before them. Projecting his voice, he announced, "In witness of you all, he states his oath to me and the gods whose Power he will inherit in time."

Edwyrd went to one knee as he had been instructed to do so during the days leading up to the ceremony, when they had rehearsed the event. Guardian Crevon's gloved hand on Edwyrd's bent shoulder, he continued. "As apprentice and future Guardian of the Core, do you accept the standards and regulations set in place by the Twelve? If so, say, I do."

"I do."

"Then, Edwyrd Eska, repeat after me: I, Edwyrd Eska..."

"I, Edwyrd Eska ..."

"Hereby declare that I will serve Gladonus to my fullest potential ..." Guardian Crevon paused, waiting for Edwyrd to repeat the words.

"That I will remain impartial to the needs of any one particular nation ... And that the Power bestowed to me on the day of passing ... By the Twelve, of who have First Blood ... will remain mine and mine alone ... through the abstinence of love and marriage and heirs ... To all of this, I swear ... in the presence of the Ancients, the Twelve, and the families in power."

Edwyrd finished. There were no regrets in his mind, only victory. He had succeeded. Against all odds, he had become apprentice. A beaming smile came across his face.

"Edwyrd Eska, rise now as my apprentice." Guardian Crevon moved his fingertips over to Edwyrd's other shoulder and then to his forehead. His left hand was no longer gloved, and as the fingers made their way to each of his shoulders, a white light trailed behind like a comet's tail.

Edwyrd stood. The Guardian withdrew a blade one and a half times the length of a longsword. It was smoky gray with amethyst lines traveling up the blade's body. Upon seeing it, Edwyrd's mouth hung slightly slack. *Adonis. The Guardian's blade. A blade made of pure Ether.* He had only heard of it in fables, and had remembered reading about it in the library, but now he finally got to see it up close. The Guardian held it up to the sky and let the light that shot from each of the nation's pillars condense at the tip and slowly sheath the sword. The pillars at the four corners of the stage shot out lights of red, yellow, blue, and brown—one for each element. It combined with the light from above and sharpened the glow from Guardian Crevon's Ether Blade.

Then, while still holding his sword upright, Guardian Crevon carefully pushed his left hand up, letting a light from his palm mix with the Power of the elements. Blue overtook red; brown blotted them out, and the amalgamation that appeared afterward looked nothing like what Edwyrd had ever experienced before. It surpassed the magma oceans of Pyre and the deepest blues of the sky, vacillating between the two in a miniature cloud of Power that coruscated like a cylindrical wall encompassing him and the Guardian. Here, enveloped within this wall of Power, they alone were privy to the secrets of Coronation. The light rotated and swooped around them, circling them as if checking them from every single angle to see if they were worthy enough. Soon languages were spoken that Edwyrd couldn't comprehend.

The Guardian sheathed his sword. "Edwyrd, hold out your hand."

Edwyrd did what the Guardian told him. His heart pounded. Sweat slid down his brows even though it wasn't hot, but just the thought of being here so close and connected to the soul of everything made his body react in ways unexpected. Awe numbed him. The cylindrical wall glowed in a light of purple and pink and blue.

The faint outline of an object started to appear. It formed in front of Edwyrd's eyes, taking the shape of a dragon with wings outstretched, silhouetted by a sun that was the backdrop. It breathed fire into the sky, as if it were ready for anything. The object dropped into Edwyrd's hands, hot to the touch and solid, too. Metal as if it literally had just been forged before him. Edwyrd looked up, meaning to look at the Guardian, but instead his eyes focused on two faces pushing against the cylindrical wall, like a person pushing his face against a bed sheet. Edwyrd looked towards Guardian Crevon, who appeared unaffected. *Does Guardian Crevon see them?*

The two voices collided in perfect unison. "Fate has chosen you, Edwyrd Eska."

The cylindrical wall stopped. Power ceased and Edwyrd and the Guardian stood once again before the families in power. Edwyrd twisted his body back and forth, looking around for some semblance of the beings that had just called out to him. *Who were they? Where did they—*

A grand applause tore Edwyrd from his thoughts. Everyone was on their feet. Edwyrd was now officially the Apprentice of the Guardian of the Core. A hand pinched his left shoulder and Guardian Crevon gestured that Edwyrd should wave, so he obliged.

In the midst of the applause, Edwyrd turned his head back downwards to the object in his hand, turning it over in his fingers. *A brooch.* Although the design was different, it was similar to the Guardian's own, and it was also the Guardian's sigil. Was this to be his sigil as well? Edwyrd flipped it over again, examining the dragon spewing flames in the setting sun. Or was it rising? Or could it be both? Was he the beginning or the end? And, if so, what kind of life and responsibility did that bring with it?

CHAPTER 27

L ight and pain hit Victor simultaneously as the world once again revealed
itself to him in the form of the adored's arm, bent like a crane working its
way around his head.

"Aahh."

"Hold still now."

The adored gripped his chin and tilted his head back. Liquid flooded his
eyes in a momentary wave of relief. Vision blurry, the wrapping was peeled
from his face like an excess layer of skin. One circle. Two circles. Three. The
adored continued looping his arm around Victor's head, the lights and shadows
coalescing in a rhythmic dance. The water in his eyes kept him from focusing
on the pain and irritation he felt as each bandage was unwrapped.

Then he felt his neck.

And by the time his hands were being unwrapped, he had regained full vision
again. A quick glance at his fingers revealed salmon-colored skin. His neck
tightened, inducing slight pain and irritation. He ignored it. "Let me see my
face."

"My good sir, are you sure you don't want me to finish with—"

"Let me see my face," Victor demanded.

Adored Jayr sighed. "Very well, sir."

The lead adored disappeared for a little while, and another adored, a female,
replaced him and continued to unwrap Victor. With each peel, he saw more of
his salmon-colored skin below the bandages. Adored Jayr returned carrying a
hand-held mirror. He passed it to Victor, who greedily snatched it from the
man.

Victor clutched the mirror and continued clutching it as his mouth hung
slack. His hair had disintegrated, leaving him nothing but a bald pate. His
eyebrows had vanished as well. Crags of black burns hung underneath his

lidless charcoal eyes, making them look more sunken and sullen than they had ever appeared before. Some parts of his skin were smooth, glossy even and of the same salmon tone of what he had seen of his hands. Other parts were redder, bumpy and consisted of swollen blisters. *My...* Victor tried to lift a hand to his face, to feel what remained of his skin, if he could even call it that anymore, but he was still strapped into the bed.

"I thought you were healing me?"

"We *have* healed you, sir. The skin that you see has been cultured and cured with the best of our equipment here."

"Do better."

"It is impossible."

"But surely there must be more that can be done?" Victor's chest tightened, his eyes dried as he looked intently at the adored, hanging onto his every word. "My father..." He couldn't finish his thoughts. He understood now why his father wouldn't want him to help build the Web. Why, when he returned, he would be relegated to the shadows. He was hideous.

"Your father should be thankful you are alive. You, as well, should give the Ancients your praise."

"But you don't understand, I—"

"Victor," the adored cut him off. His eyes held sympathy for Victor. He sighed and reached out and took Victor's hand in his own. "It has been nearly two weeks in this apothecary. This is the Central Core. This is the best apothecary in the system. We have access to nearly every element here. We have used the Katarh Flowers from Acquava, along with maro nectar from the woodlands of Epoch, and aloe vera from the forests in Chaon. We have taken out of our collection of germs, bacteria and fungus mixed together to help you culture skin when applied with the previous ingredients. Even Guardian Crevon himself helped in guiding your recovery. Believe me when I say this is the best we can do."

Victor slunk into his bed. The mirror fell from his hand into his lap, and was quickly taken away by the adored. As the bandages kept being unraveled from his body, he was numb to everything else around him. Did anything else really matter? His father and brother hadn't even returned to see him after Coronation. Even with the bandages covering him, they saw him for what he was. What would they think of him without the bandages? And Edwyrd, he had never even shown at all. Did he even feel a pang of guilt for what he had done to him? Did he even realize the monster he had created?

Guardian Crevon came into the apothecary just as the adored were finishing dressing Victor in silken clothes, the red and black of his house's sigil. "Victor, you look charming."

"Charming? Are you insane? I look hideous!" Victor looked at himself in a full-length mirror near his bed.

Guardian Crevon stood alongside him. "It isn't how we look on the outside, Victor. It is what matters on the inside." The Guardian touched his own heart.

Victor looked at his hand, pockmarked and slightly purple. He brought it up towards his chest, but instead of pointing to himself like the Guardian had done, he clenched it into a fist. *If only that were true.* He let his arms fall to his side. "May I also get a robe that has a hood and long sleeves?"

"If you insist. Of course. I understand you still need time to adjust to your new skin. I will have something sent to you before dinner tonight."

"Dinner, my Guardian?"

"Yes. You'll have one last meal with my conseleigh, Edwyrd, and I, and then I will take you home."

"If you insist, my Guardian."

"May I show you to your room?"

Victor shrugged. "Sure." Victor continued hobbling down the hallway, acclimating himself to the slight discomfort he felt with every step.

"Things will get better, Victor."

Victor ignored him, continuing to hobble until he noticed the portrait of Guardian Raule on the wall. "Were your own Trials the exact same?"

"Mostly the same, yes. They were chosen by the Guardian and tested the same abilities. Although I do believe the riddle was different."

"And it played out the same?"

"My Trials were not as fatal. Those competing understood their limits."

"So your opponent in the final trial didn't end up like me?"

"No. He forfeited before it ever escalated to such violence."

"Should I have?"

"Only you can answer that."

"Would you have?"

"I would have not."

Victor took the words for what they were. That was something, at least. He had acted accordingly; it was a mere intervention of fate that had thwarted Victor. Nothing else. *Take away the dragon and Edwyrd would be nothing.* "What were you fighting for when you competed?"

"You are asking me for my why?"

"Yes."

"I came from a family of educators. My parents were tutors to the lady of Mistral."

"Mistral, the sky nation?"

"The one and only."

"How does it work? The islands I mean."

"There is an element that has just recently been discovered. It's called anitron. Have you heard of it?"

Victor shook his head.

"You will in time. I am sure it will revolutionize transportation in this system. Instead of relying on the power from the suns, this would allow transportation to be more frequent and less meticulous and risky, not having to leave in the day and arrive in the day.

"Anyway, back to my story. Spreading knowledge has always been a part of my family and so that became my why as well. And what better way to disseminate knowledge than in a position such as this?"

Victor remained quiet. He clenched the railing as he made his way down the stairs. *A position that should have been mine.*

"Victor, I know you are angry now. But do not let this be your downfall."

Victor's grip tightened on the railing. He wanted to rip it out. Face scrunched, he turned to Guardian Crevon. "If you were meant to win, but lost to some random act of fate, how would you react? The same fate that didn't even give me the decency to die an honorable death, but to live out the rest of my days like... like this!" He spat on the ground and continued walking, faster this time hoping to get away from the Guardian and his attempts to console him.

"Victor, anger may fuel you now, but it cannot always fuel you. Turn this into your own purpose and why."

Victor stopped at the sentiment. "My why..." he muttered. He turned around and stared up at the Guardian. "My why? My why was this!" He jabbed his finger towards the Guardian. He sniffled and tilted his head up, forcing the tears that had wanted to leave his eyes to retreat. "It was becoming your apprentice and the Power that came with it. The Power to not die to fate. To live."

Guardian Crevon came to meet him on the same set of stairs. "And it seems you still have that, do you not? Are you not still alive?"

"I am, but I might as well be dead. Don't you see that?" Victor pinched the bridge of his nose. When the tears passed, he continued. "I've disappointed my family. How can I even go back to them like this?"

"They will learn to accept you. You will learn to accept you. Not doing so, and living in this past, never overcoming the fact that Edwyrd became my apprentice and not you, will lead you to your ruin. Accepting it will save you."

"So, he gathered the votes?"

"He did."

"All of them?"

"Eight out of ten."

"Where is he now?"

"You will see him tonight at dinner."

"Pah." Victor spat and turned.

"Before you stalk away from me another time, realize I am only trying to help you, Victor."

Victor got to the bottom of the stairs. "The Guardian of the Core just watches. He helps no one." Victor began hobbling across the lobby floor.

"Edwyrd beat you because he learned to use the pain in his past as fuel for his strength. He turned his pain into Power and that Power was strong enough to overtake even you. It is commendable, and I hope you can see that from an outsider perspective."

Victor stopped. He seethed. Again and again he clenched his hands into fists, wanting nothing more than to ignore what the Guardian said, but knowing he should respect his words at the same time.

"Moreover, I hope you can take that as a lesson for yourself. What you feel now, turn it into your own strength. Do so, and you will see success in whatever path fate leads you."

As cavalier as he could be, Victor turned to Guardian Crevon. With a curt nod, he said, "Thank you, my Guardian." Victor then retreated from the lobby.

Inside his room, Victor looked at the mess. He had never bothered organizing his clothes, figuring he would have all the time in the world once he won the Trials, but how his plans had changed. He picked up a t-shirt from the floor and grabbed the bag he had set on the chair he had dragged underneath a painting. Putting the shirt inside the bag, he looked at the painting—a red spiral moving downward to infinity. The artist had drawn it in such a way that the spiral never stopped, each loop getting smaller and smaller until Victor couldn't see it. He had never given it a second glance. It was just decoration. But suddenly, it stood out to him. It spoke to him. It told him that things never ended, that lifelines, which he thought the red symbolized, went on forever.

"I should have died," Victor breathed, repeating the adored's words. He looked at the salmon skin of his hand and rubbed raw fingers over it. He turned from the painting to look at himself in the mirror. Touching his face, he felt each blister that pimpled his skin, each patch of smooth, glossy skin that sat alongside the blisters seemingly at odds with them. Together they produced a landscape much like a desert, the smooth sand giving way to cliffs and dimples like gullies. He let himself feel everything Edwyrd's dragon flames had given him. "But I didn't."

The realization of that spurred something in Victor's heart. It told him his purpose wasn't over yet, that he was meant to live. He had something yet to fulfill. Like this line in the painting, his life was meant to continue until infinity, in a future so distant he couldn't yet even fathom it.

Victor cloaked himself in the robe that his wing's servant had brought for him to dinner that night. He didn't know how he looked in it. Hideous, most likely. He had made it a point to turn around all the mirrors in his room so that he couldn't see himself. Constant discomfort and itching accompanied him like ticks on stray dogs. No matter how he scratched, it kept itching. Cream the apothecary provided him with, along with a briefcase filled with other tonics and ointments, were there to placate his discomfort. All of it was just momentary relief, though. There were elements he had never heard of from the nation of Acquava and roots and plants from Chaon that he could only imagine having to find himself. Regardless of how many balms or potions the apothecary here could give him, it couldn't give him what he wanted. Guardianship. Nothing could get rid of how he felt. What he lost in that fire.

Hood draped over his face, he sat across from Edwyrd. The conseleigh and the Guardian sat at the head of the table. Before going to dinner, he had taken a vial of liquid that helped numb and cool his body from the itching that had increased as Victor had finished packing his bags. The morphine, as it was called, relaxed him and allowed him to eat at dinner without the slightest sense of discomfort, except what he felt under Edwyrd's lingering glances. To combat this, he challenged him with a flat gaze under his hood until Edwyrd looked away.

"Victor, how are you feeling?"

Victor turned towards Guardian Crevon. "I am getting used to this new skin of mine slowly, my Guardian," he lied, returning to his meal. It was good, but the food lacked the same vitality and deliciousness that it once held. His taste buds must have been affected as well.

"Do you have plans of what you will do when you return to Myoli?" Conseleigh Juniper asked.

"Not really."

Victor still couldn't understand how Conseleigh Juniper was influenced by the Sages as well. How deep did their influence go? If he had succeeded here in the Trials, what would have happened?

"That is a shame. You should try traveling, opening your horizons. The south of Empora is great. Or even Chaon, if you dare to wander its depths."

Victor held the spoon of tomato soup in his hand. He blew on it again. And then again, in a superfluous blow to give him time to think. She knew. She must have known. Or was it merely coincidence? He swallowed the soup and then turned his head towards her. "The south has always been a dream of mine to visit," he lied. As he had explained to Iris, there was nothing in Verimas besides marshlands and low hills. It was a rather boring, but perhaps such an interest in it by these two meant there was more to it than met the eye.

Throughout dinner, Edwyrd stayed obscenely quiet and when it was time for Victor to leave, Guardian Crevon, Edwyrd, and his conseleigh came with Victor to the lobby. The servant assigned to him already waited with Victor's bags in hand as well as the briefcase given to him by the adored.

Still hidden underneath the hood, Victor received the condolences of all the conseleigh personally. Then Edwyrd came to him, stepping out from the presence of Guardian Crevon.

"May I see?"

"Why?"

"Because I want to know."

Victor hesitated. "You want to know?"

"Yes."

"This is what you've done to me."

Victor pulled back his hood and revealed his face to the others for the first time. *Where is your shock? Where is your sorrow? Your sympathy? Show me it!* He glared at Edwyrd, and Edwyrd stared back at him. "Can you accept what you've done to me?"

"I didn't mean—"

"No. Of course you didn't." Victor grunted. He snatched Edwyrd's hand and put it to his own face. "Do you feel this?"

Edwyrd frowned. "I do."

"This is what I will have to live with now." Victor's eyes burned into Edwyrd's. He hoped to find terror there, but he couldn't. If anything, he could only find remorse. Genuine remorse. And that made Victor even angrier. "Aren't you going to say anything?"

"I'm sorry. Is that what you want to hear?"

"Sorry will not heal my skin."

"I know it won't."

Victor spat on the ground. He wanted to hate this man. He wanted this man to be terrified of him. To feel guilt. But he sensed Edwyrd didn't feel any of that. He felt sympathy. Drawing away from Edwyrd, he inhaled and broadened his chest. "It doesn't matter. I will carry on. That is what survivors do."

"And you are meant to survive."

Victor didn't know how to respond to Edwyrd's statement, so he merely addressed the Guardian instead. "I am ready now."

"Then let us go."

Guardian Crevon took off his reimaje and pushed Edwyrd behind him. He threw the black cloth on the floor and the blackness swirled about until it revealed the compound of the Web. Victor glanced once more at Edwyrd and then to the conseleigh, eyes falling upon Conseleigh Juniper last. She gave him a subtle wink that only he saw. Guardian Crevon extended his hand out for Victor to take. Together they went into the wormhole the reimaje created, leaving the Core, the Trials, and the past behind.

CHAPTER 28

Victor had left angered, but Edwyrd couldn't blame the man. Disfigured as he was now, his life would be a continual trial until he learned to appreciate the beauty of living instead of the vanity of what he lost. When Victor had pulled back his hood in the lobby, Edwyrd did his best not to recoil, and luckily his own past endeavors numbed him slightly to the physical impediment that Victor now struggled with. But that didn't mean what had happened, what he had caused held any less gravity.

When he had returned to his room for the night, that painting haunted him again. In that fiery spiral, he saw not only Cyrus, but Victor. He saw Vesel. And he saw everything that the flames had devoured in front of him. Logic told him to turn the painting around, to cover up his wounds and scars, hide them from himself. But his heart told him otherwise. Halfway through flipping the painting around, he stopped and let it hang there. What would his life be if he ran away from his problems? Could he truly call himself Apprentice now? Guardian later? No. So he let the painting stare at him, stare deep inside his soul, and make him come to grips with everything in his past because if he couldn't honor his past, then what glory would he bring his future?

It was to his fortune then that Guardian Crevon planned to take him back to Pyre in the late afternoon the day after Victor's departure. The Guardian knew that Edwyrd wanted to see his parents and tell them of what he had accomplished, and there was still the other matter of unfinished business with Lord Omyon. After breakfast, he spent the better portion of his morning planning what he would say to his parents. How much he would tell them. And when he finally decided to himself that he would tell of his bond with Vesel, he looked once more at the painting.

Vesel?

Edwyrd blinked. The silhouette of a dragon that he had seen had vanished. Only the yellowy, red, and orange fire remained. That fiery upward spiral. And he stared at it for a long while, observing his thoughts with an open mind, until he realized what he must do. If he truly wanted to overcome his past, to not be a victim to his guilt, then he would have to make amends with it, and that meant he would have to confront Cyrus's parents.

During lunch, Edwyrd told the Guardian of his plans, and the Guardian commended Edwyrd on his revelation. An hour after lunch concluded, Edwyrd and the Guardian entered the reimaje and stepped out into the fiery lands of Therus.

The streets of Fernis were cobblestone and the buildings were made of a red clay with roofs made from either thatched straw of red-colored firewood or black and made of clay. There was an occasional outlier that was made of stone with black mortar holding it together, but these only marked the armories and guardhouses. Lord Arco's castle at the back was the exception to everything the city offered, having an estate ten times the size of the largest building, and being built in its own area of town, across a great drawbridge that served as the only way to bypass the moat of magma surrounding it.

While walking with Guardian Crevon, he learned that the Oraine family usually lived in Brimstone, as that is the area where Cyrus's father governed as a marquis. That is where they would go next if the house in Fernis wasn't where they were currently, but Guardian Crevon had a feeling they would be in their southern home as Lord Haco had just returned home from Coronation.

"Why would that matter?"

"Lord Haco would have just met you. The man who killed their son. They will want to know the type of man you are and whether he lent his support to you or not."

"Oh." He felt stupid for asking. "He didn't vote for me. He will tell them I'm unfit."

"And you'll learn, Edwyrd, that words are water."

Edwyrd glanced at the Guardian, eyebrow raised.

"It's an Acquavan saying. Probably not appropriate on Pyre. But it means that words can take any form they need to. The second part of that saying goes 'actions are ice.'"

"Because they're solid. They can't be shaped on a whim."

"Very good. Exactly. You showing up here to meet them face-to-face is ice. And it shows the type of man you are."

Edwyrd nodded and continued taking in the sights and smells as he walked. Unlike Nova, the men and women here were garbed in lesser clothes, clay-colored togas that covered only half of their body. Others wore tunics and pants that came only to the calf. Edwyrd assumed those were higher class people. Meat vendors hung dead lizards and other creatures from their awnings, fruit and vegetable shops offered mostly Braeburn apples, ambrosia, dragon fruit, fireflowers, and fire squash.

After an hour's walk through the city, he and the Guardian stopped before a large red and black clay house located near the lord's castle.

"This is it." Guardian Crevon pointed.

With one hand, Edwyrd patted down the wrinkles in his outfit. He cleared his throat and examined the painting in front of him.

"I've been wondering why you brought that with you," Guardian Crevon said.

Edwyrd blushed. "Why didn't you ask me sooner?"

"I figured you'd let me know in time."

"I wanted to give it to his family. Something to remember him by. It was a topic in our first conversation. Do you think they will like it?"

"I think they will appreciate your sentiment in coming here to deliver it personally to them."

Arms outstretched in front of him, he glanced quickly to the door and sucked in a big breath of air. *This is it.* He tucked the painting underneath his armpit, walked to the door, and knocked. Moments later, a woman came to the door, ten years younger than his parents. Ash hadn't started to settle into her ginger hair yet, and she had the eyes of the fireson, the same orange that flared with intensity upon encountering something new.

"Yes. What is it? May I—"

"Maya, who is it?" Another voice called and soon enough a burly man with cropped brown hair and muscles that bulged out from underneath the largest clothing Edwyrd had seen appeared. The man could have broken Edwyrd in two, snapping him as easily as twigs snapped under the weight of feet. Perhaps he should have brought Vesel.

"Maya and Agni, it is nice to meet you. My name is Edwyrd Eska."

They both looked at him with blank faces.

"I was a contestant against your son, Cyrus, in the Trials—"

"We know who you are." Agni rolled up the sleeves of his cloak and stepped forward. "You are the one responsible for Cyrus's death."

"I didn't come to cause any trouble, sir. Cyrus was responsible for his own death. He could have stopped at any time."

When the man didn't halt, Edwyrd stepped back further onto the porch. Agni glanced from Edwyrd to the sole onlooker.

"Guardian Crevon?"

Edwyrd let out a sigh of relief. He looked back. The Guardian had taken a few steps forward.

"Marquis Agni Oraine, a pleasure to be here."

Agni cleared his throat. He put his hands behind his back. "It... it is a pleasure to have you here, my... my Guardian." The man bowed his head, hiding his blushed face. "I...I didn't expect you to be here."

"And if I wasn't? Would you have taken vengeance out on Edwyrd?"

"I..." Agni shook his head. "I apologize. My fireblood takes me sometimes."

"And it took your son the same way. Edwyrd is here to show his condolences." Guardian Crevon nodded to Edwyrd.

Taking control of the situation again, Edwyrd said, "Yes. I came to say that I am sorry for the loss of your son. It need not have happened, and when I am Guardian, I will make sure something like this doesn't happen again." Edwyrd spared a glance at Guardian Crevon, who eyed him in curiosity but remained silent. "This is for you." Edwyrd handed them the painting.

"A spiral."

"It is more than that," Edwyrd corrected Agni. "It was the first topic of conversation your son and I had while on the Core. I want you to have this as something to remember him by."

"What does it mean?" asked Maya.

"What do you think it means?"

Maya stammered, blushing a little. "I... Well, let me look at it." She took the painting from her husband's hands and examined it. "Why it shows that we continue upward, that life doesn't just stop at the borders. It spirals into the afterlife."

Edwyrd stayed silent. It was beautiful, and he wondered if the nostalgia of their deceased son had any effect on that interpretation. Wanting to add more to the conversation, Edwyrd said, "And I believe Cyrus is surely there in Axiumé, looking down on both of you now. He had a soul that spiraled up, and his Power was great as well, as was his intelligence; you should be proud of his accomplishments. Fate merely intervened on my behalf."

"What do you mean?" Agni asked, taking his eyes off the painting as well.

Vesel. Are you here?

I've only been waiting for you to call me.

Edwyrd backed up, placing himself on the steps. He looked up and saw a streak of silver flames in the sky. His heart pounded. Energy rushed inside of him. He loved the feeling and hated it at the same time because he knew what would come later, and he dreaded it. But for the moment, he watched the skyline, hearing his dragon roar as they reconnected once more.

Agni and Maya rushed past him, out from the porch and down the steps. All the people in the surrounding area did the same. Each one pointed upwards to the sky as Vesel flew low enough to the city to be seen, but not low enough to be a threat.

Agni turned to him. "Lord Haco mentioned you had bonded to a dragon."

Edwyrd went to stand alongside Agni and Maya. "I have," Edwyrd muttered. He did his best to rein in the restless fingers, tapping his side and the nausea starting to roil in his stomach as he looked at how magnificent and regal the dragon glided in the air.

Agni hugged Maya closer. "Truly amazing."

Maya turned toward Edwyrd. Painting cradled underneath her arm, she held out the other hand. "Thank you for coming to us, Apprentice Eska. I look forward to your time as Guardian."

He pulled his attention away from Vesel and focused on the couple. "Thank you for understanding." Edwyrd shook her hand.

Agni offered a handshake as well. Edwyrd gripped it, firm and strong. "How did you bond with a dragon?"

"In a bath of fire," Edwyrd pushed out, recalling that day more vividly now that he was back on the planet.

"A bath of fire?"

"A dragon's kiss. It was fate..." A tear began swelling in Edwyrd's eye. He looked upwards, hoping it would return to where it came from. Vesel had already left. Could he sense something was wrong?

"Die by fire, die with honor. Living in Pyre, nothing is higher." Agni beat a hard fist to his chest.

Edwyrd wiped the tear from his eye and did his best not to dry heave after the sentiment. How could he know that had been the last thing Cyrus had ever said?

Edwyrd shook his head and smiled, not wanting the moment to sour. There would be plenty of that still to come. "I will remember your son forever, Agni."

"How?"

"The painting I gave you."

"Those are the colors of my sigil. Gold to represent the first place that your son should have had, and to represent my victory as well. And the red to represent our bond as brothers born in fire."

Agni looked at Maya and then back to Edwyrd. "You will make a fine Guardian someday, Edwyrd. Thank you." He stepped back alongside Maya.

Edwyrd stepped away from them both and came back to stand alongside Guardian Crevon. "I'm ready to go."

"Then let us go."

With deft precision, Guardian Crevon threw his reimaje onto the ground, calling up the lands of Nova that were just beginning to bask in the light of day. Before entering, Edwyrd looked up at the sky, knowing that he wouldn't see Vesel there. Heart heavy and distracted, Edwyrd stepped through, feeling only slight discomfort at the tugging on his body.

CHAPTER 29

Nova looked the same as it always had. Cracked veins of ground ran along the earth. Bubbles made from elements encompassed them in domes, protecting them from the suns, heat, and dragons that prowled the sky above. The suns had just started shining over the eastern mountains that separated Nova from Therus, washing the city in a splendent magenta hue.

The Guardian had taken him directly to his doorstep. Nostalgia washed over him as he looked upon the humble dwelling.

Eagerness building in him for this part of his return, he entered, calling out the names of his mother and father. Confusion became exclamation as his parents understood what was happening. Their son had returned home, and within a minute, they had woken from their slumber to embrace him in a warm hug in the living room. It was there Edwyrd told them about the Trials. Everything. He told them the truth behind Alicia's death, his bond with Vesel, and the success and failures of the Trials.

"How long are you back for? What happens now?" His mother wiped a tear from her eye. "Do you have time for breakfast?"

Edwyrd looked around the room. "My Guardian, can..." He stopped his sentence short. Guardian Crevon was absent. "He was here." Wasn't he? Edwyrd stood up. "Just a second. I have to find the Guardian." He walked outside, expecting him to be where they had first arrived. But he wasn't. *That's odd.* Edwyrd turned around and re-entered the house. "Have you seen the Guardian anywhere?"

"All we've seen is you, Son," his father said.

"Where could he be?" Edwyrd murmured.

Edwyrd went around the house and found the Guardian near the flowerbed where his family had planted the remains of his sister. "My Guardian?"

Guardian Crevon turned to look back at him. "Edwyrd, did you finish with your family?"

"I... well, yeah... but I was wondering if we could stay for breakfast?"

"Of course. After this, you won't be seeing them for a little while."

Edwyrd turned to leave, but then paused. "Why are you down here?"

"Admiring the beauty."

"Edwyrd, did you... Oh, you're down there. What are you doing down there?"

"I hope I am not intruding, Misses Eska. I left Edwyrd so that he could spend time with you, and I saw the beautiful flowerbed down here. It reminded me a little of home."

"Home? They have flame lilies on Mistral?" His mother came down to meet him at the flowerbeds and his father joined in time as well.

Guardian Crevon chuckled. "No. Not the flame lilies. Here. These three." The Guardian pointed to the flowers that Lord Omyon planted along with Alicia's remains. The orange hibiscus, red anthurium, and yellow tulip. "North of where I was raised on Mistral, there is a place called the Rainbow Fields. The area is one big garden colored in the likeness of the rainbow. This reminded me of that. How long have you had them?"

"Lord Omyon planted them just before Edwyrd left," his mother said.

"And they've grown to show their colors already?"

"He mixed the soil with crushed ard leaves to help them grow faster," Edwyrd explained.

"How unique," Guardian Crevon murmured. "Shall we eat and be off, then?"

Edwyrd nodded.

Breakfast was full of questions from Edwyrd's parents about what happens now that their son was apprentice. Guardian Crevon answered as best as he could, in turn answering Edwyrd's own questions. What did happen now? After they returned to the Core, Edwyrd would undergo training in Power with the Sages; he would train with the Guardian's conseleigh and eventually with the Guardian himself. The scaling of his training protocol would take a handful of years, after which he would then spend a year on each nation building rapport with the citizens there as well as the families in power, but most importantly, understanding their culture. As Guardian, he would need the ability to empathize with everyone, although he could show no allegiance to any.

"And eventually," Guardian Crevon concluded. "He will take my place after the Passing occurs."

"What's that?" Edwyrd's father asked.

"I'm afraid I cannot divulge that to you, Max."

"Will Edwyrd be able to bring his dragon along to the Core?"

Edwyrd's neck tensed at his mother's question. "Mom, it's okay... I've thought about it—"

"He will."

"What?" Edwyrd twisted around to Guardian Crevon.

"You will bring your dragon back to the Core with you, Edwyrd."

"But... here... he has his home. His dragons. His—"

"Here he is weaker without you. There you are weaker without him. And separate, you two are liable to be each other's greatest weakness. The Core will be safer for him. And, in turn, it'll be safer for you as well."

Edwyrd sighed. What was going to be hard enough as it was just became harder. Edwyrd shifted in his seat. He contemplated the options left to him, but deep in his heart, he knew the Guardian was right. Alone, they were each other's greatest liability. Together, they would be stronger. Even stronger than what he experienced during the Trials. And that frightened Edwyrd because he didn't know if he could learn to control that strength.

As Edwyrd stared upon the castle that had been his second home for years, he didn't know what to think or feel. This is where it had all started. Ever since he had unconsciously said 'emotions' were elements. How little did he know then? How much did he know now? And how much more would he learn under the tutelage of the Guardian of the Core? Regardless of what he would know, there was one thing even the Guardian didn't know. Who was the Recluse?

Edwyrd walked forward, ready to hear the answers to the catalyst that had thrust him into this life. After being allowed entry by the lord himself, they met him in the open courtyard in front of the castle that was the home of many Power sessions Edwyrd had in his earlier years. The old man looked between the two of them with cautious eyes.

"Is this farewell?" his mentor asked, hands behind his back.

Edwyrd nodded.

"I am proud of you, Edwyrd. You did well. Better even."

"Thank you for believing in me and pushing me."

"It isn't me who you should be thanking." Lord Omyon smiled at Edwyrd and then turned to Guardian Crevon. "Edwyrd has an insatiable curiosity. I hope you are ready for questions, my Guardian."

"I've already learned this myself. But it is we who have questions now for you."

Lord Omyon's mouth dropped. "Is that so?" He hummed. "And what kind of question is that?"

"You promised me that if I became Guardian, you would tell me who the Recluse is."

"And are you Guardian yet?" His eyebrow arched.

"No. But I am, Garrett. And it's interesting that you keep something hidden, even from me."

Lord Omyon squeezed his eyebrows together. He muttered something under his breath, huffed, and his shoulder slunk.

"He is a Smith, isn't he? Plato?"

Lord Omyon pushed his lips to a side and tsked. "Yes, Edwyrd, he is."

"Are there any more?" the Guardian asked.

Lord Omyon shook his head. "He is the last one."

"His shield that he has. It's an Ether Weapon too, isn't it?"

Lord Omyon's eyes went wide. "Where did you learn that?"

"In the Guardian's library."

"And Edwyrd told me that you gave him an Ether Weapon of his own. Why would someone need two Ether Weapons?" Guardian Crevon stepped forward. If he had hoped to intimidate Lord Omyon, he failed.

"Why do you think?"

An interminable silence sat between them. Edwyrd sorted through his thoughts in rapid fashion, always coming back to one singular idea. "He is guarding something, isn't he? That's why he has two Ether Weapons. That's why he lives alone in a territory overrun by dragons!" Edwyrd's heart rate escalated. He was onto something. He knew it. "What is it?"

Lord Omyon chuckled. "Perhaps you won't have anything to teach him by the time he trains with you, my Guardian."

Guardian Crevon looked at Edwyrd and offered a slight nod. Then he flicked his gaze back to Lord Omyon. "So, what is it? What is he guarding out here?"

"I can't tell you that."

"But you said—"

"I promised you I would tell you who he is, Edwyrd. But it seems you've already figured it out."

"I demand as Guardian of the Core that you—"

"Do not use your title to me, Matthau!" Lord Omyon stared down the Guardian of the Core. Both of them looked at each other in a show of superiority. One in title, the other in blood.

Before it escalated any further, Edwyrd cut in. "Why can't you tell us?"

Lord Omyon killed his gaze. "Because the prophecy isn't fulfilled yet."

"Prophecy?" Guardian Crevon muttered.

"What's that?" Edwyrd looked between the two.

"Would you like to..." Lord Omyon gestured towards Edwyrd.

"Edwyrd, part of our duty as Guardian is making sure that the prophecy doesn't get fulfilled."

"But what is it?"

"The Smiths said it to the Twelve a long time ago. After the Great War, before this position was even established."

"How does it go?"

Guardian Crevon cleared his throat. And with serious eyes, the most intense Edwyrd had ever seen him, he said:

"Chosen will be blood from all five domains.
Hope they will bring through chaos, anger, and pain.
Twelve will lose favor, four will regain form.
Bringing with them more death than the Great War."

Guardian Crevon turned to Lord Omyon. "And this Smith guards something related to the prophecy?"

Lord Omyon nodded.

To Edwyrd's surprise, the Guardian didn't push further. He turned to Edwyrd. "Then we are done here. Call your dragon and let us be off."

"That's it?" Edwyrd asked, part of him curious as to why such a matter was dropped but the other half hoping to stall time from the inevitable.

"If this man has something related to the fulfillment of the prophecy, then it isn't our duty. Our duty is to make sure it doesn't get fulfilled in the first place. And if there ever comes a time that it should be fulfilled. Well, now, I suppose it is only us three that know it." Guardian Crevon flicked his eyes towards Lord Omyon. "Is that true? We are the only ones?"

"Yes."

"Then what was learned here is bound by our oaths as Guardian. Edwyrd, do you understand?"

"I understand, my Guardian."

"Very well. Let us be off. Now call your dragon."

"Here?" Edwyrd squeaked.

"Yes. Why not? I would like to see him. And I'm sure Lord Omyon feels the same way."

"But the barriers?" Edwyrd asked.

"Edwyrd has a point. Let's go outside. I would like to see him too."

His two mentors began walking away, and reluctantly Edwyrd followed with slumped shoulders. *Vesel?*

No response.

Edwyrd took a few more steps. *Vesel?*

Nothing.

Terror began seizing Edwyrd. What was wrong? Why had Vesel gone? This isn't how he had planned things to go. Not like this. Never like this. Thoughts frantic, he cried out in his mind. *Vesel? Where are you? We are leaving. I need—*

So, you do want to see me?

What made you think—

We are bonded, Edwyrd. I can feel your emotions. They told me you are ashamed of me.

Not ashamed. Just... Edwyrd sighed. *Can we talk? Can you meet me outside the barrier by the castle?*

I will be there shortly.

By the time they reached the barrier nearest to the castle, a large silver alpha male dragon waited for them. Edwyrd introduced Vesel to everyone and everyone to Vesel. Guardian Crevon and Lord Omyon looked at Vesel in awe. They even asked Edwyrd if they could examine him closer and touch him, and of course, after getting Vesel's permission, he obliged their request. All the while the two elders petted and examined Vesel, Edwyrd forced a smile on his face, and he looked longingly as his dragon. His heart pounded, yet shattered at the same time. It was like forbidden love, a guilt that gnawed at him from the inside, yet one he indulged in all the same. A vice, yet a strength. When the two finished examining Vesel, Edwyrd asked them to give him some alone time with Vesel, and so the two retreated into the bubble barrier, leaving Edwyrd alone to face the silver dragon by himself.

Vesel looked at him plainly. Like usual. Could he know what was coming? Certainly, his dragon felt something amiss, but could he possibly know?

After a long interminable silence where Edwyrd only stood staring at the dark red eyes of his dragon, the same eyes that his sister had had, he finally got the courage to say, "Vesel."

The dragon snorted silver plumes.

"I..." Edwyrd sighed. "I..." He tried again, only to fail. "I want you to say thank you for saving my life in the Trials. Twice, actually."

But? Praises do not take so long to give. What is it, Edwyrd? What is bothering you?

Edwyrd put his hands on the back of his head and paced to and fro, avoiding the topic for as long as possible. Until, that is, Vesel caged him between his silver wings. Staring into the eyes of his bonded dragon, Edwyrd knew this was where it ended for them.

"I appreciate you. And I love you." Edwyrd petted his dragon's nose. "But, I..." Edwyrd closed his eyes, inhaled, and exhaled deeply. As fast as he could, he said, "I wish for you to stop speaking to me."

Stop speaking to you? What have I done?

Guilt gutted Edwyrd, but he needed to stay strong. "Vesel, my Power with you is unimaginable. And I owe you my life. I owe you this apprenticeship I have. But you've also caused me more guilt and grief than I can bear. Alicia died because of you. Cyrus died because of the strength you gave me. And Victor now curses and resents me with that same strength."

Vesel cowered back, the talons on his wings dragging on the terrain.

"I've seen what the strength of a dragon can do. And I'm afraid of it. I'm afraid to call out to you. Who else's life will I ruin next?"

Vesel blinked down at him. His throat growled.

"I want to honor their memories and their sacrifices as best as I can. And I believe honoring them means I must cut ties with you. I am unsure if you can understand. I'm not even sure I understand, but it's something I feel I must do. Unless I tell you specifically to speak to me, please do not."

Edwyrd looked deep into Vesel's eyes. Had tears formed in his as well? Did his giant dragon heart beat like Edwyrd's? Did he accept Edwyrd's proclamation?

"Do you understand, Vesel?"

Yes, Edwyrd. I hear. This will be the final thing I say.

"Thank you. We leave here for the Core. It is... it is best you come with me, but I understand if you never wish to see me again."

Vesel snorted silver flames and lowered his body to the ground as much as he could.

"You want me to ride you?"

Vesel grumbled.

"Well... okay..." Still timid at mounting an animal that was at least ten times larger than him, Edwyrd propped himself up on the dragon's back, holding onto the silver spikes on the back of Vesel's neck.

"Are we finished here then, Edwyrd?" Guardian Crevon came back into the scene, Lord Omyon trailing behind him.

"I think we are."

"Direct your dragon into the reimaje then, and I will see you on the Core."

Vesel took to the sky. Hot air washed over Edwyrd's face. Off to the distance, to the west, he saw the blue of Dragon's Falls. The Recluse was there. Somewhere. Guarding something of such importance that even the Guardian of the Core wasn't privy. He had solved the mystery his sister had been trying to solve, only for his knowledge to be obscured with yet another mystery. How many more things would he learn during his time as Guardian? He didn't know. How many more lives would he hurt? He didn't know. How would fate continue guiding his life? He didn't know.

What he did know, though, is that a new life awaited him. Training awaited him. And in time, his training would teach him to control the Power that swelled inside him. Time would mend his past wounds, grant him wisdom, and allow him to look at the Trials objectively and change them, rewrite their scripts so that none had to suffer the guilt he had to. Hopefully, they would walk away with their characters as clean as when they entered, and none of them would have to cheat or deceive or kill to become the Guardian of the Core. That wasn't what being Guardian was about. It was about being a role model for others. The questions asked at Coronation confirmed this for him. And as he led that advancement in technology, as access across the system broadened, cultures and stories would start to intertwine in unfathomable ways. As future Guardian of the Core, he would be at the epicenter of some of those stories, and he hoped that his memory would live on in reverence, not in infamy.

EPILOGUE

Fourteen years later...

Victor sat in the first row of the funeral procession that took place within the Web. It had been the accomplishment of his father before his death, and Victor often thought that it was his fault for his father's death. Ever since returning from the Core disfigured, he had been rejected by his family. That is why he sat by himself even now, at his father's funeral, while his younger brother Renaul sat atop the dais with his wife and three children. It was Renaul's responsibility to give the eulogy, to address the people. Not Victor's. If Victor had gone up there, people would have shivered in disgust at his marred face, pockmarked and boiled and glossy. A constant reminder of how Edwyrd Eska, the Guardian of the Core's apprentice, ruined his life.

To combat this irrefutable and unforeseeable damage to their family's name, his father had worked tirelessly on completing the Web; he had worked tirelessly on building a strong central authority in Mendeck that none of the lesser marquises would rise up against; he had worked tirelessly to build the dynasty of the Zigarda household. His brother had helped. And Victor had remained in the shadows.

It was in this way that his father had begun giving his attention to Renaul, and how the youngest soon surpassed the eldest. Not in Power, of course, Victor was still stronger than Renaul in Power, in combat, and all other lethalness, but Renaul had gained his father's favoritism. And that is why he stood upon the dais now, both hands on the onyx pedestal, addressing the marquis who had made the trip to see his father's funeral.

His brother was just finishing up the eulogy, making pretty and flowery statements, as Victor knew he would. He had always been too much of a people pleaser, and now that his father's reign would go over to him, bypassing Victor due to the fallout from his father's good graces, he made it a show to court everyone that attended the ceremony. All Victor could do was listen, arms crossed over his chest, and hope not to vomit at the hyperbolic flattery his brother gushed forth.

"... my father's greatest honor was having all of you serve under him. I know that from somewhere in Axiumé, he is looking down on this event, even now, and his heart is warm in seeing such support. Thank you for coming from Lokigh, from Aeston, from Rydel. And even a dearer special thanks goes to our truly esteemed guests that traveled leagues and parsecs to attend today. Lord Senlin Khan, thank you for coming this far north from the capital of Chaon.

"Conseleigh Juniper, thank you for coming all the way from the Core.

"And, of course, how could I forget the Sages of Gladonus? They have always been dearest to my family, and even sponsored my brother once upon a time. Sages, I hope you will see my reign the same way you saw my fathers, as an opportunity for advancement. For while one story closes, I believe my father has already written the opening prologue to the next novel, and it all begins with the Web and establishing and building the Zigarda name throughout the planet and the system, and for that, I will need the help of everyone here. Think not of this moment in melancholy, reflect upon this moment and rejoice in all that my father has done, and what we will continue to do together. Thank you."

Victor's mouth fell open. He reeled his head back and propped himself up on the chair to try and see past the crowd in attendance. *They're here?* Not being able to see properly, he got up from his seat, no longer caring about the protocol that had been given to him to not talk with any of the guests for fear of scaring them from giving the same fealty to his brother as they had his father. He had only given his agreement to that obscene request to shut up his brother and his brother's personal guard and council, but when he had been given that information, the attendance list hadn't been disclosed to him. He hadn't known anyone from Chaon, nor the conseleigh, nor the Sages would show up.

He didn't bother keeping his head low as he maneuvered against the crowd that waded forward towards the casket to pay their respects. Fourteen years and peoples' mouths still hung slack at the sight of him. But none of that mattered. At the end of the procession, he saw Conseleigh Juniper exchanging words with Cronos. By her side stood the Lord of Chaon, and near him stood someone Victor never thought he would have seen again: Iris.

Iris waved her hand, her pockmarked hand, full of scars and debts, at Victor and flashed a smile. "Hello, Victor. Long time no see."

Like he, she had aged. She had cut off her long hair to make it cropped and slanted her bangs to be like a razor's edge along her forehead. Her face was rounder and her waist was not as slim as it used to be. Parts of her black hair were overtaken by gray and her skin wasn't as golden as it used to be, but that could have also been due to the dark archer outfit she wore and the obsidian pearl earrings that pinched her ears. Without any visible weapons, she still stood smiling at him with the greatest weapon in her arsenal: intent.

"What..." Victor took a moment to catch his breath. He tried slowing his pumping heart, but this sudden blast of nostalgia wouldn't afford him any ease of his anxiety. "What are you all doing here?"

"We came to pay our respects to your father, of course," Conseleigh Juniper said. The conseleigh had aged as well, but she still remained remarkably lithe and lethal, as Victor had first noticed when he had seen her on the Core so many years ago. She walked forward and touched Victor's shoulder; she leaned into his ear. "We will meet privately after the procession finishes."

And just like that, she wandered past him, along with the others who followed her lead, and joined the crowds of individuals who waited in line to say their condolences to his brother and to pay their respect, one last time, to the late Hayden Zigarda.

It was in the middle of the afternoon, shortly before dinner, when Victor found himself in his chambers surrounded by figures of his past. Figures he thought only a distant memory, but had turned into shadows stalking him from behind.

"Victor, is it true that your brother will be ruling in your stead now, due to..." She paused for exaggeration, Victor was sure, not to find the right word. "Due to your, well, you know."

Victor didn't respond. Instead, he looked towards the Sages. "You told me that I would win."

Cronos clutched his Ether Staff, that looked like an eye with long pointed eyelashes sticking out from it. The other Sages, like usual, stayed silent behind him. He wiped his hand over the eye on the top of his staff and gave a long, serious look to Victor. "I did say that, and it would have been true. Fate intervened for Edwyrd; you know that as well as I do."

"Everyone knows that," Conseleigh Juniper said. "Edwyrd should have been burned by the fires you deluged him in, but it was that dragon of his that saved him."

"When I observed all the contestants who had been noted as entering, he wasn't bonded with a dragon at that time, meaning it must have happened sometime shortly before the Trials began. I did not steer you wrong, Victor."

"You were meant to win. The Sages were meant to train you, and then all of us together would have been enough to overcome the Guardian and see the masterpiece fulfilled."

Victor inhaled deeply and exhaled. He had no idea what Conseleigh Juniper droned on about, but he knew that she and Cronos were right. He very well should have won that duel, but Edwyrd's bond with that dragon had caused everything to end up against him. *Why hadn't I seen that earlier? How could I have? There was no dragon on the Core, and he never gave any impression of being bonded.* Victor battled his conscience.

"Sure," Victor agreed. "I should have won. But there is nothing that can be done now about it."

"That isn't entirely true." Cronos tapped the ground lightly with his staff. "And besides, you have some debts to pay."

Iris smirked. "Yes, he does."

Victor ignored the temptation to look at his hand. He didn't need yet another reminder so blatantly in his face as the woman before him.

Cough.

And then another.

Victor put his hand to his mouth to stop himself. His coughing had persisted ever since returning to the city from the Core. The adored in his father's apothecary had told him it was brought about due to the onset of his condition and the mixture of the pollution that was fueling the city's progress and the advancement of the Web. Even when bringing this news to his father, though, his father had ignored it, not willing to halt the advancement of his plans to secure the health of his already disfigured son. Victor couldn't blame his father for that, so he never complained about the cough, but it had grown to be a part of him just like his shadow, always lingering, insidious, and a reminder just like the people who surrounded him. In some ways, it even helped him remain connected to the father that had estranged him and worked himself to his grave. The last years of his life, it had been mostly Renaul who had completed the finishing touches on the Web. And it had been Renaul to guide him through the three main buildings of the Web and the underground interconnected tubes linking all of them. Renaul had shown him the dungeons, the apothecary, the armory, and the other various locations. It had been a moment Victor had been excluded from.

"I will get my brother to do something about our little deal." Victor flashed a gaze at Iris.

"It is us who care about Verimas, Victor. Iris was only our tool to mention it to you during the Trials, but we very much need that city."

"Why?"

"Don't you remember our little tour, Victor?"

Victor glanced at Iris. "How could I ever forget?"

A sly smile spread across her face.

It hadn't even been a year since he returned from the Core when Iris reached out to him through his telecommunicator and told him that he should meet her in Verimas. Nothing but an afterthought of his father's attention at that point, it was easy to go there, telling his father he would oversee the construction of the Great Bridge for a while.

She had met him at a modest inn. Nothing special about it, except for the fact it looked like a cottage and was the closest living space near a set of rolling hills with little caverns cut into them. She had taken Victor to those caverns and introduced her to something that shouldn't have existed. At least, his conscious, his studies, and all his thirty-four years on the planet told him it shouldn't have existed. A shapeshifter. Her husband.

He had introduced himself as Zalos. His wrinkled and furunculous skin made him a monster, same as Victor. Gray eyes with flints of amber in them allured Victor. But what enthralled him was when the man had stood beside Iris and had wrapped his arm around her. White puss had excreted out of his body, and he had stepped back from her, wiping the puss all over his body. A slight hissing sound, like acid burning through wood, had prickled Victor's skin, and before he knew it, a clone of Iris stood in front of him, minus the clothing. Victor had coughed, like usual, given his condition, and the noise echoed throughout the cavern. Then he had heard it. The crying of an infant. And Iris had introduced him to her newborn son, not even a few months old.

"Why do you live in here?"

Her husband had answered. "My kind has been living in shadows for generations. Just like the shadows you live in now. Don't you already know the answer?"

Iris added. "The moisture of the cavern is good for their skin, too. It helps with ensuring their ability passes over."

"And you?" Victor asked, now wondering if he had truly understood Iris at all during the Trials.

"No. My father was. Mother wasn't... Ability didn't pass on to me."

"Then how come..."

"I was born in too dry of a climate. Mother ran off when she knew. Father had tracked her down, killed her right in front of me. Took me back, raised me in his ways. Got me into the Bonded Guild and from there the rest is..." She paused, looking for a word. "history. Isn't that how they call it?" She giggled. "Just like what we are about to make..."

Victor had stared at her, dumbfounded by the extent of information she had given him. If she could so casually tell him that, then there weren't many boundaries she couldn't cross. Killing him in a cavern alone being one of them. He had gulped and shaken his head. "I can't give you Verimas yet... I—"

"Understand." Iris smiled. "I just wanted to remind you about our debt." She waved her scarred hand at him.

Victor shivered. "How could I forget?"

"I haven't the faintest idea. We will keep in touch. Or my husband will keep in *touch* with you." She giggled once more, knowing the discomfort she caused him by the way she played with the words.

Victor had looked from her to the other Iris, who morphed back into his original form within a minute. He flashed a wicked smile and crossed his arms over his chest.

She had guided him out, and he hadn't heard from her again until the year that Edwyrd had lived in Empora, six years after the Trials. His father had slowed his progress on the Web during that time, making sure the apprentice was accommodated, for that was his duty. Victor's duty had been to make sure that Edwyrd never went to Verimas, and so he had spent an awkward and elongated time with Edwyrd. Time in which they never spoke, even though Victor could tell that Edwyrd had wanted to say something to Victor. After a month of it, Edwyrd had gone off to explore other parts of Empora, and Victor was once again free to return to his life as a silent shadow in an intricate web.

"So, what brings you here today, then?"

"Today is when you fulfill your promise."

"Fine, Verimas is yours." Victor waved his hand, wanting to be through with his Blood Oath to her.

"Is that it?"

"What do you mean? That is what we agreed upon."

"Don't you want more, Victor?" Cronos's amber eye gleamed and flashed.

Victor coughed. "What do you mean?"

Cronos strode forward and produced a vial of bright blue liquid from the satchel on his waist. "Take this."

Victor eyed the liquid, then Cronos, the blue almost as blue as the other bi-colored eye. He took it and gave it a swig. Instantly, he felt better. His skin felt not as itchy. A coolness slid over his body as if he was under the constant trickle of a waterfall. "What... What is this?" Like a greedy fool, he looked for a name on the vial but saw nothing.

"It is called youthwater."

"Youthwater?"

"It is only produced in Acquava and is a byproduct of Pearl's lifeforce. Only the lord of Acquava can get that for you, and with it, you can continue living, not succumbing to old age. I'm offering it to you in exchange for helping with my plan."

Victor eyed him incredulously. "What plan?"

"A plan that will reopen Gladima. A plan that will see you triumph over the Guardian of the Core. A plan that will see the rebirth of a people. A plan that will take more than a century to complete. A plan that will bring about change."

His words seeped into Victor, like the youthwater coursing through his veins. Something about the sage's words invigorated him. If not for fate, Victor would have been Guardian, yet here he was on a different doorstep of immortality. He swirled the blue liquid in his hand.

"How does this plan begin?"

"It starts with Verimas," Cronos said. "Everything starts with Verimas." He massaged the top of his Ether Staff.

Victor got lost in the nostalgia of seeing his first shifter in those caverns. His skin shivered thinking about them, but he did know how they felt. How it was to live in the shadows of others.

Something sharp poking into his chest brought him back to reality. Iris stood in front of him, dagger extended. How she had gotten it inside the premises with the security for his father's funeral was beyond him, but he knew Iris to be competent enough to always have something up her sleeve.

"Here," she said. "It's tipped in venom, so only unsheathe it when you plan to use it."

"Use it for what?"

"Use your imagination." She gave a small wink, and then returned to Cronos's side.

The dagger felt weighted in his hands. He felt its intent. And he realized what they wanted him to do with it.

"Like I said to you before, Victor, you have something the other contestants didn't possess. You aren't afraid of bloodying your hands. Sometimes change requires sacrifice."

What will become of the blood feud between Victor and Edwyrd? How will the system change when Edwyrd becomes the next Guardian? Find out the answer to these questions and more in the series, <u>The Guardian of the Core</u>.

About the Author

Michael E. Thies is an English educator and Holistic Health Coach currently living in Suzhou, China. He is a child of God and is a proud member of the Church of God Ministry Jesus Christ International (CGMJCI) and draws much of his inspiration from the Bible.

www.ingramcontent.com/pod-product-compliance
Lightning Source LLC
Chambersburg PA
CBHW032124170626
46808CB00006B/2096